FITNESS JUNKIE

FITNESS JUNKIE

LUCY SYKES AND JO PIAZZA

DOUBLEDAY

NEW YORK LONDON TORONTO

SYDNEY AUCKLAND

www.doubleday.com

DOUBLEDAY and the portrayal of an anchor with a dolphin are
registered trademarks of Penguin Random House LLC.

Jacket photograph © George Baier IV
Jacket design Emily Mahon

LIBRARY OF CONGRESS CATALOGING-IN-PUBLICATION DATA
Names: Sykes, Lucy, author. | Piazza, Jo, author.
Title: Fitness junkie : a novel / Lucy Sykes and Jo Piazza.
Description: First Edition. | New York : Doubleday, [2017]
Identifiers: LCCN 2016035896 (print) | LCCN 2016045702 (ebook) |
ISBN 9780385541800 (hardcover) | ISBN 9780385541817 (ebook) |
ISBN 9780385542968 (open market)
Subjects: LCSH: Weight loss—Fiction. | GSAFD: Humorous fiction.
Classification: LCC PS3619.Y544 F58 2017 (print) |
LCC PS3619.Y544 (ebook) | DDC 813/.6—dc23
LC record available at https://lccn.loc.gov/2016035896

MANUFACTURED IN THE UNITED STATES OF AMERICA

3 5 7 9 10 8 6 4 2

First Edition

For all those fierce and fabulous fit bitches—you inspire us personally and professionally every single day.

Dedicated to Euan Rellie, the fittest husband—and Dad—I know. You inspire me to be the most Fit Person I can.

—LUCY SYKES

Nick Aster. Maybe we'll work out more next year.

—JO PIAZZA

"I'd rather smoke crack than eat cheese from a can."

—GWYNETH PALTROW

"Food is an important part of a balanced diet."

—FRAN LEBOWITZ

FITNESS JUNKIE

CHAPTER ONE

⌒

can't believe you ordered that."

Beau Von B. narrowed his brown eyes at Janey Sweet's French toast. He reached under the table and into his leather satchel to pull out a small metal plate.

"What's that?" she asked, taking the opportunity to pop a perfect square of buttery French toast smothered in raspberries and powdered sugar between her glossy lips.

"It's a scale," Beau said shortly, as though the fact were self-evident. He placed the device flat on the tabletop and laid a single strip of turkey bacon across the mirrored surface. Beau's eyebrows lifted when the small dial barely twitched to an ounce. Only then did he allow himself to begin nibbling, like a very delicate bunny, on the end of the strip of meat.

"Sugar is the devil, you know," Beau whispered to Janey as if he were conveying a very dirty secret to a very stupid child.

Janey poured a tap of syrup onto her plate and made her voice equally low and mysterious. "So they say." She refused to let Beau irritate her this morning. She was busy enough the rest of the day with things that could cause actual stress—a couture dress fitting with that bothersome model with the high-pitched voice, a meeting with investors about brand expansion in Asia, and yet another call with her divorce attorney to finalize the details of the fairly large settlement she'd soon have to hand over to her almost ex-husband.

Beau continued his lecture on the merits of eliminating sugar from one's life. Her business partner loved few things more than telling other people how they could improve themselves.

"Not everyone totally gives up sugar. I did, of course. It was the right thing to do. Sugar is just a health-food faker *and* a big tummy maker," Beau expounded. "But I do know a lot of people who are just giving up on recreational sugar these days. Maybe you should think about trying that."

All around them, Manhattan's fashion world breakfasting elite—hipster e-commerce entrepreneurs in their factory-dyed organic denim, the *Man Repeller* blogger crew, all the European fashion editors who still had time for meals outside of the office—took no notice of the woman enjoying her French toast or the man fretting over his bacon. The Horse Feather was the kind of place you came to for breakfast if you wanted to be seen eating breakfast, not if you wanted to enjoy it. The portions were notoriously small, the service slow, but the lighting was fantastic and made everything look lovely on Instagram. It was Beau's favorite restaurant for that very reason. His #avocadotoast posts from here always got more than a thousand likes. It didn't matter that he never actually ate it. No one ate it. The décor of the Horse Feather could best be described as hunting lodge chic. Along one wall sat shelves of succulents, while tasteful taxidermy adorned the exposed whitewashed brick. Two full-sized Joshua trees, imported from Southern California, took up residence in each western corner. The once wooden floor was painted a shiny white to match the exposed beams overhead. Paparazzi regularly waited outside to catch a shot of Gwyneth Paltrow or Amal Clooney walking through the grand wooden barn doors.

"*Recreational* sugar? You say that like it's a *drug,* Beau."

"Sugar is a drug," Beau insisted with all the seriousness of Nancy Reagan.

He'd only eaten half the strip of bacon before putting it onto the saucer next to his triple espresso. She wondered why he'd bothered to order the bacon at all.

"Janey-boo, we need to talk."

"I'm listening," she said, letting an edge creep into her voice. Beau only brought out the baby talk when he wanted to discuss something she'd find irritating.

"Have you seen this morning's *Fashion List Daily* yet?"

She hadn't. She'd taken an Ambien. Okay, maybe an Ambien and a half last night, which caused her to wake up just ten minutes before this breakfast was supposed to take place, forcing her to forgo her morning inspection of *FLD*, Twitter, Instagram, the Skimm, and the *Wall Street Journal*. And though her morning data check was typically a sacred ritual, it had taken a lot just to put on pants that morning. Because of that Ambien and a half she also found herself feeling cloudy and unfit for the fight Beau was so clearly looking for. And speaking of meds, Beau seemed like he was on something new; he was all amped up, his beady eyes darting left and right. She looked hard at him. Beau had always been too thin, but only recently had his face and body become all forty-five-degree angles with no round edges at all. Each month some new quack told Beau something else he shouldn't be eating—fat, carbs, oil, gluten, now sugar. This meant that Beau just kept subtracting from his diet without ever adding anything back in.

"Of course," she lied. Lying to Beau was a professional obligation.

"Please don't lie to me, boo-boo. You're a shitty liar. I *know* you haven't seen it because if you had you'd be as mortified as I am." Beau pulled his iPad from the bag and tapped it before turning it around to face Janey.

"You're all over Instagram too . . . un-Facetuned," he said in a superbitchy voice that went high on the last syllable and was beginning to make her light-headed. Facetune was Beau's favorite new app. It let you retouch any picture before you posted it on social media, making it possible for every normal human to look like Cara Delevingne all of the time.

She squinted at the screen. This particular photo of Janey must have been taken at a show for a capsule collection for Stone Fox Bride yesterday morning. The presentation had been packed, since everyone was obsessed with Stone Fox and their genuinely foxy founder, Molly Guy, so even the snooty fashion editors who couldn't give a damn about what was happening in the bridal world accepted the invite. There she was, sitting between the new editor in chief of *Brides* magazine (she could never remember her name) and Linda Fargo, the beloved women's fashion director of Bergdorf Goodman. Her face was large on the screen and she was biting into a bruffin, the new pastry fad created by that sexy French chef down on Spring Street (the one who never buttoned his shirt all the way) that was supposed to be the love child of a brioche and a muffin. They were delicious—both pastry and chef.

There was nothing wrong with the picture as far as she could tell. As the CEO of B, the couture wedding dress company she and Beau ran together, Janey was photographed all the time sitting in the front row of fashion shows. She'd gotten so used to it that she'd perfected her "very serious yet playful CEO face" for the cameras. She tilted her head to the right and smiled with her mouth closed, her nose slightly scrunched as if she were about to break into a laugh. For Janey, being photographed was part of the job. For Beau it was a passion. He regularly courted young paparazzi to ensure his most fabulous nights out in his most outlandish outfits would find their way into the party pages of *Vanity Fair* and *Town & Country*. Janey had once discovered that the majority of space on Beau's hard drive consisted of two decades of Beau's high-resolution press photographs sorted by date and the designer of his outfit.

"Do you care to explain what is happening in this picture, Janey?" Beau said in his best kindergarten teacher voice.

Do I care to explain myself? Not even a little. God, she was tired. This coffee was not giving her the wake-up buzz she needed. Janey felt a tickle begin at her collarbone and reached up to scratch it. A bumpy rash had begun to form, a physical manifestation of the anxiety Beau's questions were causing her. A low level of angst in her stomach was the norm on most days. The rash was the next level of unease.

Janey sat taller in her chair and willed herself to channel her inner badass. It didn't matter that it was ridiculous that she even had to do this as the CEO of their company. It didn't matter that this wasn't fair. This was going to be her morning.

"I was at Stone Fox. The dresses were gorg . . . if a little over-priced. They're boho perfection. If I ever get married again *and* if we didn't make our own wedding dresses for a living, I'd wear their second-skin silk Lucinda dress. You should've been there too, but I believe you needed to go to Ashtanga yoga instead. Or maybe it was Bikram. I get them confused. Which one gives you an orgasm when you put your leg over your head?" They'd come to a tacit agreement years ago that Janey would be the one to attend early morning meetings, fittings, and fashion shows since unless an appointment involved shirtless yoga with a fit nineteen-year-old yogi, Beau was unlikely to make it out of bed before ten a.m.

Janey continued, allowing her irritation to seep into her voice. "I'm eating a bruffin in this photo . . . banana nut I think."

"Exactly! You're *eating* in front of one hundred people!"

Janey paused and waited for some sign that he was kidding, but his expression never changed. She stifled her own laugh and glanced left and right at the crowded dining room.

"Shit! I'm doing that right now too." She feigned mock horror and put her hand to her chest. "Should I stop? There might even be fifty people in this restaurant. And they're all . . . watching . . .

me eat. Careful— They're watching you too. Maybe we should hide? Shall we take our plates underneath the table?"

Now that Janey stopped to really look around, she realized she didn't actually *see* anyone else noshing on French toast. The waiters, all of them irresponsibly handsome struggling actors, were serving veggies with Crayola-colored dips for thirty dollars a platter and twenty-dollar thick dark green smoothies. The two elegant women at the table next to them had nursed the same espressos for more than an hour, their eyes wide and alert from caffeine and hunger. Janey was complicating the temperament of the Horse Feather by devouring her carbs, an item that had only been placed on the menu for the benefit of the odd tourist who happened to find his or her way into the restaurant.

As Beau sighed, his baby blue ascot wiggled like a genie shaking free of a claustrophobic bottle. He held up a single bony finger too close to Janey's mouth to signal her to pause their conversation for a moment while he made eye contact with the waiter.

"Where's this bacon from?" Beau asked the handsome young man.

"I believe it came from a turkey," Janey muttered under her breath, glancing up to see if Beau's question was met with disbelief equal to her own. She briefly wondered what type of "slash" this waiter was. Was he a waiter/actor or a waiter/model? He was too handsome to be a waiter/poet. Those guys did better in Brooklyn anyway. She settled on actor, certain he'd been one of Marnie's boyfriends on *Girls*.

"Oh, it's a local heirloom turkey," the young man said without missing a beat. Heirloom food was all the rage these days, but Janey had no idea what that even meant. She thought it was the food equivalent of vintage clothing. But did that mean it was old?

"How local?" Beau pressed, forming a steeple with his two index fingers beneath his chin.

Instead of rolling his eyes, which Janey believed to be the only proper response to this kind of question, the waiter paused and nodded earnestly.

"I'll check on that for you. Right away."

Talking about the turkey reminded Janey of the first time Beau spent Thanksgiving with her family back in Charleston. It seemed like a thousand years ago. Beau was more than just her business partner. They were best friends, the oldest kind, able to date their friendship before the onset of puberty. As a kid, Janey had lots of friends. The other children treated her friendship as a prize, since she was practically royalty in South Carolina. Her daddy owned the Sweet Chocolate company that employed half the damn county. From a very early age Janey realized everyone in their town was the same. They talked the same, liked the same things, hated the same things, wore the same clothes, and had the same ambitions. Janey observed the other kids at school with the same curiosity she used for the adults and found that the boys and girls adopted their southern parents' stereotypes early on. The little boys wore sherbet-colored polo shirts, worshipped at the altar of the Gamecocks, and were a peculiar mix of chivalrous and misogynistic. The little girls arrived at school with perfectly coiffed hair and Lilly Pulitzer sundresses covered in excited crabs and petulant seahorses. They adopted their mamas' turns of phrase—"Not to be a gossip, but . . ." and "God bless her heart."

Beau came to their school in the third grade, and from the start he kept to himself. He was smaller than the other boys, and when they went off to play at recess, he sat under the willow tree timidly eating his own lunch out of a brown sack. Janey couldn't help but watch him. For weeks, she had no idea he was watching her too.

"Hello, Jane Sweet," she heard a high-pitched voice say one afternoon while she sat reading on the bench outside school waiting for Mama to pick her up.

"Hi, Beau," she responded cautiously.

"Do you think it would be all right if I drew you?"

"Excuse me?"

"I want to sketch a portrait of you." The words didn't belong in the mouth of an eight-year-old.

"I guess so. Wanna come to my house before dinner?" she asked. "It's meatloaf night. I'm sure you can stay. Mama makes too much. There'll be pie too."

His hair was slicked back and parted perfectly on the left side, and he had the longest eyelashes Janey had ever seen on a boy or a girl.

"I'd be delighted," he replied.

From then on, Beau came over every day after school and it felt like the most natural thing in the world.

"You're my muse," he told her.

She looked up the definition of "muse" in her daddy's dusty old Webster and decided it was an acceptable thing for the pretty little boy to call her. He was sarcastic and funny and self-absorbed but also obsessed with Janey in a way that made her feel more special than her parents could ever make her feel. Her parents *had* to love her. Beau *chose* to love her, and when he turned his light on her she felt she could accomplish anything and be anyone.

At first Janey assumed Beau's perfectly pressed khaki pants, starched white button-down shirts, and pocket squares were the result of his having a meticulous southern mother just like her own, Miss Lorna Sweet, a legend in Charleston society and a paragon of motherhood. Beau and Janey had been inseparable for six weeks when she learned the truth: Beau was practically raising himself. His daddy was long gone and his mother, who worked as a clerk in a gas station at the edge of town, spent nearly every night with a boyfriend. Each morning Beau ironed his own clothes and packed his own sack lunch.

The Sweet family were happy to bring Beau into their fold, due mainly to his undeniable charm. "I love that little pansy," Reginald Sweet, Janey's conservative southern father, said after his second sazerac. Reginald never realized you weren't supposed to call little boys pansies, even if they liked to wear your daughter's dresses and makeup.

Swiftly the two were a pair. That first Thanksgiving Beau's mama took off for Knoxville to spend the holiday with yet another new paramour, leaving Beau with a neighbor she'd given a twenty-dollar bill and a frozen Sara Lee. Janey invited him to the Sweet house for the first of ten turkey holidays Beau spent with them. Janey was an only child, but the Sweets had a large extended family that stretched from South Carolina to Texas, and they hosted at least forty people each year. While Beau was quiet with other children, he was anything but around adults, especially adult women. He pulled Janey aside before the guests arrived that day and told her his plan.

"Let's play a secret game of pretend all day. Only we know about the game. We can't break character. We'll be a very fancy lord and lady from the British countryside. We don't have any children but we do raise excellent foxhunting dogs. For all of dinner we can only talk about our manor house, hounds, Victorian politics, and how difficult it is to manage the servants." Janey hadn't been able to keep a straight face when Beau spent most of the pudding course explaining the intricacies of hound breeding to her Aunt Lois from Lafayette, Louisiana. Their childhood fantasies of this ilk could stretch for days and sometimes weeks at a time.

When Lorna found out how much Beau liked dresses and design she insisted on showing the two children Princess Diana's wedding, which she had recorded on a VHS cassette and kept in the bottom drawer of her nightstand. Royals, Miss Lorna insisted, weren't any more interesting or special than regular folk, except for Princess Diana. That wonderful woman was something distinct, and Miss Lorna felt a certain kinship with the princess of Wales since they both married young and became mothers within a few years of each other. Beau curled into Miss Lorna's side on their old chesterfield sofa, barely breathing for the entire ceremony. He wholeheartedly agreed with Lorna that Diana's wedding dress was one of the most beautiful dresses ever created—though he'd later bitch with outrage over the crumpled taffeta.

Janey liked remembering Beau as a child because he'd been so much more likable then.

By the time they turned eighteen, half the town expected they'd just get engaged and elope somewhere exotic, like Hawaii, despite the fact that Beau was so clearly what wealthy conservatives below the Mason-Dixon Line liked to refer to as a "confirmed bachelor." Besides, Janey hadn't had a mess of boyfriends. She found the jocks and meatheads on the football team distasteful and boring.

Beau hightailed it to Manhattan the second he got his diploma with a scholarship to FIT. She went to Princeton, hoping proximity would keep them close, but the seventy-five-minute ride on New Jersey Transit proved too long for Beau's rising star. Those were the days right before email and well before Facebook, which meant it wasn't as easy to stay friends with someone who wasn't standing right in front of you on a daily basis. Even though they didn't speak often during those years, Beau remained her constant companion in her head. She'd see a plain girl from West Palm Beach wearing a poorly chosen beret in her economics class and create a wild backstory about how it landed on her head through an accidental affair with an elderly French tourist. She heard Beau's voice instead of her own when she made wry asides about ironic facial hair to her girlfriends after drinking too much bourbon at speakeasy-themed parties. Beau made her funnier and more interesting, even when he wasn't there.

She went from Princeton to Philadelphia, where she finished an MBA at Wharton with a thesis on the market penetration of the single-serving candy bar, the bite-sized treat that changed Halloween as America knew it. She'd been recruited by banks and consulting firms to do a dozen different things involving algorithms and spreadsheets, but none of them were appealing. She'd only gone to business school in the first place to make her daddy happy. "My little gal is smarter than every man in this county," Reginald would tell anyone who would listen. His goal, she knew, was to groom her to take over the Sweet business one day, the first Sweet woman to be the president and CEO.

Meanwhile, with his thick southern drawl peppered with devious wit, perfect porcelain skin, and wedding dress designs that garnered attention from New York City's most outrageous socialites and editors, Beau was the fashion world's new darling. At twenty-four he won his first CFDA award and landed his first stint in rehab. He'd been having way too much fun to call Janey for those six years, but once again, he needed her.

"Help me" was all he had to say.

To his credit, Beau was scared out of his mind and ready to take all of her hard-earned business school advice as gospel. She asked her daddy if she could have a reprieve from coming down to work at Sweet. Not forever, just long enough for her to try out living in New York and get Beau's wedding dress thing off the ground. When Janey arrived in New York, Beau was living in a ridiculously expensive loft in SoHo, paid for by a much older boyfriend/investor. His designs were brilliant, but his business was not. He'd spend two thousand dollars on materials for a dress and then sell it for a thousand. It took Janey a month to streamline everything, and by the end of the first year all the pieces fell into place.

"I want half the company," she said then, high on being a newly minted MBA and the one person Beau could turn to for real help. She wanted him back so badly, but she wanted him to earn it too.

Besides, she knew she'd deserved it. She'd gotten them in Barneys' famous display windows and on the Hollywood wedding circuit. And though Beau Von B. had added two syllables and gotten rid of his real last name (Matthews) when he came to New York City, Janey insisted they keep their brand name simple, just B.

B was for beautiful, for bride, for beholden, even though she let

Beau keep thinking it was a B for Beau. Just like that B became the sum of her life with just a few subplots. For the most part she loved what she did, enjoyed the wedding dress business. There was something special about making a bride feel like the most beautiful woman in the world. B dresses weren't for everyone. They never talked about it, not out loud anyway, but for the past couple of years the B designs, with their sultry silhouettes and clingy lace, were best suited to slender women, very slender women. And even though B never publicized the fact that they didn't make a dress above a size 6, it was well documented in the fashion press that "shedding for the wedding" took on an entirely new meaning when a woman purchased a B original. You'd think that would limit their selling potential, but it did the exact opposite. It made them seem more luxurious, more aspirational. Janey wouldn't have been able to fit into a B wedding dress. For her own wedding Beau designed something custom, and she'd never even thought about what size it was.

Janey was jerked out of her nostalgia and back to the Horse Feather by Beau's moody whine. "You're eating a muffin in the front row of a fashion show in front of hundreds of editors and bloggers and buyers and cameras." The expression on Beau's face as he said the word "muffin" was akin to the one people made when they said the word "pedophile." His entire mouth shifted to the right side while his eyes danced left. Janey was tempted to stand up, leave the restaurant, and go to the office. Let Beau's tantrum pass. They always passed.

"It's a bruffin, not a muffin," she said, using the tip of her index finger to swipe the remaining maple syrup from her plate. The knot of anxiety deep inside her stomach demanded she put more food into her mouth even though she felt full. As predicted, the act of licking the sweet liquid off her fingertip soothed her. She studied the picture again and tried not to laugh. She looked fine. Maybe she had a slight double chin, but it was probably just a bad angle and that chin (chins?) was framed by her lovely long shiny black hair. She was starting to regret the bangs, but they weren't her idea, they were Beau's. "You'll look so Parisian!" he'd exclaimed after gushing over a spread of Isabelle Huppert in *Vanity Fair.* "And besides, then you won't need to get Botox as often." So she'd asked her hairdresser to try the bangs, but instead of looking French she looked like a forty-year-old woman trying too hard to look like a twenty-year-old woman, like those people on reality television.

"Janeyy, Janeyy-boo! Are you listening to me? Do you hear what I'm saying?" Beau waved the gnawed piece of bacon in the air like a wand. His voice became firmer.

"No, Beau. I didn't hear you," Janey said sarcastically, grabbing the piece of meat from his hand and putting it into her own mouth. He wasn't going to eat it anyway.

"I can't have my CEO eating, especially in the front row of a runway. It's all over Instagram. Everyone is talking about it. I don't even want to read you the comments, but somebody compared you to the Stay Puft Marshmallow Man."

He couldn't be serious. No one would compare a grown woman at a fashion show to the Stay Puft Marshmallow Man. No one who wrote about fashion shows was old enough to have seen the original *Ghostbusters.*

"This is so bad. So bad, Janey! We sell wedding dresses. We sell dreams of perfect, slim, beautiful brides and here you are looking all . . . 'eff.' Everyone is calling you 'eff.'"

"Excuse me? Looking all what?"

"Eff. The F word. Don't make me say it, Janey; you know that word makes me gag."

"Say it, Beau," Janey growled at him.

"Fat," he whispered.

"Fashion fat?" She cracked a smile. It was an inside joke between the two of them, created back in the days when they still had inside jokes. They'd hear their models, their size 0 models, complaining about how fat they were and report back to each other about which girl incorrectly thought she was a cow that week. She was "fashion fat," an absurd term they created that meant anything larger than a tiny size 4. They'd elongate and soften the "a" so that it sounded vaguely German. *Faashunvaat.*

But Beau wasn't smiling. "No, Janey," he said without blinking. "Fat."

His words stung like a slap. "Seriously, Beau?" She'd gained a little weight in the past year, but who was counting? Beau was, apparently. She knew she could lose a few pounds, but she was far from fat. So what if her skinny jeans didn't fit anymore. She wasn't a teenager. She didn't wear crop tops no matter what *Elle* said about how they were making a comeback—FOR ANY AGE! Her backside had a bit of jiggle, but who cared? It had been a tough year. Besides that, she was a forty-year-old woman, not a teenager. People gained weight when they got older. When her standard uniform (beautifully cut black blazer, black trousers, crisp silk shirt for day and an array of soft simple T-shirts for night) began to feel tight she simply ordered the next size up on Net-a-Porter and tried not to pay attention to the numbers. She'd done that three, maybe four times in the past twelve months.

"I'm not fat, Beau!"

He crossed his arms in front of his petite chest.

"I'm not saying you *are* fat, but other people are saying it. You're the face of my brand, Janey. You have to be aspirational. That's part of why this works. We're both so cute."

Beau was the kind of person who said things out loud that other people would only think to themselves.

"I'm pretty sure this works so well because I know how to make you money, Beau," she growled. "What do you want me to do? Go on a diet? Are you seriously telling me to go on a diet?"

"Janey, you aren't hearing me! We cannot work together anymore right now." Janey looked down at her empty plate and then back up at Beau. Something had changed. She didn't know what.

This was no longer a simple breakfast. This would mark a turning point in their thirty-year friendship and their business partnership. She began thinking of all the times Beau had failed to show up at company functions, bailed on important meetings, forgot the date of their own fashion shows. *She* was not the problem with this company. Her chest tightened. Her cheeks burned. She was angry, and she never got angry with Beau. Not when he borrowed money and never paid her back. Not when he canceled plans at the very last minute or just didn't show up without an explanation. She let him get away with murder because she loved him like a ridiculous younger sibling or an eccentric guileful pet, and because she'd given him the better part of the last two decades of her life. She spent more time with him than she spent with her parents or with her almost ex-husband. That was part of the reason Michael was out of the picture, for good. He'd been sick of playing second fiddle to Beau all the time, and she didn't have enough energy for both of them. Along with her anger would come tears. But she wouldn't let Beau see them. Janey bit down hard on the inside of her cheek to keep from crying.

"Are you on drugs again? Are you actually high right now? I thought you stopped taking pills on weekdays."

"We need a break. We need some time off. I need you to get your priorities straight." Beau carefully poured half a saltshaker over the remaining items on his plate and placed a napkin over the mess, pushing it away from himself

"My *priorities*?"

"Yes. Who do you want to be, Janey Sweet? Who are you on the inside?"

She bit down harder. "I'm the same Janey who turned you into a multimillion-dollar brand. I'm the one who makes you look incredibly good on a very regular basis."

Their waiter couldn't have known he was choosing such an inopportune moment to return with an enormously pleased smile on his face.

"The turkey was raised on a rooftop farm in Brooklyn, the Gowa-nus neighborhood, fifth floor with a view of the Statue of Liberty." He allowed his gaze to linger on Beau before looking down at his handwritten notes. "She was humanely slaughtered by a farmer named Kristen on September first. We have a live feed of the tur-keys available on our website if you'd like to check it out later." Janey could see a flirtation brewing between the two handsome men. She was momentarily distracted from her own situation by the revulsion at the thought of a herd of turkeys (were a group of turkeys called a herd?) being live-streamed from a roof in gentrified Brooklyn, coddled by hipster farmers who believed a view of the Statue of Liberty was a turkey's life goal.

"I'll definitely take a look tonight," Beau said with an odd affec-tation. "Bookmarking now!"

"I can tell you where your potatoes came from too," the waiter offered. "We know so much about the dirt!"

"Please!" Beau said. "You know I only eat food that comes from the earth. And I love dirt."

"Oh shut up," Janey interjected. "What do you want, Beau? What exactly do you want me to do? How can we end this ridicu-lous conversation right now?" Janey massaged her temples, her fin-gers warm and soothing from clutching her coffee cup.

"Janey, darling, I want you to stop stuffing your pretty little face. I get it. This year has been terrible. Your parents. The divorce. But is that really an excuse to become an addict?" he said in an exag-gerated whisper.

Janey had quit smoking and drinking more than three cocktails in a single evening in her early thirties. She could count on one hand the times she'd indulged in anything more mind-altering than a Red Bull, while Beau had experimented with every pill and powder he could get his hands on.

"An addict?"

"Sugar, Janey. You're a sugar addict."

"Okay, so I'll go on a diet." Agreeing with Beau was always easier than fighting with him. He'd be off on some new tangent by the end of the day.

"That's a start. But I don't think it's enough. Take some time off. Why don't you take three months and get into shape before the start of next season? We'll call it a hiatus." He switched to a whimsical tone. "Don't you love the word 'hiatus'? It's so much fun to say. It sounds like a holiday. Hiiiiiiiii-ay-tooooos."

Janey cracked a false smile to cloak her growing insecurity with the situation and spoke slowly through gritted teeth. "You can't ask me to do that. I own half this company. Stop behaving like a child. We have a busy week."

"Forty-nine percent. Not half," Beau shot back. "Besides, it's in your contract." Beau wouldn't meet her eyes.

It infuriated Janey when Beau went from irrational to logical. "What's in my contract?"

"That you stay the size of a fit model. In the contract we made when we first started working together. When you *were* my fit model. Way back. When you were still yummy. Yummy with no tummy," he added with an exasperating wink, unaware of how hurtful he was being.

"I was twenty-four. Things have changed since then, Beau. I haven't been your actual fit model for more than a decade." Her eyes narrowed as she recalled the terms of that long-ago contract in her head. He wasn't wrong; she had promised to be something ridiculous, like a size 4, but it was a document written in their twenties over three bottles of champagne in someone's sister's cousin's beach house in Sag Harbor. Their twenty-something selves did a lot of questionable things. She'd also added a clause to his contract back then that he needed to stay away from the underage party boys and keep out of rehab, and one that they would always live within three blocks of each other, have a baby together if they were both single at age thirty-five, and that they would sell the business at forty and retire to an island off the coast of Madagascar.

She needed to get out of here. She reached down to grab her purse from beneath the table, taking the opportunity to swipe away a tear. "Beau, just tell me what you want." Janey stood.

"You're out until you drop thirty."

CHAPTER TWO

~

WOMEN'S HEALTH
By Electra Ellis

Forget the coconut water and kombucha. This spring is all about H2BROC! We're talking about the all new broccoli-infused water available exclusively at Complete Foods. The brainchild of supermodel India Ellsworthy and her entrepreneur husband, Alex Goldblatt, H2BROC provides all the nutrients you need for a meal in a single drink.

"After we had our twins we set out to devise a pure and healthy alternative to the chemical-filled drinks out there. We wanted something our whole family would enjoy," Ellsworthy told us. "We loved broccoli and we loved water and so we thought, 'Why not make broccoli water!'"

Now the real secret to H2BROC is in how you serve it. The drink is best served in a mason jar, and not just any mason jar, but a mason jar manufactured before 1957.

Why? Nineteen fifty-seven was the time that mason jars ceased containing cadmium. Cadmium reacts with the free radicals in broccoli to pull all the nutrients out of the vegetable and directly into your bloodstream.

Not only will H2BROC fill you up, it will also absorb into your skin to reverse the process of aging. Super food doesn't get more super than that!

W here's your scale?" CJ asked, rooting around in the cabinet beneath Janey's sink. "I see European toothpaste, a bottle of Penhaligon's aftershave, Laundress delicate wash powder, and a jar of Moroccan oil. No scale."

"I don't have one," Janey shouted to her best girlfriend from the kitchen of her apartment. She leaned precariously out the window as she took turns puffing on a mint cigarette and sipping a Diet Coke. Janey gazed out over the perfectly manicured Gramercy Gardens. She'd never actually gone inside them. She was always too busy working.

CJ strode out of the bathroom and down the hallway of Janey's two-bedroom prewar apartment that Michael was currently contesting in their divorce proceedings, despite the fact that she put in the bulk of the down payment and paid the entire mortgage for the past two years.

"Who doesn't own a scale?" CJ was incredulous. "And what the hell are you doing?"

"I've never had a scale. My clothes fit or they don't fit. They usually fit. Right now . . . ehhhhh," Janey groaned, pulling in a drag of the herbal horror and thumbing her phone. She'd been googling "lose weight fast," "fat removal," and "crash diet." She still couldn't believe Beau was doing this. Janey toggled to her Facebook feed, which these days was filled with photographs of artfully arranged fruits and vegetables, articles extolling the virtues of a raw diet, and inspirational quotes like "You are not going to get the butt you want by sitting on it" and "Keep calm, get skinny." She leaned against the wall to steady herself. The cigarette made her light-headed.

"I'm dieting," she yelled back at CJ. "Diet Coke and weird cigarettes. It kept me skinny in my twenties. Remember? You too!"

CJ sighed and snatched the cigarette out of her hand, stared at it, took a drag, and crinkled her nose before stubbing it out into the porcelain kitchen sink.

"It didn't keep me skinny in my twenties. I've never had your luck . . . or your metabolism. Come on! We need to weigh you. We need to know what we're dealing with."

CJ, short for Chakori Jeevika (her Indian immigrant parents were insistent that an Americanized nickname would help their daughter fit in at school), had been her best girlfriend since college. Back then, CJ tacked photos of Kate Moss to their miniature dorm fridge as "thinspiration," coveting the look of the androgynous model in those Calvin Klein ads from the nineties where everyone wore the same unisex white tank top and sullen expression.

"Why don't you ever have to diet?" CJ whined, and Janey would shrug. She was lucky, she guessed. But she wouldn't stay that way forever. She had pictures in her apartment of her mom and dad from their early twenties and thirties, both slim and fit. But as they aged their waistlines grew in a direct correlation to Reginald's love for Lorna's buttery, sugary cooking. The most exercise she'd ever seen them do was walking eighteen holes on the golf course.

CJ and Janey became truly close during what Janey now referred to as her Beau-free period of six years of university and graduate school. They'd bonded over being away from home, having anxiety attacks when they tried to smoke pot, and using coed bathrooms for the first time. They were both aliens at Princeton. CJ grew up in a first-generation bubble, her social life limited to aunties, cousins, and friends of her parents who spoke Hindi at home and had no use for outsiders. Janey's deep southern accent and use of the word "y'all" made the northern girls giggle, not in a mean way, but enough to make her feel strange. The two girls were also both only children, so they agreed it was weird to see boys in the bathroom plucking at their nose hairs with tweezers and leaving disgusting specimens in the shared toilets. Neither of them liked eating cafeteria food when they were both so used to their moms' home cooking. CJ's mom and aunties sent her to school with giant containers of samosas and pakoras, not understanding the limitations of their dorm room mini fridge or the fact that CJ was embarrassed when she made the entire building smell like cumin. But rather than throw them out, CJ would eat only samosas for days until they were gone and then starve herself for the rest of the week, which made her hungry and crabby and unpleasant to live with.

As long as Janey had known her, CJ Goldberg née Lakshmi had been a varsity-level dieter, sometimes juggling two diets at a time. She applied the same mathematical precision she used in her old job as a hedge fund analyst with $5 billion under management to calculate her caloric intake. She could rattle off the amount of saturated fat in nearly any food product and knew to a tenth of a mile how much she walked in a day. And yet none of the dieting made CJ any skinnier for longer than two weeks, except for that month the two girls spent mucking about in India after senior year, traveling from Mumbai to Jaipur to Delhi and finally Rishikesh, when they both contracted giardia and lost fifteen pounds each. CJ still talked about it, nearly twenty years later, in dreamlike tones.

"Wasn't that just the best diet ever?" she liked to recall. "It was even better than Atkins."

"Fixing" herself was CJ's only irrational habit. In the rest of her life she was practical to a fault. She'd married a lawyer, had adorable twin boys, and sat for Shabbat dinner with her mother-in-law every single Friday night even though she didn't believe in God. CJ began working part-time after she had the babies, but she never quite got into the rhythm of being a stay-at-home mom, so she was constantly piling on new projects and programs. Janey couldn't blame her. It felt strange to be sitting around her apartment on what should be a work day.

"What diet are *you* doing right now?" Janey asked her.

"Clay."

"The Dr. Clay diet? Never heard of him. Does he work uptown?"

"No. I'm eating clay. Just clay," CJ asserted in her husky and calculating voice. "Clay for breakfast, clay for lunch, clay for dinner. Everyone's eating clay. Karlie Kloss and all the girls do it before the shows."

"Clay? The stuff you make pots and ashtrays out of?"

The smell of kitty litter permeated the room as CJ pulled a plastic Tupperware container from her purse and removed the lid. She grabbed a bottle of Pellegrino from the fridge and mixed the fizzy water with a brown-grey powder. She produced what looked like a baby spoon from a Ziploc bag and without hesitation began shoveling the dirty soup into her mouth.

"It's better if you add some stevia," she said, swallowing with intention. "Clay is high in iron and folic acid. Traditional tribes use it to cleanse the body of toxins. This one was harvested from a hundred-year-old termite mound in Ethiopia. Not only does it soak up all your toxins, but the clay swells up to twelve times its original size in your stomach so you always feel full. It's magical." CJ looked up, a mustache of grey liquid glossing her upper lip.

"It's dirt!" Janey replied.

"Technically it's volcanic ash."

"What's it cost?"

"I'm paying a thousand dollars for nine days."

Before Janey had time to question spending a small fortune on edible kitty litter, CJ cracked open Janey's laptop.

"I'm signing you up for SweatGood," CJ said as she daintily blotted her lips with a baby wipe.

"Is that a diet?"

"No, it's a class pass."

"Like a gym membership?" Janey had a gym membership. Who didn't? She'd been dutifully paying the monthly dues at FLEX! since about 2006 even though she couldn't remember the last time she'd gone to the gym. She had the membership because her ex signed the two of them up on a family plan with her credit card and it kept renewing, even after her marriage ceased to do so.

CJ looked at her with a mixture of pity and perhaps jealousy.

"No one just goes to the gym anymore. How did this whole fit revolution just pass you by?"

Janey recognized the benefits of eating healthy and being active. But that wasn't always so easy when you worked eighty-hour weeks. She'd noticed the younger girls in her office taking clients out for juice instead of cocktails, yoga classes instead of dinners. But she'd never been one to indulge in any of the latest health fads. "I've been a little busy."

CJ sighed. "No, you've been a skinny bitch who had the metabolism of a high school cheerleader for too damn long and men threw themselves at your feet so you never had to think about cellulite. Sorry. Mean."

"Yeah, mean," Janey said indignantly.

Her friend rambled on. "So SweatGood is a pass that gets you into the very best workout classes all over the city. You pay one fee and you can sign up for everything. If you didn't have the pass you could spend up to fifty dollars for a single class. This way you get a big discount everywhere. And you can manage it on an app right on your phone. It even has this geolocator so you can find out the soonest, closest workout to you anywhere in the city at any time of day. Haven't you ever walked out of a big gross lunch and been like, 'I need to take a spin class right now'?"

"No."

"You're in the minority."

Janey leaned over her friend's shoulder to look at the computer.

"Look at this schedule. You can take spin, underwater spin, spinoga—that's spin and yoga together. There's trapeze ballet, hula yoga, hot Pilates. I hear hot Pilates is all set to hard-core rap. It's all 'Yeah bitch mothafucka . . . I put my leg ovah my head. I put my leg ovah my head.' Oooo yes. I've been scared to try this one . . . but I'll do it if you go with me. It's conscious pole dancing."

"Did you just buy two SweatGood passes on my credit card? Why do I need two?"

"Well, I bought one for me too."

"Don't you already have your own?"

Her friend's fleshy cheeks were the color of Chanel's Rouge Allure Velvet lipstick.

"I had one and then Steven made me cancel it and if he sees another one on our credit card he's going to get pissed and I don't want to deal with it. Marriage is about finding ways to avoid conflict."

Steven very rarely got pissed at CJ. Her friend's husband thought she walked on the Hudson River, and while he poked fun at her off-the-wall dieting practices, he was shockingly supportive and sweet for a criminal defense attorney who spent all day every day dealing with the very worst Manhattan had to offer.

CJ continued. "I *had* my own SweatGood pass and I got so pumped about it I started signing up for everything. Everything! I wanted to make sure I got a spot in every new class. Most of them fill up a week ahead of time. But then *my* schedule got busy. Meetings with potential clients, hair appointments, Botox, waxing, sugaring, playdates, shitty mummy things, and I would have to cancel. But what I didn't realize was that they charge you a 'motivation tax.'"

"What's that?" Janey asked, with genuine interest about anything related to finance and not dieting.

"They charge you the full price of the class when you cancel and donate it to something awful. When Steven saw our credit card statement he lost his mind. There was a three-thousand-dollar donation to some group that wanted to speed up climate change and another thousand to the KKK."

"Shut the front door." Janey sank into the couch. "The Ku Klux Klan?"

CJ nodded. "Direct to David Duke."

"I can't do this. What happened to diet pills? What happened to fen-phen?"

"Honey, I think those made the flipper babies. Come over here. Come on." CJ stretched her short arms out to pull Janey up to standing and then placed her hands on her shoulders.

"I need you to do something for me. I want you to close your eyes."

"No."

"Come on, close them. Close them. Please!"

"Fine." Janey closed her eyes.

"Now I want you to hop up and down five times. Like a bunny rabbit."

"What the hell are you trying to make me do?" Janey had only been awake for three hours, but somehow she was exhausted, and CJ was starting to get on her nerves.

"You need to learn this exercise. Sara Strong is telling everyone to do it. There was a story about it in *Women's Wear Daily*."

"Who's Sara Strong?"

"Only the most important fitness instructor and health guru of right now. She's the reason Madonna doesn't look a hundred and seven. Sometimes she writes a column for the SweatGood newsletter. Come on. Hop. Hop. Like a bunny. Soften your shoulders and jaw. Relax your belly. Feel all of your tension just shake off your body." Janey hopped, but not at all like a bunny. She barely came off the ground. Hopping was a funny thing to do when you were no longer five years old. She felt silly and tense, her body resisting the hop.

"Your feet have to leave the ground."

She bent her knees a little deeper and pushed into her feet a little harder.

"Okay. Now I want you to stand very, very still. Suck in the biggest breath you can take, and I want you to scream."

CJ demonstrated by opening her mouth as wide as a cantaloupe and stretching her tongue down toward her chin.

"PAHHHHHHHHHHHHHHHHHHHHHHHHHHHHHHHHHHHH!!!!!!!!!" The wail echoed off Janey's high ceilings.

"I have neighbors."

"PAHHHHHHHHHHHHHHHHHHHHHHHHHHHHHHHHHHHHH!"

"Someone might call nine one one."

"PAHHHHHHHHHHHHHHHHHHHHHHHHHHHHHHHHHHH!"

"Fine. Fine. Fine. I'll do it if you'll stop. PAHHHHHHHHHHH-HHHHH!"

With the primal scream lingering in the air, the doorbell buzzed.

"Who's here?" CJ looked miffed to have her shouting session interrupted.

"Ivy, I think."

CJ made a face in defiance of her Botox. "Is she as hot and young and perky as ever?"

"She's not that perky anymore, to be honest," Janey whispered as she walked to the door. "Young and hot, yes. Perky, no. In fact, she's completely different now. I think you might like the new Ivy."

Ivy was Janey's gorgeous younger cousin by way of marriage. Just twenty-six, Ivy had been a ballerina with the New York City Ballet until she was hit by the M34 bus riding her bike to Lincoln Center and put into traction, her hip shattered, shoulder dislocated, ankle crushed, and her dream of being the next Misty Copeland kaput. One day another ex-ballerina visited her in the hospital to tell Ivy how she'd reinvented herself doing PR for a place called SoarBarre, "a radical new spin studio for strong women looking to co-create their future selves." Through a mixture of charisma, charm, and a fuck-all perfect body, Ivy became the star SoarBarre instructor of NYC. She was the poster girl for radical change after *Today* did a segment on her recounting her terrible accident, expulsion from the ballet world, and subsequent reinvention.

Ivy *used* to be polite and perky. As a teenager she was one of those girls who peppered each sentence with an affirmation. She was crazy with approval.

Wow, you look amazing, Grandma! Can I borrow those earrings?

You have the best taste ever! What number Benjamin Moore is this absolutely perfect white paint?

Can I ask you a huge, huge favor . . . would you mind awfully passing the milk? I love your eyebrows.

Isn't the sky the best ever shade of blue today?

Ivy had been an exceptionally good child and a particularly wonderful niece to Lorna—always offering to help Lorna with her DIY projects when Janey was away, things like constructing an air plant garden on the sun deck or adding banana leaf wallpaper to the downstairs guest bathroom. Lorna Sweet was Pinterest before Pinterest existed.

Ivy's classes now had a wait list, and she was on the cover of *New York* magazine's "Fit New York" issue two months ago—a teensy GI Jane flexing her biceps in a sports bra and microscopic SoarBarre boy shorts under the headline "No Pain, No Gain . . . Bitches." *Self* magazine had her writing a column called Hurt Yourself to Love Yourself. Her bosses at SoarBarre encouraged her to be mean, even abusive to the clientele. They loved it when she shot water guns in their faces as they pedaled up pretend hills. The nastier Ivy behaved, the longer the wait list for her classes. No one in New York City wanted a positive life-affirming spin instructor. Her clients, the ones paying fifty-five dollars for an hour-long class, wanted to be abused. They wanted to be screamed at and tortured, and it went against every sweet cell in her body. Being a bitch at work took a toll on the formerly kind ballerina. She'd allowed it to bleed into her personal life, and made her hate herself.

"Today sucks," Ivy announced as she walked through Janey's door. The words sounded incongruous coming out of the mouth of the little blond fairy. "Everything about today sucks." Janey's cousin gave her a hug as Boo Radley, the half-blind wirehaired dachshund Janey inherited from her mother, moved between her feet, causing her to stumble.

"Boo Radley is still alive?" Ivy asked incredulously. The dachshund with the incredibly unfortunate name (Janey constantly told

Lorna that she must not have fully understood what *To Kill a Mockingbird* was actually about) was now eighteen years old. Despite losing his eyesight, most of his hearing, and his ability to walk down stairs, Boo remained in good spirits.

"He's like a roving shag footstool." Ivy looked down at the dog and finally nudged him aside with her toe to give Janey a hug.

Ivy was skinny, but not in the way Beau's runway models were skinny. Her muscles were tight and taut, her triceps like hard little peaches, and her butt a perfectly round melon. She had these unbelievably long eyelashes and corn silk white hair, always pulled into a high ponytail. She wore the perfect amount of smudge-free makeup to work out, eyeliner *and* sweat-proof mascara.

"So what happened? He told you that you weren't allowed to work because you're fat? You're not fat. That's fucking stupid." Ivy drummed her turquoise fingernails on Janey's countertop. "What do you weigh? You look great. Much tighter than some of those obese bitches in my classes." Ivy clasped her hands over her mouth and collapsed into a chair, a heap of despair wrapped in six hundred dollars' worth of moisture-wicking performance fabrics. "Listen to me. I'm a gross asshole. That word, 'bitches,' was never even in my vocabulary before I started working at SoarBarre. When did I get to be so mean?"

Janey couldn't help but smile at this new Ivy. Her cousin *was* a whole different person now. Just a few weeks ago she'd given Ivy the number for her longtime shrink, Ron, to try to help her with her anger.

"I hate Beau," Ivy spat. "He's a shady little troll. I've always thought he was a shady little troll. I don't even feel bad saying that." Ivy pulled a large bottled water out of her purse and began to unscrew the top. A stalk of broccoli was suspended in the container.

Janey sighed. She wouldn't let Beau force her out of the company she'd built from nothing. Right after she'd left their ill-fated breakfast at the Horse Feather she called the B general counsel, a birdlike woman named Natasha, a disciple at the Temple of Beau.

Beau won Natasha's heart when he paid for her honeymoon to Malta. After Janey reached out, Natasha immediately sent her a memorandum explaining that "in light of her publicly disgracing the brand, the founder and president of the company, Beau Von B., believed it in the best interest of B for her to take a leave of absence of three months' time." She could almost hear the polite restraint in Natasha's legalese.

"I ATE A GODDAMNED BRUFFIN!" Janey screamed into Natasha's voicemail, since Natasha was the kind of lawyer who knew better than to ever answer her phone when she could bill twice as much for having to listen to a voicemail and then draft an email response.

She consulted her family's attorney, Ronald Applebaum, who read through the memo, left Natasha his own voicemail, and went back and forth several times with her disembodied messaging system at *his* steep cost of five hundred dollars per hour, all to come to the conclusion that Beau, with his 51 percent stake in the company, could indeed ask his CEO to take a leave of absence if he felt she was "disgracing" the brand.

"What about sizeism? I can sue him for being sizeist, can't I?" Janey pleaded.

"That's not a thing," Ronald Applebaum drawled, coughing once on his own cigar smoke. "Anyway, this sounds like sibling rivalry to me." He was making a joke. All of the Sweets and the people who worked for them considered Beau to be family. They *were* like siblings, and that was one of the things (one of many) that made this situation so intolerable and made Janey feel like even more alone.

The attorney was clearly finished with the conversation. "May I ask how much you weigh?" he asked uneasily.

"I don't even know." Janey had hung up the phone determined to do whatever it would take to lose whatever weight she'd gained as quickly as possible, go back to work, and take the entire goddamned company from Beau.

Janey walked over to the fridge to grab another Diet Coke. She looked at a photo strip of pictures of her and Beau, ripped it off the fridge, and tossed it into the trash bin.

Ivy changed the subject. "Are you dating? Maybe you need to take your mind off work for a little."

CJ answered for her. "She hasn't had a date in six months."

"I've been busy." Janey's fists began to clench.

"You've been lazy," CJ continued. Janey never thought it was fair for CJ to appraise her personal life when she'd been happily married to the love of her life for the past decade.

"The options are limited."

"You haven't even looked at the options."

Ivy interrupted the spat between the two women. "I'm seeing someone. It's new. I met her on the bike. You know, at SoarBarre. I know it's probably not great to be hooking up with clients, but it is soooooooo much easier than Tinder, and sometimes these girls just throw themselves at me after class. She's a kindergarten teacher on the Upper East Side. Every time I curse she makes me put a twenty into this jar she keeps on top of her fridge. At this rate we'll be able to go to Jamaica for Easter based off my filthy, filthy mouth."

"When did you become a lesbian?" Janey asked, surprised only because Ivy's daddy was a very well-known Baptist preacher.

"I'm not full gay yet. I just identify as LGBTQ right now." Ivy shook her high ponytail. "Anyway, I'm having the best sex of my life with a chick and she's wonderful. I think maybe everyone is a little bit gay these days. I know a lot of divorcées who go gay."

Janey found "divorcée" an irritating label, one that denoted failure and marked her as the kind of person who wasn't very good at things. Janey considered herself one of the most, if not the most, capable women she knew, and she despised the idea that she wasn't good at something, even if it was something she hadn't much enjoyed. She was always surprised to notice, however, that remembering her ex-husband, Michael, didn't trigger any kind of emotion for her. She knew she was supposed to be sad, to miss him, or to hate him, have any really strong emotion. She'd read somewhere that losing a spouse, through divorce or something worse, was like the severing of a limb. For Janey it was much more mild, maybe a sprained ankle. There were little things she missed. He made her English muffins with cheddar cheese when she worked late at night. She liked the way their feet touched beneath the blankets in the morning. But she didn't ache for him.

On the surface there was nothing wrong with Janey's husband. Just the opposite. He was good-looking, tall, handsome, a young Cary Grant in a perfectly cut suit. They first hooked up after meeting at the Cap and Gown eating club, just one week into her junior year of college. CJ was home with the flu or food poisoning or a wicked hangover and Janey found herself scanning the room for a place to sit. Michael caught her eye, and even though they hardly knew each other, he raised a friendly hand and beckoned her to join him. He had a joke ready to break the ice. "How do you pronounce the capital of Kentucky? Lou-ah-ville or Loo-ee-ville?" His eyes sparkled waiting for her answer. But Janey was one step ahead of him. "Neither," she replied, unfolding her napkin onto her lap. "Frankfort is the capital of Kentucky. Try another one."

They broke up a couple of weeks before graduation. *We're too young. We should see other people. We should see the world.* After college he went to work with all the other upwardly mobile Ivy League graduates on Wall Street. They reconnected at a benefit to save the western Congolese gorillas from going blind at the Museum of Natural History, where he made her smile with his Louisville joke all over again. They dated for three years before getting engaged and had a lovely society wedding in Charleston. Everyone she knew married the guy they were dating at age twenty-nine. It was just what you did, and Lorna desperately wanted to throw her only daughter the wedding of her dreams. Lorna's dreams, not Janey's. Janey felt so bad about disappointing her parents when she didn't come home to work at Sweet Chocolates that she felt obligated to give her mother this one thing.

Michael's only aspiration at the time was turning other people's money into more money, and Janey cared about little else besides making sure Beau was pleased with her work. But when banking became less glamorous after the housing market crash, Michael wanted to be an entrepreneur and join the armies of young men marching down Silicon Alley with their ideas for apps and widgets and e-commerce companies.

"We'll be fine on your salary," he'd protested with too much confidence, and without consulting her quit his very well-paying job at Morgan Stanley to learn how to code. Janey didn't mind being the breadwinner exactly, but there was something uncomfortable about his assumption that she'd simply take to it. It also annoyed her that being a tech entrepreneur seemed to involve a suspicious amount of video-game playing on the part of her thirty-five-year-old husband.

Their union was nothing like the one Janey had grown up watching. She loved Lorna and Reginald's love story. They were completely captivated by each other from the day they met at the Charleston country club, where Lorna was wearing a near-skin-colored one-piece working as the lifeguard. A practically nude bathing suit was acceptable to Lorna even though a bikini would have been unheard-of. Reginald, home from Vanderbilt for the weekend, pretended to drown in order to receive mouth-to-mouth from the buxom blonde. The Sweets were conservative in everything except showing affection. From that day forward her parents were constantly cuddling, kissing, and holding hands.

Lorna worked as the communications director for the Charleston mayor for the first three years after the wedding and then decided she would do much better in the position of CHO, chief household officer. And that's what she called herself. She even had custom stationery drawn up with the title, and she never let Reginald forget that she ran things at home. She also practically ran Sweet Chocolate from their marital bedroom, since he asked her for advice on every major decision he ever made for the company. Lorna never accepted computers, email, or smartphones, preferring instead to complete all her correspondence in handwriting on Smythson stationery. In a single week Lorna could pen ten separate notes to her daughter, varying in length from a couple of lines to several pages.

Her first year working at B, Janey had dragged Lorna's wedding dress out of mothballs and begged Beau to re-create it for their line. It became an instant best seller. She'd never believed someone could die of a broken heart until her mother passed away last year from fast-moving colon cancer. Just a month later, behind the wheel of his fifteen-year-old Mercedes during the ten-minute drive from his office to their now empty house, Reginald slumped over the steering wheel, dead of a heart attack. The death of both her parents so close to each other shook her to her core. Since Beau knew Lorna and Reginald better than anyone, she'd moved into his loft and curled up on his couch. Beau bought a giant screen and a projector on which he looped old photographs and home movies of Janey's parents. The two of them cooked their way through Lorna's handwritten cookbook. Janey devoured giant platters of shrimp and grits, buttered honey-glazed biscuits, fried okra, and blueberry cobbler. Beau watched.

Janey believed she gave her marriage the old college try, but Michael didn't agree. "You're married to Beau," he'd say to her. For the first few years she'd laugh it off, but truthfully, she *was* much more attracted to Beau's ridiculous humor and charisma. Michael had tried and failed to join their little world of two. He accepted Beau's joining them on long weekends out to the Hamptons. He never complained about their regular slumber parties, where he'd come home to find his wife and her business partner sitting up side by side in his marital bed wearing matching sleep masks and rewatching a DVRed version of Prince William and Kate Middleton's wedding. He even tried to cultivate his own inside jokes with Beau, testing out a few affectionate nicknames and inviting him on long-distance bike rides out to the North Fork, but Beau rebuffed her husband's friendship.

She remembered being in therapy around that time.

"Tell me why you hate your husband," the analyst asked her.

"I don't hate my husband," Janey replied evenly, telling the truth. She didn't hate her husband. She didn't hate anyone. Of course the shrink did the shrink thing and just stopped talking, leaving Janey's last words lingering in the air in one of those little word clouds, so that she eventually had no choice but to fill the space.

"I'm just bored with my husband," Janey finally admitted. She had no interest in his new plans to launch a website that would predict what was missing in your pantry using some kind of bar code technology and automatically deliver it to your door with a drone.

Michael sensed it of course.

"We could leave New York," he'd say sometimes without prompting, desperate to find a way to please her. Sometimes he mentioned the possibility of moving to San Francisco, which she silenced with a single look. They didn't wear high heels or mascara there. Other times, he concocted wilder schemes, clearly just meant to get her attention. "Why don't we quit our jobs and open a hotel on the beach in Zanzibar?" Janey would force herself to smile at him and avoid mentioning the small fact that he didn't have a proper job to quit. Besides, Michael would never live at the beach. His mother was a ginger, and he sunburned too easily. She could, however, imagine running a hotel with Beau in Zanzibar. It would be all whitewashed walls and Byzantine blue tiles. They'd start serving ginger lime cocktails at sunset and bring in the most fabulous DJs who would play until the sun came up. Everything was more fun, more real, better than real, when Beau was there. Despite his drawbacks, Beau had the ability to make any situation a dozen times better. But with her husband, she knew she would just continue to be bored on another continent.

Janey wasn't one of those hard-core "childless by choice" chicks, the ones who told anyone who would listen that their uterus was not open for business. In her thirties she just didn't feel she had the time for kids, kept telling Michael they would wait until B had expanded to China and then until they hired a new marketing officer to take some of the pressure off her. After that she worried their apartment wasn't big enough for three of them. They should wait until the housing market slumped again. In their last uncomfortable year of marriage she'd promised to go off the pill. She did for six months, and for six months she didn't get pregnant. Every time her period came she felt like a failure.

She started taking birth control again without telling her husband. Michael found the pack of pills where she'd hidden them, in an empty quart of Sweet chocolate ice cream in the back of the freezer. He left the empty ice cream container on the counter with the pills sitting on the bottom when he moved out of the apartment.

She knew, from Facebook, that his new girlfriend was due to give birth any day now. All she felt was relief that he was with someone else. And soon enough, after she wrote a large enough check, they wouldn't have any connection at all.

Ivy continued her diatribe against modern dating. "It just sucks. Everyone lies on his or her dating profile. Not a single person has any basic communication skills. It's all texts and emojis and abbreviations. Tinder is truly the worst. The worst! One time I thought I was going on a date with this hot yoga instructor and I got there and it was his dad. His dad was there to go on the date with me. And then when you finally find someone you like, you go out once or twice and they just ghost. They disappear without a word as if you never existed. Dating is impossible for me and I'm young. I can't imagine what it would be like if I were fifty."

"I'm forty!" Janey objected with horror. Forty today wasn't her parents' forty. She was just heading off to college when Lorna turned thirty-nine. In fact, Janey believed, forty today wasn't even the forty of ten years ago. It wasn't even considered old anymore. But, no matter how much you rationalized it, this was one of those milestone years, and the birthday *had* put Janey on edge, until it came and went without any fanfare at all. She woke up the morning after her fortieth birthday and felt exactly the same.

Her cousin looked at Janey with a mixture of sympathy and skepticism. She began scrolling through her phone.

"Wow. Forty, getting divorced, and out of a job. It's like you're the poster girl for sadness." Ivy got a faraway look in her eye. "That would be a great name for a girl band . . . Poster Girl for Sadness. Anyway, what do you actually weigh?"

"I think Fiona Apple already was the poster girl for sadness back in the nineties, kid. I have no idea what I weigh," Janey said, flopping into her overstuffed armchair. "CJ wants to weigh me, but I don't have a scale."

"We can go to SoarBarre to find out," Ivy said.

"There's a scale there?"

Ivy rolled her eyes. "Are you kidding? There are like six scales. I'm teaching a class at five anyway if you wanna join."

"Is the class free?" CJ chimed in. "Do we have to sign up? Is it included in SweatGood?"

Ivy just shrugged. "Sure it's free. Be my guests. It'll be my good deed for the day. Dr. Ron has me doing a good deed every day. He's all 'what you put out into the world is what you get out of it.'"

Under her breath she added, just loudly enough for Janey to hear, "Namaste, bitches."

CHAPTER THREE

oarBarre franchises had become as omnipresent as Starbucks in neighborhoods with large populations of high-achieving women. That meant there were two within a five-block radius of Janey's Gramercy Park apartment.

The three women set out together, Ivy in the lead. She placed earbuds in her ears and ignored the others, chanting positive affirmations as they marched single file through Fifth Avenue's late-afternoon crowds.

I am peacefully allowing my life to unfold.
I take the time to show others I care about them.
I am fun and energetic and people love me for it.
I like other people. I like other people. I like other people.

Passersby gave her a wide berth on the sidewalk, the kind usually reserved for men with face tattoos. Nothing about these words made her less angry. And she hated being angry. Growing up, her family had always put a premium on niceness, and Ivy prided herself on being the nicest one out of all her four siblings. It wasn't the fake kind of nice, either; she'd derived a genuine joy from making other people smile. But her bosses at SoarBarre didn't want her to make people smile. Their customers paid more when she made them cry.

She did feel good about helping her cousin out, even if it was ridiculous that Janey needed helping at all. Janey Sweet came from what people in Charleston liked to call the "fortunate side" of the family, while Ivy was part of the "less fortunate" relations. Since Janey didn't need a job, Ivy couldn't understand why she was so upset about losing this one. Sure, no one wanted to be called fat, especially by her best friend, but Beau wasn't ever a good friend to Janey. It was so obvious that Beau loved Janey's money and status and not Janey.

She was a teenager when Janey married Michael, too young to be a bridesmaid and too old to be a flower girl. At their big fancy wedding she'd just kind of wandered around trying to find somewhere to fit in when she discovered Beau, who was Janey's best man, smoking a cigarette with Michael behind the gazebo. "Are you sure you want to do this?" she overheard Beau say to the groom. Who asked their best friend's almost husband if he was sure he wanted to marry her?

Ivy never mentioned it to Janey. It was such a weird thing to tell someone and especially hard because she was so much younger than her sophisticated older cousin. She glanced back at Janey. She wasn't fat, not by any stretch of the imagination. She was taller than average, with broad shoulders, but not thick. Ivy always told Janey that she could be Anne Hathaway's older sister with her shiny dark hair, killer cheekbones, large brown eyes, and bright red lips that never needed any lipstick.

SoarBarre was carved out of a massive neocolonial bank building from the turn of the century. The architects of New York had once given the best real estate to the places that held America's money. Now those spaces had been given over to a new obsession. The façade had its windows blacked out with a high-gloss black paint, written over in gold lettering declaring the studio's mantra: "Pain is gain." Above the entryway two massive yellow angel's wings stretched across the sidewalk toward the street, beckoning visitors to join them in this fitness heaven.

When Ivy came here for the first time she'd been intimidated and overstimulated, but now it was just the plain old place she worked. Some people worked in a cubicle and she worked in this fitness industrial complex. Some people wore suits. She wore spandex. Plenty of people would envy this life of hers, so why did she hate it so much? Huge steel doors opened into an enormous raw space where bare copper pipes and exposed air conditioner ducts formed a maze on the ceiling and a DJ perched conspicuously in a booth playing Euro-trash trance. The owners had designed the studio space themselves, and each of the locations was nearly identical, with brutalist concrete walls straight out of Communist China painted in brightly colored graffitied phrases:

PAIN IS GAIN
HURTS SO GOOD
REDUCE, REVIVE, REVITALIZE
IT'S YOUR BODY, BITCH

Giant steel stationary bikes dominated the rooms like metal insects from a steampunk future. A doctor wearing a white lab coat operated sleek metal machines in the corner. He was a recent addition. All new clients were now given a full blood analysis and genetic testing to figure out the most effective type of workout for their bodies.

"Hi, Kim." Ivy waved to the birdlike woman sitting behind the reception desk. "This is my cousin Janey and her friend CJ. They're my VVIPs today." Ivy turned to Janey and muttered, "They want everyone to feel special here so all the members are called VIPs. When we have guests we call them VVIPs or very, very important people. Makes you feel nice and squishy, don't it?"

Kim placed both her palms down on the onyx countertop, her face sour.

"Welcome to SoarBarre, Janey, CJ. And Ivy, my name is Kimberly now. Remember? I came into my wholeness last Tuesday and rediscovered my full name. We talked about this." Kimberly, formerly Kim, seemed to distrust the words as they came out of her mouth. She spoke tentatively, like a middle school teacher confronting a class of juvenile delinquents for the first time. Kimberly was one of those customers who worked behind the front desk to earn free classes. It was a brilliant scheme that could only work in the fitness world, where almost everyone except for the instructors, from the women who cleaned the bathrooms to the receptionist, provided free labor.

Ivy rolled her eyes and tried to stifle her irritation. Kim was also one of the front-row bitches, the women who clambered to sit directly in front of Ivy and delighted in her vitriol and insults. This was a person who needed much more than a name change to be happy with herself. "Yeah. Sure. Kimberly." She led the two women down a dark hallway toward the locker rooms. "I came into my wholeness today because I didn't have anything better to fucking do after my husband left me for my manny," she muttered under her breath. Kim's husband had indeed left her for their children's male caretaker last month, and since then Kim had been working double shifts and taking four SoarBarre classes a day.

Ivy caught herself and yelled over her shoulder. "You do you, Kimberly! You're a warrior queen! You're a fucking redwood." Ivy saw Janey and CJ exchange a horrified look.

"What do these classes cost?" Janey asked the two of them.

"Fifty-five dollars for a one-off spin class, a little less with a membership or the SweatGood pass," CJ answered in her know-it-all voice. "There's a sliding scale for the barre classes that starts around thirty-five dollars. There are also the new hybrid classes that are part spin, part barre, part ballet, and part kickboxing. Those are fifty dollars. But we'd be crazy to do those. The women who do those classes are out of their minds."

As usual, the locker room was packed with impossibly fit women storing high heels in tiny lockers before donning their identical SoarBarre socks (fifteen dollars at the front desk) and strapping their feet into spin cleats that resembled tennis shoes with fangs while finishing off the last drops of a sludgy maroon liquid from oversized mason jars.

Ivy was momentarily distracted as she wondered who had dictated that everything these days had to be drunk out of a mason jar. Then she saw her cousin tentatively approach a thin glass scale in the corner of the room. Janey stepped onto the delicate-looking glass, inspected the number, recoiled in horror, and stepped off before anyone else could see. Ivy walked over to pat Janey sympathetically on the back. "So how much weight do you think you've gained since the last time you weighed yourself?"

"I honestly don't know. Maybe thirty pounds? I get weighed at the doctor, but I never pay much attention. And I don't think I've gone to the doctor"—Janey ticked off time on her fingers—"in about three years."

CJ hugged her. "I'm so sorry," she said solemnly.

"My god, CJ. It's a double chin and a bit of a tummy, not a death sentence," Janey said.

"I know. I know. But I'm here for you. You're all signed up for SweatGood. I'm going to help you find the perfect organic artisanal food delivery service. I've tried them all. We've got this. The first ten will be easy. The second ten will kill you. The third ten will be the hardest thing you've done in your entire life."

Ivy liked CJ. She was funny and loyal and meant well. "Are you bitches coming to class? It's about to start and I can't keep the fatties away from the back-row bikes I saved for you for very long."

A plump girl in a too-tight green jumpsuit looked up at Ivy with adulation.

"Yeah. You're fat," Ivy said to her simply. She hated doing that, but she knew the girl would write her an amazing review later on Yelp and probably tweet how inspirational she was right after class. Why did these women want to be abused? It was so messed up.

CJ scampered behind Ivy, pulling her friend along. But Janey lingered in the doorway.

"Why the hell did you fat sluts bother to come here today?" Ivy climbed onto the pedals of her own bike, surveying the crowd with a scowl. She didn't work out during these classes or even break a sweat. She just stood high on her pedals and screamed into her headset. The bike was essentially a stage for her daily unmannerly performance. She made a few taps on her iPhone to start playing Dr. Dre's *Chronic* album. Nothing got a roomful of middle-aged white women up a hill faster than gangster rap out of Compton. "You don't deserve to be here. If you slow down I swear I will spit in your eye. SPIT IN YOUR EYE. Do you bitches hear me? Do you hear me? Do you think you're special?" She sucked a breath deep into her belly and thought about her mantras.

I am peacefully allowing my life to unfold.
I take the time to show others I care about them.
I am fun and energetic and people love me for it.
I like other people. I like other people. I like other people.

In front of Ivy five rows of women and the odd man huffed and puffed on spin bikes. The ones in the front were the ones with the fuck-off bodies who didn't need to be in a spin class that cost fifty-five dollars. They took their Fabletics halter tops off about two minutes into the class to make sure everyone saw all six of their abs as they went in for Ivy's special breed of crunches.

"It should feel like you're being punched in the gut. Banish your belly fat. You chubby bitches need to work harder," Ivy yelled. "Go faster. Be better. Embrace your pain."

CHAPTER FOUR

J aney let the substantial door of SoarBarre slam behind her as she walked into the crisp January air, trudging through slush puddles and letting the salt settle in patterns on her weathered Chanel motocross boots. Her tummy rumbled. She needed an action plan and a stop at that delicious crêperie on West Twelfth.

On the way downtown she thought about what Ivy said back at her apartment. She'd gone on a total of three dates since her separation, the most recent of which *was* six months ago. It was an acquaintance of Steven's from the boxing gym, a guy described by her best friend's husband as the "Iranian George Clooney."

"He's a professor at NYU, literature, I think . . . or maybe philosophy. Owns his own place in Williamsburg, forty-two, never married, perfect for you."

He *was* incredibly handsome with a strong jaw and a caveman's brow, which worked for him, and very cerebral. They spent one cocktail talking about Hegel, the second discussing Janey's expansion of the B brand around the world. He seemed impressed by her and she was almost ready to order a third drink and an appetizer when things took a left turn.

"Want to get some coke?" he asked nonchalantly.

"Excuse me?"

"Want to grab some cocaine?"

Janey *was* tired. "I think I'll just go home," she said and collected her jacket.

Ivy wasn't wrong. Everything about dating *was* terrible, but Janey didn't think it had anything to do with her age. She just thought finding the right person was hard and harder still when people were married before and had kids and baggage and inappropriate drug problems in their forties, despite having very nice hair and an apartment on the good side of Williamsburg.

She pulled her rabbit fur hat down over her ears. It felt nice to walk. She never did it much anymore since she was always in such a rush to get from one meeting to the next in a taxi, where it was easy to be on a conference call with the Japanese while in transit. Walking at a leisurely pace, it still took Janey just five minutes of strolling down Sixth Avenue before she crossed Fourteenth Street. Without warning large droplets of rain began falling from the sky, sending pedestrians scrambling for stores and the subway. Men selling umbrellas seemed to materialize from nowhere, now perched on upturned buckets on the edge of the sidewalk. "Eight dollars, eight dollars. For you, seven dollars," they entreated damp passersby. Janey actually liked walking in the rain, even though she couldn't remember the last time she did it. She tucked her leather Mulberry satchel beneath her jacket to keep it dry and enjoyed having the sidewalks all to herself.

The lights were dim inside the crêperie that had never had a name, and it was clearly closed. Had she ever come here before seven p.m.? Or by herself? A shop called the Wandering Juice next door appeared warm and inviting. Hadn't she promised CJ she'd keep an open mind about fitness and juice and even kale?

A kind-faced Rastafarian held the door of the Wandering Juice open for her. The small space was crowded with people trying to escape the rain. As she stood in line, a puddle formed around her on the sawdust-covered wooden floor. The interior of the juice shop was straight out of a Pinterest board for a rustic barn wedding. Reclaimed wood dominated the small space. Chairs were replaced with actual bales of hay, and the counter was constructed of five oak wine barrels. The room was lit with those old-timey lightbulbs with exposed filaments hanging from what looked like the tines of a pitchfork. A grand map dominated one wall with multicolored pins dotting the surface indicating how far a particular fruit or vegetable had traveled to end its life here in a Vitamix. Was that a chicken coop in the corner? The menu was a simple chalkboard perched precariously on the counter.

Green, Red, Orange. Those were the only options on the menu. Twenty-three dollars apiece.

"You look lost," the juice guy working the register said. She admired his blue-black curls and oddly shaped nose.

"Shouldn't you be charging more for your juice?" Janey asked, shaking the water out of her hair. "I hear Whole Foods is getting at least twenty-four dollars a bottle."

"I should just go work at Whole Foods then." He grinned, making an adorable dimple appear in his left cheek. "It gets even better. If you bring your own reusable mason jar for your juice the price gets knocked down to twenty."

"I love price discrimination. You could go work at Whole Foods, but then you wouldn't be able to raise these lovely chickens. *Are* those chickens in that coop?"

"Guinea fowl, actually. Chickens are very 2015."

"Of course," Janey said, amused by his earnestness and warmed by his cheery expression. Upon closer inspection Janey noticed distinct white polka dots on the black feathers of the caged fowl. Designer chickens! "Well, what should I order? I've never requested juice by the color before." Janey peered at the selection of fruits and powders displayed on a large tin shelf in what looked like the kind of beakers she'd used in high school chemistry class.

"What do you need juice for?" Juice Guy asked.

"Excuse me? Does juice need a purpose?" Her enthusiasm for juice was building.

"Hell yeah." He nodded, and Janey couldn't tell if he was in on the joke or the butt of it. "The juice business is built on aspiration fulfillment."

Did he just wink at her? Did anyone wink anymore?

"Do you need more energy, an immune boost, want to cure a hangover? Looking to stimulate your creativity? Some juices are even the culinary equivalent of Viagra."

A woman behind the counter with sleeves of tattooed ferns climbing both her bare arms piped up. "Try the Red. It will give you a B-vitamin blast, help feed your skin, and support hormone production. If you want a real yummy treat I can't say enough about these activated cashews. They're serious brain chemistry magic. Chase them with a shot of pressed turmeric root in freshly squeezed lime juice." Janey squinted to make out the phrase on her artfully faded tank top: "Kelp is the new kale."

"What she said," the guy agreed.

Janey let the faintest of smiles touch her lips, pleased he seemed to be taking the piss out of this. "I'll take Green."

"Good choice. Kale, broc, spinach, arugula, collards, cucumber, mint, and a little bit of basil. But the basil is my secret, so don't tell anyone."

She resisted wrinkling her nose. "Sounds lovely." The truth was that she had put *way* worse things in her mouth.

She reached for something else to say to continue the conversation. "What's with the name?" she asked coyly, chewing on the side of her bottom lip. "Wandering Juice?"

"It's a play on words. Like the wandering Jews?"

She raised both eyebrows.

"In the Old Testament of the Bible. The Jews wandered in the desert for forty years. It's also a popular houseplant. You probably have one and you don't even know it. They're very leafy and they grow like guinea fowl, which is to say very fast, as long as they have a lot of water and light."

"So you're religious and clearly into botany and exotic poultry . . . what a combo!"

"Nah. I'm a mutt. A halfie. We grew up with a Christmas tree and I got eight presents. I just like Jew puns. I went to Penn. You can major in Jew pun there."

"Ahhh, I went to Wharton."

Juice guy did a little bow. "Then you were much more sensible than I, a poor history and geology major."

Out of the corner of her eye Janey could see the young woman at the other end of the counter, the one who couldn't get enough of activated nuts, glaring at her.

Lust is in the air at the juice shop, Janey thought. Who could blame her? It was the first conversation she'd had with a man in months that she didn't want to end. But she wasn't the kind of girl who chased after someone who might be taken. She shot Fern Tattoos an honest smile to show she had no interest in intruding on her territory, took her cup of Green, and bid the cute juice guy good-bye. As she turned she felt a delicate touch on her inner arm and heard someone say, "Hello darling."

The stroke was soft and sent a tingle through her arm, but the voice was so deep Janey was surprised to see a beautiful woman standing next to her instead of a man.

"Oh my goodness, I am so sorry," the straight-backed woman said. She had the largest green eyes Janey had ever seen. "I thought you were my friend Alli. The two of you have the same black leather bomber jacket and cute ass."

Janey nodded to the stranger to show no hard feelings, but the stunning woman continued.

"Would you like to share a bit of my matcha powder for your juice? I took out too much and once you expose it to the air it begins to lose potency. I always drink it around this time of day to calm my monkey mind. I'm Stella by the way." She stretched a slender palm toward Janey but didn't stop at her hand, instead grasping her forearm.

"Strong pulse. A lot of life in there."

Janey couldn't help but smile at her before she tried to guess the woman's age. But for the first time in a long time she had no clue. Stella had the ageless face of a Ralph Lauren model, glowing, unlined, and seemingly airbrushed. In one ear hung a beautiful turquoise peacock feather that implied a certain whimsical youth, but other than that Janey couldn't tell if she was twenty-five or fifty.

"Do I look like I have a monkey mind that needs calming?"

"Yes," Stella replied matter-of-factly, rummaging around in a leather satchel for her wallet.

"Hi, Stella."

The girl behind the counter lit up. "I just read your latest blog post about harnessing the power of the new moon this month. So, so good. I sent it to everyone I know. And I took your quiz to find out my spirit animal. I'm a turtle. Do you want the usual?"

Stella nodded serenely. "I'm also going to get some of the yummy bee pollen and sit for a few minutes." She looked at Janey. "Have you had bee pollen? It's just the perfect everyday superfood!"

For the first time in as long as she could remember, Janey was in absolutely no rush. No husband. No job. No email to check. Boo Radley didn't even need walking. After wearing her busyness like a shield for so long, it was strange to admit she had all the time in the world.

"I'll join you." What did she have to lose? The two women migrated toward two empty bales of hay. The seat felt scratchy through Janey's thin cotton workout pants.

"Tell me your journey," Stella said, stirring a fine green powder that Janey assumed was the monkey-mind-calming matcha into both of their green juices.

There was something about Stella that was so peaceful and so compelling Janey suddenly felt like spilling everything: her anxiety over her career, her split with Beau, her nightly dreams about publicly humiliating Beau, her guilt at being a forty-year-old woman who didn't want kids or a husband.

"I feel like we've met before? What do you do? Are you in fashion?"

"We don't know each other yet. You can call me a healer or an intuitive. I've been called a shaman. I prefer alchemist, but no one understands what that means." She shrugged, her cascade of long hair moving in a ripple around her face. "I know things. And I help people."

Shaman? Seriously? Janey had a tendency to shudder at things her father would have referred to as "new agey hippie bullshit," and it wasn't a career choice you heard every day. It had the ring of "poet" or "adventurer," careers that rich kids with trust funds chose in order to avoid telling people they were actually unemployed.

"How do you become a shaman?" Janey was genuinely curious.

Stella lowered her voice. In whisper form it became even more husky and seductive.

"When you're eight years old you're taken away from your family and left out in the wilderness. After three days with no food or water you turn into a glorious bird with large wings and fly up above the land, shedding all of the trappings of the earth. When you return, naked as a baby, you begin your training."

"Really?" Janey felt herself starting to lean away from Stella, carefully reaching for her handbag to make a quick exit if necessary.

"No, that's a shaman joke. I grew up here. On the Upper East Side, started modeling when I was sixteen. I went for a shoot in the Peruvian Amazon, fell madly in love with the local shaman, the medicine man from an ancient Incan tribe. He taught me everything he knew and then he disappeared. Maybe he turned into a bird. Kidding! I've been traveling around the world as a healer ever since. I like marrying science with the spiritual. That's why I love this place. I feel like they're channeling the spirit of Maimonides into their juice! How about you? Wait! Don't tell me. Can I read your palm first?"

Janey raised an eyebrow. "Seriously?"

Stella's touch once again sent a tingle down Janey's spine as she grabbed her left hand in her right one. "Please. I'm still learning from this incredible astrologer and palm reader from Nepal."

Oh, what could it hurt. "Go ahead."

The woman began tracing the lines of Janey's palm with her index finger. It tickled and felt almost sensual. "What an amazing life line. This goes on forever. You are going to accomplish so much." Janey tried to keep her amusement and skepticism off her face as the shaman looked up at her. "You're so young. But this tells me you've already had two marriages. Both finished?"

A shadow of concern crossed Stella's face as Janey snatched her hand back.

"I'm sorry. Too personal?" Stella apologized with genuine sorrow.

Janey shook her head. "Just one marriage." *Unless you count Beau,* she thought to herself. But that was just ridiculous. "And yes. It ended last year. We're in the middle of finalizing the divorce."

"Ugh. Awful. Sorry again. How about we try this the normal way." Stella let go of her hand, but the warmth of her touch remained in Janey's palm. "So what do you do?"

Janey chose her words carefully. "I work in the wedding dress business, on the finance and marketing side. I recently decided to take some time off. I've been working nonstop for more than fifteen years."

Stella leaned in to listen to her. "Burnout is a real thing, love. I get it. The Internet is frying our brains. I only allow myself online for an hour in the morning and an hour in the afternoon. And can I tell you a secret?"

"Tell me."

"I get just as much accomplished as the days I used to spend staring into the abyss of my laptop. You're not alone. Everyone I know who takes time off ends up with grand intentions to write the great American novel or take a yoga teacher training class, but most of them just binge-watch Netflix or get pregnant."

"I'm getting in shape," Janey lied carefully. "I've been working out a lot."

"Great. Have you tried The Workout?"

"Which workout?"

"The Workout."

"Which one?"

"Sorry. No. It's just called 'The Workout.' A client of mine started it. Very hush-hush actually. Invite only, but, pardon my presumption, you look like the kind of girl who could probably get herself an invite."

Janey was sure this was something CJ could tell her about later. "What is it?"

"It's everything and it's nothing. It's the best workout you'll ever have and it's not a workout at all."

Stella pulled a small vellum card from her large bag. On it, in stylized type, were the words "The Workout" and an address in the financial district.

"It moves locations, but this is where it is this month. Every morning at six a.m. and every night at six p.m. The address will change again in March. I have to fly to Nairobi to work with a client tomorrow, but I'll be back next week if you want to meet me at the Tuesday morning class?"

"Sure." Janey hoped she hadn't said it too eagerly. It was a strange thing to make a new girlfriend in your thirties or forties. CJ had been a part of her life for more than twenty years and Beau even longer. They had a group of girls from school, but many of them had moved when they had kids. Janey could count on one hand the number of new friendships she'd made in the past ten years.

"Should I text you?"

"I gave up texting for the lunar New Year," Stella said, standing and tossing her juice cup into a compost bin. "Don't worry, I'll find you." She was gone as quickly as she'd appeared, leaving behind her the faint scent of magnolias. Janey turned, hoping to see the cute juice guy one more time, but he'd disappeared, leaving Fern Tattoos with her permanent scowl in his place.

Janey shook the remaining raindrops off her jacket, pulled it back on, and made for the door. She'd been so busy talking that she had only finished half the Green. Janey was worried Fern Tattoos would judge her for throwing away perfectly good juice, so she held on to the cup for the walk home. She was halfway there before she noticed that Juice Guy had scrawled his number in black marker on the side of her cup.

~

CHAPTER FIVE

**SweatGoodDaily—We Aren't a Newsletter,
We're a "Better You" Letter**

FREE THE NIPPLE YOGA WILL CHANGE YOUR LIFE

By Eden Storm Ellis

Who's sick of spending way too much money on the latest Fabletics? Why not ditch the sports bra altogether and set your nipples free—just the way Gaia Mother Earth intended.

SweatGood is so excited to announce a new member of our class pass family. Meet Elizabeth Madden. You may know her as the Naked Yogini who brought her Venice Beach style of bendiness to the West Village with her Monday night Free the Nipple Yoga class. This topless yoga class will literally change your life. Promise. Pinkies!

"Free the Nipple is all about creating a safe space for both women and men to love their bodies, and of course it's also about decriminalizing breasts. We welcome breasts of all shapes and sizes. At the end of each class you'll feel freer in every possible way. Burn your bralette and join us!" Madden said.

End class with a savasana rubdown with the Naked Yogini's juicy therapeutic-grade essential oil blends of floral waters and a yummy Kundalini meditation.

Sessions start promptly at seven p.m. in the ZenRiot space on Bank Street. There's a wait list, so make sure to sign up as soon as possible!!

Janey knew plenty of women who loved not working, but she wasn't one of them. It was only five days into her "hiatus" and she was bored out of her mind. When she wasn't attending SweatGood classes—aquatic spin, cardio tai chi, hip-hop Pilates—she paced around the apartment, puffing on the horrid mint cigarettes and going over various ways she could spend her time. Maybe she could go back to school. But what would happen when she started working again? She already had an MBA and didn't have any real interest in pursuing another degree. She could take a much-needed vacation, but everywhere she wanted to go was a delicious foodie destination—Paris, Tuscany, Barcelona— which would be counterproductive to losing weight in order to keep her job. Going to Paris without cheese, Tuscany without pasta, or Barcelona without paella was like walking into Barneys and buying gum. Everyone seemed to be knitting these days. She could make Boo Radley adorable little lamb's wool sweaters. Then there were the more serious options. When her dad passed, Janey was given a controlling interest in Sweet Chocolate. Her dad's right-hand man helmed the company, but he was in his sixties and preferred the golf course to the boardroom. He'd give the job to Janey in a heartbeat if she'd come back. For the past year she'd been listening in on conference calls once a week. It could be a seamless career transition, but she didn't know if chocolate was her future. And leaving New York now, a single woman, to settle in her hometown surrounded by happy families felt like giving up or the start of a Lifetime movie.

Blargh! She just wanted to go back to work at B.

Janey's only communication from Beau over the past week came through the delivery of a brown parcel with two smaller packages nested inside. There was no note, but Beau's home address was scrawled on the upper left-hand corner in his childish script.

One of the packages contained a terribly impressive and technologically advanced scale like the one from SoarBarre. The second—smaller and lighter—contained a slender magenta band. It was called a FitWand. CJ went gaga over it as the two women walked through the West Village to a yoga class on Monday night.

"That's the newest version. It's way better than mine." She raised her arm to show Janey a nearly identical bracelet. "It tells you pretty much anything you want to know about your body . . . weight, cholesterol, BMI, BGI, BMNOB." CJ eagerly rattled off a half-dozen acronyms. "It counts your steps, your calories, measures your metabolism, tells you how well you are sleeping. It can even tell you when you're ovulating."

"Who even knows if I still ovulate." She'd started making jokes about her dwindling fertility when she turned thirty-five. It was a defense mechanism that had become a habit. "Why do you think Beau sent these over? Do you think I should call him?" Janey asked, knowing CJ would roll her eyes, which is why she didn't admit she already *had* called him and had prepared a curt but witty little speech about the presents. She tried him three times, but he never answered. Sending her the gifts, no matter how insensitive they were, meant he was thinking about her and that meant something. Didn't it? It had to mean that this was something they'd get over.

Janey couldn't help but be a little impressed with the petite bracelet. Now that she thought about it, she'd seen these things on women's left wrists for the past year, but she assumed it was meant to support some kind of cancer charity. "I don't know if I programmed it properly. It keeps beeping and announcing things in a British accent."

On cue, the bracelet began speaking in a mechanical voice that bore more than a slight resemblance to Dame Judi Dench.

"You have only completed two hundred steps today." How was that possible? She'd walked downtown to meet CJ. That had to be at least three thousand steps? She was walking everywhere these days. Ivy had kindly dropped off a pair of bright yellow SoarBarre-branded Nike sneakers. "Good deed for the day," she'd said and rushed off. Without anything else to do each morning she just left the apartment and began walking. She must have walked the length of the High Line ten times already. There are few things more perfect than the High Line early in the morning, well before the tourists arrived. She'd dug up a book called *City Walks of New York* Lorna had sent her last year. Her mother had helpfully dog-eared the walks she thought Janey would find culturally interesting (The Museums of Fifth Avenue, A Ghost Walk of the Upper West Side). She'd placed it on her desk in a special Lorna pile, which also included interesting articles sent to her from the *Charleston Dispatch,* three cookbooks of Low Country cooking guaranteed to please your man, and photographs of Boo Radley from two months to fifteen years. Until now, she hadn't bothered to crack the spine, but now, placing a check mark next to each of Lorna's suggested walks was a satisfying way both to start the day and to remember her mother. She downloaded language apps to her phone and started learning rudimentary Chinese and French during her walks and slow jogs.

"How do I make it stop?" Janey asked CJ, tapping on the bracelet in search of an off button that didn't exist.

CJ looked perplexed. "I'm not sure. Mine doesn't talk. We'll google it later and try to figure it out."

"What kind of yoga are we doing tonight?"

CJ shrugged. "White person yoga."

"You need to walk nine thousand more steps to reach today's goal," Janey's bracelet reminded her.

As they got closer to the ZenRiot studio on Bank Street, Janey made a declaration. "I'm not taking my shirt off tonight."

"They say it's optional," her friend replied matter-of-factly. "You do you. I'm personally excited for someone to look at my bare breasts and not try to suckle."

"I don't even see the point of topless yoga, except to allow creepy hippie men to ogle my breasts in downward dog," Janey complained.

"No, no, no." CJ shook her head. "Everyone is talking about it. This is the hottest yoga class in the city right now."

"Of course everyone is talking about it. It's filled with naked women. The only thing New Yorkers like to talk about more than naked women is brunch," Janey said with confidence.

"I heard it's so much more than that. It's not about being naked. Well it *is* about being naked, but not in the way you're saying. When you don't wear a shirt the instructor can make sure you're properly aligned and then adjust you correctly into the poses. They also turn the thermostat way, way up so you are sweating out all your toxins. If you sweat when you're wearing cotton then every single chemical that has ever been used to clean your clothes sinks into your pores and poisons your nervous system. It makes so much sense when you actually think about it."

"None of that is true," Janey replied, rolling her eyes.

"It is. I read it on Goop."

She wanted to ask when the editors at Goop had become experts in neurological toxicology but decided to change the subject instead. If CJ read something on Goop there was no changing her mind.

"You're limping," Janey said, staring down at her friend's left foot as they sped up to beat a yellow light crossing Greenwich Avenue.

"I'm not." CJ winced and stepped up her pace.

"Now you're just limping fast. What's going on?"

Her friend sighed. "I have SoarBarre foot."

"Excuse me?"

"SoarBarre foot . . . it's like tennis elbow, but from spinning too much. I went to the doctor last night. It's the new normal. He says he's seeing at least six cases a week. It's not broken or anything, the nerves have just gone into stasis."

"Stasis?"

CJ gave a resolute shrug. "Like a coma. The nerve endings go to sleep. The foot feels tingly. It's hard to put weight on. Totally no big deal."

Janey watched her carefully as CJ began making a concerted effort to put weight on the foot, grimacing with each step and finally grabbing the crook of Janey's arm to steady herself.

"I don't believe this is a thing."

"It's a thing! But it isn't a big deal," CJ said at the same time Janey blurted out, "You can't feel your damn foot. You shouldn't be walking, much less coming with me to yoga. Come on, let's just go home. We can grab takeout and eat with the twins."

CJ sped up again, her hobble more pronounced as she rounded the corner. "No! Absolutely not! We'll be charged the motivation tax. This week they're donating to Donald Trump's next presidential campaign. I am *so* fine. And I need to bikini tone before Steven and I go to St. Barts next month. That's not happening just eating clay."

The Naked Yogini's class was on the second floor of a posh West Village townhouse. Janey allowed CJ to grasp her elbow so she could drag her immobile SoarBarre foot uselessly behind her as the two women climbed the staircase.

Elizabeth Madden, the yoga instructor, greeted the two women at the door, wearing dark brown leather booty shorts and no top. Her breasts were tiny and taut, her nipples alert. A thin gold band ran from her slender neck, down between her breasts, and then looped back around her skeletal midriff. Her exposed skin shimmered with some kind of gold glitter. A beaded headband held her blond curls off her high forehead.

Janey tried desperately to maintain eye contact. She couldn't explain it, but these yoga instructors, gurus, and fitness mavens all intimidated her just a little bit. Anytime they approached her she felt an immediate and irrational sensation of desperately wanting them to like her.

"Welcome to Free the Nipple. I honor you," the instructor said in a serene Australian accent. "Feel free to place your bags in the back. You may hang your coats and your shirts up on the rack in the corner. I have something for you." The woman grasped Janey's hand and opened her palm, placing a smooth white stone in it with no explanation.

Tall, willowy white curtains framed floor-to-ceiling windows. Janey looked at the rows of colorful mats, each one occupied by a topless human. There were more than thirty people sardined into the room, not a single speck of floor between the foam. A large mahogany Buddha with a fuchsia face and shiny bald head took up residence in the corner, his own bare chest and big belly set in a smile.

"You said it was optional . . . taking off your shirt," Janey whispered to CJ. "Everyone in here has his or her shirt off. I think I see Anderson Cooper over there without his shirt on. I can't have Anderson Cooper seeing me topless."

"They're all exercising their option," CJ hissed back as the two women moved through the room, keeping their eyes glued to the floor. "What are you so worried about? You have great boobs. I breast-fed twins. I have udders! And Anderson Cooper is in the front row. There's no way he'll see you. Also, you're not his type."

Janey slowly removed her shirt, pulling one arm in and then the other, letting it hang around her neck for a moment, before finally lifting it over her head in submission to peer pressure. She hated being naked in front of strangers. It was one of many reasons she'd never gone to Burning Man, even after it became trendy for fashion designers and tech billionaires to attend the desert festival and exercise their right to take mushrooms and have sex with strangers without judgment.

"Let's put our mats in the back." Janey found enough room for two yoga mats in the very back corner next to an electrical outlet, above which was painted the word RECHARGE.

"Fine by me." CJ patted her belly. "I'm wearing control-top leggings to cover most of my stomach. Same ones I used when I was pregnant."

Janey's shoulders involuntarily curled in toward her breasts to provide them shelter, but no one paid her any mind. Their eyes were already closed, their mouths set in composed lines. There were only four men in the class, and none of them was obviously a pervert. Besides Anderson Cooper, they each had hair that hung below their ears and tattoos in Sanskrit. The women's breasts came in all shapes and sizes, and Janey couldn't help but examine them. There were round nipples and oval nipples. There were nipples in the shape of Idaho. Some breasts hung low, others pointed in two different directions.

"Excuse me, excuse me," came a shrill voice attached to the woman with the mat next to Janey's. She was wearing a black T-shirt that read KINDNESS IS MY RELIGION. "Her mat is touching mine. Your mat is touching mine," Kindness shrieked at the woman on the other side of her, a slight girl with frizzy auburn hair. "I can't get settled while your mat touches mine. I can't get my fucking zen! Move it. You need to move it now!" The girl's face began to crumple as though she might burst into tears. She slowly shifted her mat, and Kindness sank down to the ground and removed the mantra T-shirt, revealing two surgically altered domes.

For some reason the lyrics to "La Vie Bohème" from the musical *Rent* popped into Janey's head right then. She'd seen the show on Broadway with Beau four times. *To yoga, to yogurt, to rice and beans and cheese* . . . Neither bohemia nor bonhomie was alive in this room.

A very pregnant woman pulled her mat in front of Janey's. "Congrats," Janey whispered and smiled.

The woman grinned beatifically back. "You too. How far along are you?" The woman was staring at Janey's stomach.

Don't be rude, Janey thought. "Just a couple of months," she whispered back.

Elizabeth Madden slid gracefully to the front of the room. "Can we all start in a comfortable seated position? I know all of you are anxious to begin. But before we do let's review the pillars of confidence. First off we must have a poised posture as we take to our mats. Shoulders back and down. We set our gaze with intent. Focus your eyes like you mean it. Tap into the primal power of your body as you move. And remember, this is a safe space. You may feel vulnerable in a new and unique way. Embrace it! This is a place to eradicate all of your fears."

"Can I tell her I want to eradicate my fear of my inner thighs rubbing together in shorts?" Janey whispered.

CJ considered it and nodded. "It's valid." CJ looked up at Elizabeth Madden's lithe frame. "I'm so glad she's skinny. I never trust overweight yoga instructors."

Janey rolled her eyes. She had no particular antipathy toward overweight yoga instructors. It bugged her that a 200-hour certificate course made them feel and act superior to you in every aspect of life. "Being skinny isn't the point of yoga," Janey said, moving her mat inches away from Kindness, who was sitting in lotus position with her eyes closed.

CJ looked at Elizabeth one more time. "Sure, it's about balance and happiness. But if you're really balanced and happy, then why aren't you also thin?"

The Naked Yogini instructed them to close their eyes and focus on their inner child.

"We will begin together with three chants of om."

Janey sucked a breath deep into her belly, keenly aware that the instructor and anyone who chose to turn her head could see the air rippling through her chest and into her bare stomach. The air somehow became heavy with the scent of jasmine.

"Ommmmmmmmmmmmmmmmmmm," the entire class chanted together in unison.

"Ommmmmmmmmmmmmmmmmmm."

"You have walked twelve hundred steps today. You are at only ten percent of your goal. Your heart rate is below average," came an aristocratic British voice from Janey's wrist.

Shit, Janey thought. *How do I turn the FitWand off?* This was the last thing she needed. All the peaceful yogis opened their eyes and craned their necks to stare at her. Anderson Cooper was staring at her with a confused look on his face. She fumbled with the bracelet while trying to cover her exposed nipples with her forearms.

"I'm sorry. I'm sorry. Go on—I mean go om—without me."

Janey pulled the wretched device off her wrist and laid it flat under her mat, hoping to suffocate the disembodied voice.

To her credit, Elizabeth Madden showed no trace of annoyance. Nothing could fuck up her zen.

"Okay then, one more om and we move into our downward dogs."

The FitWand continued in its condescending monotone. "Move faster. You need to move faster. You are burning no calories." Out of the corner of her eye she could see CJ teetering on three limbs instead of four before she collapsed in a heap on her pink yoga mat.

"I can't put weight on my foot," CJ whispered.

"I know. That's why you shouldn't be here."

The rest of the class was a haze of limbs and affirmations. Within five minutes Janey forgot she wasn't wearing a top, even when Elizabeth Madden came over to adjust her into a more perfect version of warrior two, squatting behind her and wrapping her own arms under Janey's armpits. Janey could feel the yogini's pert breasts pushing into her own shoulder blades as she pulled her shoulders in line with her hips. Janey could hear her mother's gravelly voice in her head instructing her to cover up. Nice southern girls were more modest than this. But here Lorna's daughter was, stretching her arms high above her head, bosom bare to the world and prime-time news anchor, feeling an intense sensation of freedom.

There was just one occasion during warrior three where she had to reach over to prop CJ up. Ninety minutes went by in a blur. Before she knew it Janey was prone on her back in savasana with Elizabeth Madden massaging her temples in a counterclockwise motion with an oil that smelled like eucalyptus. Doing this to each and every person in the class made the practice of lying in corpse pose last an additional fifteen minutes. But it was nice. Janey could feel the tension wound tight around her spine melt down into the floorboards. Her body temperature began to dip, and she shivered. Without having to say anything Elizabeth came by to drape her in a hemp blanket.

Janey felt so relaxed in her warm cocoon, she drifted off to sleep, only coming to with a startled gasp when the rest of the class began chanting their final oms. She was almost disappointed it was over.

"How are you feeling?" CJ asked her cautiously as Janey searched the coatrack self-consciously for her sweater. This was clearly the awkward bit of the class. It was like the morning after a drunken hookup. Now they avoided eye contact and hunched slightly as they rummaged for their clothing. It was one thing to be naked during group exercise, another thing entirely to be braless while you searched for your cell phone in your purse.

"I feel pretty damn good."

In response, Janey's FitWand, which had remained wonderfully silent since the start of the class, retorted, "You are not working up to your potential."

Trying to adjust the wretched device with one hand and cover her chest with the other, Janey turned directly into a man sidestepping his own way to the jackets.

"Oh hey. Fancy meeting you here, Green."

"Excuse me?" Janey looked up, startled.

"Green juice. That's what you got at my shop last week, right? I never forget a color." His dimples bounced up and down when he smiled. "You never texted me."

It was the handsome man from Wandering Juice.

"Of course," Janey motioned with her elbow for CJ to wait up for a second. "Hi. How are you? What are you doing here?"

"Yoga?" he said, raising both eyebrows.

Janey laughed. She liked the way he was looking at her and the fact that he managed to maintain eye contact. "Yeah, me too." She didn't know what to say next. "I was just thinking maybe my friend and I should stop in for a juice after this class."

He glanced behind him, looking to see if someone was waiting for him, Janey assumed. "Sadly, I won't be there. I have to go straight home. I like to see my daughter before she goes to bed."

Janey didn't know why she was surprised that he was a dad. Probably because he looked so young, definitely under thirty.

"I do have to run," he continued. "But I would love to take you out for a drink sometime. It can be any color you want. It doesn't even have to have kale in it."

Was he asking her out on a date? She remembered his number scrawled on the side of her juice cup. She'd been flattered but had ignored it because it felt peculiar to call a complete stranger. When was the last time she'd been asked out on a proper date? She knew she'd never been asked out on a date when she was standing topless in a room of strangers.

Would she have said yes to the juice guy a month ago? Probably not. She would have said she was too busy with work. But right now she could think of few things better than staring at his dimples for a couple more hours. She reached into her bag and fished out her card, letting both her arms drop to her sides and subsequently freeing her nipples. She handed it to him with a smile.

"My email's on here."

CHAPTER SIX

J aney had a perfectly awful long-term memory, but one of the earliest things she could recall was Miss Lorna catching her in a silly lie about whether or not she'd snuck downstairs in the middle of the night and eaten the cookies Lorna had baked specially for a Rotary Club luncheon. Janey was four then and was old enough to know better, but her mother's butterscotch truffle cookies were the best things she'd ever tasted. If heaven existed, the way Reverend Paul insisted over and over that it did on Sunday mornings, then it was a place filled with Lorna's butterscotch truffle cookies. Miss Lorna gave her a talking to that caused the little girl to burst into tears and Lorna's heart to melt. Her mother reversed course and pulled a Sweet chocolate bar out from the cupboard to give to the wailing child. From then on, when terrible things happened that were out of her control, Janey turned to chocolate. But Janey was a good daughter. She lived to please her parents, and the two of them had no reason to reprimand her again until her freshman year of high school, when Beau convinced her to borrow Reginald's car while her parents were away at a confectioners' conference in the Outer Banks. He'd somehow gotten the two of them tickets to a Pearl Jam concert thirty minutes outside of town. Both kids were going through a short-lived but passionate grunge phase wherein they both wished they could lose their virginity to Eddie Vedder. The problem with driving to the concert wasn't evading the eye of the Sweet housekeeper who was keeping watch on Janey that weekend. It was the fact that they were both fourteen and two years shy of having an actual driver's license. But she'd never been able to say no to Beau. Besides, she knew how to drive a car. Reginald had been teaching her stick shift in the chocolate factory parking lot since she was twelve. Being the responsible one, Janey had limited her consumption for the evening to one can of warm Bud Light, but Beau had managed to procure a plastic baggie filled with what he claimed were magic mushrooms, and on the way home he began singing and dancing along to the *Ten* album. When he began pounding on the dash and wailing, "Jeremy spoke in. Spoke in, spoke in, classssssss today," he flung an arm out in front of Janey, pretending it was a microphone, and invited her to join him for the next song. She was already distracted by the milky fog rolling in from the swamps, and trying to quiet Beau didn't help. So of course she didn't see the whitetail buck before it leapt in front of the car. When it did, she slammed on the brakes and skidded into a ditch on the side of the road, narrowly avoiding the animal and hurling them both toward the dashboard. The two of them were shaken but unharmed. The car, of course, wouldn't start, and Janey said she'd hike to the gas station down the street to call the police for help. When she'd returned Beau was nowhere to be found. He'd run off into the woods and hidden, afraid the police would arrest him for being high. The police did bring Janey into the station for driving without a license, and she shouldered the blame for the entire incident.

Reginald grounded Janey for six months after he'd screamed and yelled and cursed the fact that he had to come home from the beach a day early and missed the round robin golf tournament of leading chocolate makers from around the country. Of course, later that night Lorna came up to her room with a gallon of mint chocolate chip ice cream to tell her that even though she'd been an incredibly naughty girl, she was just happy that she was safe.

Why was she thinking about that night now? She'd always excused Beau's leaving that night. He *was* high on mushrooms. He didn't know what he was doing. But he'd still abandoned her to get into all of the trouble with her parents. He could have at least stayed and held her hand. Beau's mother never would have found out what happened. Not that she would have cared.

Janey was having a horrible time getting to sleep anyway. No matter what she did, her FitWand would not stop announcing her vital statistics at least once an hour, urging her to move more and then systematically insulting her when she ignored it.

Wasn't it supposed to help track your REM sleep or something? Didn't it know it was the middle of the night?

Janey finally hid it in the freezer, afraid if she threw it out the window it would sprout legs, find its way back to her, and force her to do burpees. And on her way back to bed she grabbed a handful of Sweets from inside the cupboard.

Even with the voice silenced, she tossed and turned. Back when they were married, Michael slept on the right side of the bed and Janey slept on the left. No matter where they were in the world or whose bed they were sleeping in, they adhered to this natural order of things. Her husband had been a light sleeper, so after they kissed good night, Janey never dared to stray to his side. Even after Michael left, by force of habit, she remained on her side of the bed. Slowly, slowly, she infringed on his former territory. Now she found herself rolling about from one side of the California king to the other. She'd thought it much too large when they bought it, but now she couldn't imagine sleeping in anything smaller. She loved this bed so much more now that she had it all to herself. She thumbed through the music on her phone until she came to Pearl Jam. When had she downloaded this? She began playing "Jeremy" softly until she finally drifted off to sleep.

Come morning Janey was so groggy she almost considered not showing up to The Workout that day, but the draw to see Stella again was strong. She'd done a little bit of Google stalking to find the shaman, and it proved harder than she'd originally suspected. How many professional shamans lived in Manhattan anyway? According to her phone there were thirty-seven—men, women, old, young. Stella was in good company. One shaman was the former CFO of Coach, another the child star of a hit eighties sitcom that did very well in syndication. It wasn't even that hard to become a shaman. There were six-week online shaman certification programs and shaman retreats to places like Peru, Brazil, Argentina, and St. Barts.

She went back and forth on the idea of staying in bed for another ten minutes and then decided that something about the bewitching stranger was more captivating than a lie-in.

She treated herself to an Uber downtown, whizzing quickly through the predawn empty streets at five-thirty in the morning. It was the one hour where the city grew quiet. The late-late-night crowd had finally stumbled into someone's bed, and run-of-the-mill early risers wouldn't be up and out for another fifteen minutes. Bleary-eyed, Janey stared at the metal buttons on a doorbell outside a nondescript building on Pearl Street, looking for The Workout studio.

Janey glanced over her shoulder. Surely someone else would be by soon who would have a better idea of what bell to ring, where to go.

Just as Janey was about to give up, her finger poised above her phone to order another Uber back uptown, three tall and slender women wrapped in near-identical black cashmere coats stepped out of a sleek town car. Janey was sure that she recognized one of them. *Was that Miranda?* It had to be. She had that characteristic gap between her two front teeth and her eyes were an unnaturally light shade of grey.

"Miranda Mills?" Janey said with confidence. "How are you? It's me, Janey Sweet."

Miranda Mills began her career as a model in the late nineties and had evolved from heroin chic to homegrown glamour girl to wonder mom to the first plus-sized model to appear on the cover of one of the major fashion magazines. Janey remembered that Miranda had been a size 22, but now she appeared to have shrunk back to a size that would be startling anywhere but New York City.

"Janey! Hi! Oh my gosh. It's been ages. I don't think I've seen you since I dropped all the weight. I must look like a completely different human now." If Janey was being honest, Miranda looked like a human covered over in another human. He skin seemed permanently detached from her face and neck, having expanded and contracted so many times it had finally given up.

"You look great," Janey said as the two women exchanged obligatory dual-cheek kisses and a mannered hug. Miranda's shoulder felt frail beneath Janey's arms.

"You're here for The Workout, right? How did you meet Sara Strong?"

The name Sara Strong was definitely familiar. Had she read about her in the SweatGood newsletter?

"Around."

Miranda nodded, indicating she also knew Sara Strong from "around."

Janey remembered Stella telling her that the location for this exercise class often changed.

"I've been in Shanghai for work for the past few weeks waiting for samples to come in," she lied. "This is a new location, right?"

Now it was Miranda's turn to nod. "Brand-new. I've only just started coming myself. Before this, though, Sara was hosting it in Kate Wells's apartment. It was so hush-hush, the two of them were like best friends, you know?"

Kate Wells was that actress everyone loved to hate. She'd grown up in New York City, the daughter of a movie producer and actress, had attended the poshest private schools, and then moved to Hollywood at age eighteen and won her first Academy Award at age twenty-three. She was blond and beautiful and married to a rock star. Several years ago she began blogging about her very perfect life on her website, Lovely, which she treated like her personal diary, complete with copious amounts of xoxoxos. The site was famous for blog posts about four-hundred-dollar flip-flops, breast-feeding five-year-olds, and how you simply cannot trust your well-tipped concierge's recommendations when you are vacationing in Milan/London/Paris. She'd recently made headlines when she announced she was giving up acting to focus full time on Lovely.

"The universe is telling me I need to focus on this twenty-four seven right now, and I can't tell the universe no," she'd laughed to Matt Lauer on the *Today* show a few weeks earlier.

"Were best friends?" Janey asked curiously.

Miranda lowered her voice. "They had a falling-out. The Workout is supposed to be supersecret, you know, but Kate cannot keep anything private. She wrote a whole essay about it on Lovely, and Sara Strong was so mad she stopped talking to her. It's very recent."

"So they've moved The Workout here to the penthouse. I think it's owned by some Saudi sheik whose wife swears The Workout changed her life. I'm so happy to see you here." Miranda pushed the button for P and the door buzzed open almost instantly. She seemed to forget the two women with her until the four of them were waiting for the elevator. Janey estimated that they were about ten years Miranda's junior.

"I'm the worst. Sorry. Janey Sweet, these are my friends from school. Our kids are in the same class at City and Country. Janey is the brains behind B wedding dresses. She runs the company." Miranda unhelpfully did not provide the women's names.

"Really?" Mommy number one, a pale woman with heavy-lidded eyes and a tiny rosebud of a mouth, was suddenly interested in her. "I wore a B gown for my wedding last year."

"Which one?" Janey gave her a polite smile.

"It was the Eliza in champagne."

There was one season where Beau went through a *Hamilton*

phase, listening to the musical's original cast recording on repeat in their office and naming all of their styles things like the Eliza, the Angelica, the Schuyler, and the Miranda, named after Lin-Manuel. Of course. With her own minor in American history, Janey got a real kick out of Beau as a burgeoning history buff obsessed with the country's founding fathers, if only for a fleeting moment.

"Beautiful dress. Wonderful choice. Where did you get married?" Janey had perfected the art of feigning interest in the intricate details of other people's weddings.

"Here in the city. At the Public Library."

"The perfect venue." It was a ridiculously expensive venue. Janey knew that it cost a mere $100,000 just to rent the space before paying for food or service.

"I kept the dress for my daughter. I can't wait to tell her I met the designer!"

"Oh, I'm not the designer," Janey said humbly. "I just run the business side of things."

This was clearly less interesting to Mommy number one, who changed the subject once the elevator doors opened.

"Do you come to The Workout often? I don't think I've seen you before."

"Not as often as I'd like," she replied.

"I know what you mean." She nodded in agreement. "I just need more hours. Right now I only get to train about three hours every day."

"Training? How cool. Are you doing the New York City Triathlon? That's coming up, right? God you're brave. There's not enough money in the world to get me to jump in the Hudson."

Mommy number two fixed Janey with a cool stare, her upturned nose making the slightest twitch. "We aren't doing a race. It's just our daily fitness regimen."

"You work out three hours a day for fun?" Janey asked as they approached the top floor. As Mommy number two's coat fell open, Janey could see that working out twice a day was probably nonnegotiable if she wanted to contain her body in her skintight soft grey ballerina-style leotard finished off with grey cashmere leg warmers.

Mommy number one grew serious. "Oh, there's nothing fun about it." She looked at Janey's wrist. "Nice. I have one just like it." The woman held up her own delicate arm to display her own rubber bracelet. "My husband loves it."

"Oh, does he have one too?" Janey asked out of politeness. This might have been the slowest elevator ride of her life.

The woman shook her head. "No. But if I don't reach twenty-five thousand steps a day I have sex with him to make up for the missing calories."

Before Janey could respond the elevator doors finally opened into a grand space. The penthouse apartment took up the entire fifty-fourth floor, with windows on all sides providing sweeping 360-degree views of both rivers, five bridges, the Statue of Liberty to the south, and Central Park to the north.

Janey craned her neck, looking for Stella, but saw only a sea of grey. Not a single person was wearing a speck of color in this room. Not even the odd white.

Miranda and the mommies took off their coats to reveal three near-matching light grey workout outfits.

Thankful she hadn't worn her purple spandex, Janey still felt out of place in her black Lulu once she removed her own camel hair overcoat. Wasn't matching outfits the step before drinking the Kool-Aid?

Janey could feel even more color rise into her cheeks as Stella strode gracefully across the room to greet her with a warm hug. She too was clad in grey tones—leggings and a long flowy top that reached to midthigh. On her hands were fingerless grey cashmere gloves that reached to her elbows.

"You made it. I'm so glad." Stella lowered her voice. "I feel terrible. I forgot to tell you about the grey. I think it's a bit silly myself. Sara Strong wants everyone in the class to wear grey. She says it's this great equalizer in addition to being color therapy. I prefer a hint of pink myself, but what are you gonna do? Let's grab a tea. Everyone starts the class with Sara's very special tea. There's nothing like it. I keep trying to get Sara to give me the secret, but she is completely mum about it."

In the corner of the room stood a beautiful hand-carved oak table on which burned a couple of huge black candles next to a monstrous iron cauldron and stacks of copper cups.

Stella expertly dipped a ladle into the black pot and poured the tawny liquid into a cup for Janey. The smell was delicately intoxicating, and the warmth radiated from her hands into the rest of her body.

"Wow. This *is* good."

"I know, right? Stella turned to Janey. "I want to introduce you to Sara, but we'll have to do it after class. We only have a minute or two now. It starts promptly at six. The door is already locked. No exceptions."

The penthouse held about twenty-five women—all of them already incredibly fit and already standing in five rows of five with an arm's length between one another.

Janey recognized quite a few of B's former couture wedding clients, all of them looking much skinnier than they had been on their actual wedding days. Other members of The Workout were actresses, hipster socialites, yummy mummies, and models.

The room grew silent as the clock struck six. A door slammed near the elevator and a tiny woman with dark brown hair extensions reaching below her tailbone strode to the front of the room. She let loose a primal scream so loud the windows rattled.

The rest of the room followed suit. It was clear that Janey was the only newbie here. There was no introduction necessary.

This was Sara Strong.

With the remnants of the scream still lingering in the room, Sara smiled, and Janey remembered CJ making her scream and hop like a bunny in her apartment the day after Beau threw down the gauntlet.

"Good morning, fellow seekers. I'm filled with gratitude that you're all here. This morning during my meditation I couldn't get some valuable thoughts out of my head. I wrote them down so that I could share them with you this morning. When things like this come to me, I know it's the universe asking me to share its wisdom with you. Here's what it told me this morning: I know we are often comparing ourselves to other women who may be younger and more fit than we are. The problem is that every year as we get older we have a larger group to compare ourselves to. Stop comparing. Acknowledge other people's greatness and you will be more powerful and centered. Others will notice and embrace your confidence. There's nothing sexier than someone who is content with herself and trying every single day to be better and improve on her own terms."

Janey looked around to see the other women nodding. One even wiped away a tear.

"Okay, Tabata time." Sara quickly shifted gears into workout mode, walking catlike on her tiptoes across the front of the room. Thus began a portion of the class that involved thirty seconds of intense activity—jumping jacks, high leg kicks, push-ups, sit-ups, squat thrusts—followed by ten seconds of rest. By the end of ten minutes Janey's heart rate was through the roof, her back drenched with sweat, and she was ready to let loose her own primal scream. It felt fucking good.

"Now plank."

The class moved seamlessly into a plank position, holding their arms and their core rigid for three straight minutes. No one groaned and fell to the floor when it was over. Sara passed part of the time with a well-enunciated reading of the Khalil Gibran poem "On Pain."

Your pain is the breaking of the shell that encloses
your understanding . . .

They dropped plank and moved into Brazilian street dance. Ten minutes of arms waving and legs kicking to the beat of steel drums. The rhythm was mesmerizing, almost magical.

"Find a partner across the room from you, make eye contact, but don't go to her. Mirror her movements. Be conscious in your dance. Release your inner little girl. She's been waiting for this moment. She wants to play!" Sara Strong commanded as she undulated her own body to the beat.

Janey felt strange. Her limbs tingled, she felt almost turned on as she followed Stella's lead, watching the shaman's long hair whip around her head as she moved in a sensuous rhythm with the drums. She didn't even break pace as she pulled her hair on top of her head into a bun.

Next they split into four groups, each moving into a corner of the room, taking turns climbing a hefty braided rope that reached to the high ceiling, the same kind of rope they had all probably climbed in middle school gym class.

As she clung to the rope for dear life, Janey began to sweat like she'd never sweated before. Below her the rest of her cohort clapped, whooped, and did squat thrusts until she made it down. Her arms shook like fragile twigs as she gripped the rough fibers.

Back on the floor, Janey found herself enveloped in hugs from complete strangers.

Suddenly, Sara Strong leapt into the air and screamed again: "YEEEEEEEEEEEEEEEEEEEEEEEEEEEE!" This time the sound was more shrill. Once again, the whole class joined in.

"YEEEEEEEEEEEEEEEEE!"

And then came CJ's favorite: "PAHHHHHHHHHHHHHHHHHHH-HHHHHHHHH!"

Nonsense words and sounds escaped the mouths of Manhattan's finest and fittest.

Sara raised her arms skyward for a final scream before dropping into a heap on the floor. The rest of the class followed suit, curling into the fetal position on their right sides. Out of the silence came a gentle melody. The sweet sounds of . . . was that "Rock-a-bye Baby"? The lullaby? Because Janey had never had kids and because she was an only child, she had probably spent less time around babies than the average forty-year-old woman. Still, she knew the sound of a baby's cry when she heard one after spending many, many evenings sleeping at CJ's when her own apartment was being redone during the twins' colicky period. She should have sprung for a hotel then, but CJ and Steven's house practically *was* a hotel with their six bedrooms, three floors, and basement sauna. At least once a night, one of the twins wailed for an hour. Just seconds after the first was comforted and quieted, the second one would steal the spotlight and begin his own solo.

But those boys had nothing on the sound Janey heard now. She couldn't help but sit up to confirm her suspicion that the sound of a baby crying was coming from the mouth of the fitness instructor in the front of the room, rocking back and forth to the tune of "Rock-a-bye Baby." As the rest of the class followed suit, making their own baby cries, wails, and snuffs, Sara Strong appeared to compose herself.

"That's right. Let your inner child out. You're safe now. You're back in the womb. Nothing can hurt you here. This is a time to become who you really want to be."

And then, just as quickly as it had all begun, the class was over.

"Wait a minute. I didn't pay for the class," Janey said to Stella as the two women put on their coats.

Stella shook her head. "You pay what you wish. There's a donation box when you walk in the door. I paid a little something extra for you today."

Janey was perplexed.

"How does she manage to make any money?"

"People *pay* what they wish. Her class works for them and clients compensate her properly for it. Trust me. Sara Strong is no longer hurting for money. I've seen clients drop hundreds in the box." They made their way over to the elevator. Janey would have liked another cup of that delicious tea, but the grand table had been removed from the room. All around them, women hustled toward the door.

"But she *was* hurting for money?" Janey suddenly wanted to know everything about this mysterious woman who had disappeared as soon as the class was over. "When?"

"She was broke." As they rode the elevator alone, Stella went on to explain that Sara was a successful banker for fifteen years, married to the equally successful owner of a tech hedge fund. After the most recent stock market crash, Sara Strong's husband had been indicted for investing lots of money that wasn't his in funds in the Cayman Islands that didn't really exist. The Feds took all their money and he was sent off to a fancy country club prison in Virginia. It didn't help that Sara was pregnant at the time. She gained more than sixty pounds during the pregnancy and then thirty more after the birth to deal with the stress of being a single mother and a pariah in the financial services industry. She sold the one thing she had left—their house in Connecticut—and dedicated herself full-time to physical fitness and wellness while living in a studio apartment with her little girl. After a year, she lost the weight, dropped her husband's last name, and completely reinvented herself. She first met up with Kate Wells one day at SoarBarre, where Kate had complimented her on her incredible triceps (even better than Michelle Obama's), and a friendship grew from there. Sara became her exclusive personal trainer and eventually corralled all of Kate's contacts into a new and intense fitness regimen designed exclusively by Sara—The Workout. Then the pair had their mysterious falling-out. Kate was banned from class, but her friends were there to stay. Workout devotees claimed they dropped 20 percent of their body weight by attending The Workout twice a week for one month.

"Wow," Janey said. "Impressive. I'm still shocked I never heard of it."

"Sara is all over Instagram, and she writes for all the major wellness outlets. She's still a top private personal trainer, but she doesn't advertise this. She doesn't have to. The secrecy is part of what keeps it special." Stella winked, pulling her hair out of its bun and transforming it into an elaborate braid. "I don't know if I buy the twenty percent of your body weight. Nor do I really care. I'll take a strong body over a thin one any day. But The Workout does make you feel great. Don't you feel so energized right now?"

Janey did. It was as though she'd already had three cups of coffee and a bar of chocolate all before eating breakfast.

"Stella!" Janey heard a calm but energetic voice call after them down the street. Wearing nothing over her grey halter top to protect her from the cold, Sara Strong herself was now chasing them down Market Street.

Up close she had an undeniable glow, Windex-blue eyes, and the whitest teeth Janey had ever seen. She didn't appear to be the least bit cold, even though Janey shivered just looking at her.

"Aren't you freezing?" she asked and pulled her own coat more tightly around her midsection.

Sara laughed. "My heart rate is so high right now I could jump in the Hudson and still be warm. Mind over matter. You feel what you think." Her accent was strange, maybe a little midwestern, but with the undertones of an Irish lilt.

Stella introduced the two women. For a moment Janey worried she'd be rebuked for coming to The Workout without a personal invitation, but Sara just smiled broadly at her.

"Janey Sweet. What a gorgeous name. Thanks for coming. What did you think?"

What *did* Janey think? Could she admit it began as sixty minutes of pure torture and that she now felt like she could lift a Volkswagen over her head?

"It was good. Your story is incredible. Stella was telling me. So inspiring."

Sara waved her hand in the air. "We all have a story. What happened to me is nothing in the grand scheme of things. I've just been lucky to have such incredible people help me on my journey. And now you're a part of that journey. Thank you. You'll be back again, I hope?"

"I think I probably will be," Janey said, knowing it was true. She felt good, and if she was able to burn as many calories as Stella claimed, she could be back to work in no time.

"Great. It's so nice to have you." She turned her attention to the shaman.

"Stella, I have a thousand details I need to figure out for St. Lucia. Can we FaceTime later?"

"Of course." The two women kissed three times, once on the right cheek, once on the left, and once more on the right, and Sara sashayed back down the street.

"What's happening in St. Lucia?" Janey asked with genuine curiosity.

"Oh, The Workout is having a retreat there. This is the second year we've done it. They call it ReVigor-8. Last year was incredible. Eight days of The Workout at the most perfect compound on the north coast there. It's owned by this wonderful interior designer and her husband. They built it ten years ago as a place for their friends and family to escape New York and it is simply divine."

For a second Janey assumed Stella was about to invite her, but the words just hung there in the air.

"When is it?" Janey pressed.

"At the end of next month. March is just the worst month to be in Manhattan. It's the perfect time to get out of town and get to the beach."

"It does sound divine."

A shadow crossed Stella's face. "I'd love to invite you, but Sara is so stingy with the ReVigor-8 invites. It's not my place. I help her out and I run all sorts of ceremonies while we're there, but I don't have control over the guest list."

"Of course not. No. I get it. I don't even know if I'm in town at the end of March. I may need to go to Shanghai to sort out some samples." *Jesus,* Janey thought, *when did Shanghai become my go-to fib? I need to stop telling everyone I'm flying off to Shanghai.*

"I should really get home. I didn't take Boo, the dog, out this morning, and he is probably very, very angry with me." She realized that she still had no way of getting in touch with Stella, but the woman answered Janey's question without her having to ask it.

"Janey.Sweet@B.com, right? I'll email you. I have something fun happening later this week."

"Great." It should have felt creepy that Stella knew her email address off the top of her head, but it didn't. With that, a black car appeared out of nowhere in a sea of early morning taxi traffic. Stella blew her a kiss and folded her long body into the car.

"I'd give you a ride, but I'm off to Brooklyn for a townhouse cleansing ceremony. Bad juju in the place. Brutal divorce. Husband is bringing me in to clear the negative energy out before he brings the kids back from boarding school. Wife is off in Paris with her new boy toy. Never a dull moment when it comes to humans. Do something nice for yourself today!"

Janey walked the forty blocks back uptown in an effort to appease her FitWand. Back at home, she googled "The Workout" and "Kate Wells" and "Lovely." At first glance, Janey couldn't see anything wrong with it. The review was glowing, almost effusive.

Now friends. I want to share with you a little secret today. I get compliments on how wonderful I look all the time. People come up to me on the street and say, "Kate, how do you stay so thin? How do I get a stomach like that? You must not eat food." I won't lie to you. It is hard work. The secret is my personal trainer Sara. Actually Sara is more my soul mate, my best friend, and my sister from another mother than she is my trainer. Her creative achievements are manifold. With her help I have managed to take control of my cravings, lose the weight from two babies (click here for more adorable photographs of Angel Dust and Hercules), and regain the energy I lose from filming for eighteen hours a day (click here to see clips from my latest movie). Let me take you into the best fitness class you'll ever visit, The Workout!

First off let's talk about the wardrobe. It's a little slice of monochromatic heaven. Sara and I both believe that eliminating color from your wardrobe is the great equalizer. It is one of the greatest democratic issues of our time. You all know my history with primary colors. I can't even get into it now. The whole class wears delicious grey clothing. It's the most wonderful mixture of Brazilian dance and jujitsu, mixed with tantric breathing, conscious muscle movement, and some old schoolyard tricks. You walk away feeling energized, thin, and strong, and I cannot tell you the benefits for your skin (click here to see my new vagina skin care line).

And, today only, seriously, today only, sign up for my Lovely newsletter, to receive a little bit of inspiration every single day, and you could win a free pass to The Workout in New York City.

How could this story cause a rift between Kate Wells and Sara Strong? She just didn't get it. Sure, it was pretentious and self-congratulatory, but it wasn't something worth ending a friendship over.

Janey began puttering around the apartment, running her fingers along the edge of her bookshelves. There was a picture of her and Beau on her wedding day. Instead of feeding her cake like a groom, he appeared to be withholding a slice from her, and her head was thrown back with laughter. There was the pair of them at high school graduation and lounging on a beach in Anguilla after some celebrity wedding. There was a photograph of Beau with Miss Lorna when she was still young and healthy and Beau was a wild-eyed teenager. The Sweet family really had been Beau's only family. God, she loved this one. It was a picture of the two of them at her debutante ball just a few months before everyone left town for college. Janey hadn't cared about the formalities of "coming out" to Charleston society, but Beau convinced her to embrace the silly tradition so that he could design her the grandest deb dress in all of South Carolina. "Think of it as *my coming out,*" he'd said with a snigger. Janey hadn't seen the dress during the three months that Beau designed and crafted it. He'd sent it to her just an hour before the event. Looking at the two of them standing on her front porch still made her sick with excitement after all these years. The dress was a white satin corset (très nineties Dolce), with an enormous tulle skirt. She swore she saw tears in Beau's eyes when he first saw her in it. "Janey Sweet, you are a swan," he had said to her. They walked arm in arm practically the entire evening. It was one of the most romantic nights of her life.

. . .

The adrenaline high from that morning's exercise was beginning to fade, causing a dull ache just behind her eyes. She must be dehydrated. She poured herself a glass of water from the bathroom sink and looked at herself in the mirror. This bathroom had very good lighting, *Today* show lighting, Beau liked to call it. "It can make Matt Lauer look twelve years old," he would say. "And I know Savannah has more wrinkles around her eyes than what we're seeing in HDTV." Janey still genuinely liked what she saw in the mirror. There hadn't been many new lines around her eyes or mouth for ten years, and since she stopped working some of the navy crevices beneath her eyes had begun to fade back to a nice normal beige. The flesh beneath her chin was certainly softer and looser, and she had a pair of parallel lines between her eyes that only used to appear when she squinted. Now they'd taken up permanent residence. She pulled up her shirt to inspect her belly, gave it a poke, and watched the soft flesh jiggle. She pinched her stomach between all four fingers and her thumb and then let the flesh flop unceremoniously over her elastic waistband like a jellyfish surrendering onto a beach. This wasn't a huge cause for alarm. She'd never had the abs of a sixteen-year-old Britney Spears, but then again she'd also never had a tummy that flopped quite so easily. She looked down at the clock on her phone. It was only 8:30 a.m. What was she going to do with herself for the rest of the day?

—◡—

CHAPTER SEVEN

www.twitter.com
@BJaneySweet

Wall Street Journal @WSJ 10m
New study confirms red wine causes weight gain in women.

Women's Health @WomensHealthMag 1h
Confirmed: 2 glasses of red wine before bed can help you lose weight.

SoarBarre @SoarBarre 2h
Join this month's FAT BLAST challenge and drop two dress sizes. #hurtssogood

Mindbodygreen @mindbodygreen 2h
Nail Reading: What Your Fingers Can Tell You About Your Health

Skin & Body Renewal @SkinBodyRenewal 4h
Freeze that **fat** off! **Cryo-**Lipo, ideal for stubborn pockets of #BodyRenewal #fattydeposits

BuzzFeed News @BuzzFeedNews 4h
This Man Proposed to His Boyfriend with the Cutest **Spin Class** Flash Mob Ever.

Mindbodygreen @mindbodygreen 4h
What Everyone Should Know About Energy Healing

Glossy @Glossy 4h
Can this shaman change your life? Meet Stella Bard, the shaman to the stars.

The Zoe Report @thezoereport 5h
9 reasons detox juice cleanses are the BEST idea

Good Housekeeping @goodhousemag 5h
9 Reasons Detox Juice Cleanses Are a Stupid Idea

Sara Hopkins @Sayhop Feb 29
We can stop this together. Friends don't let friends over-**Facetune**. (W/@robbyjayala)

Now I circle your fat."
"Excuse me?" Janey stammered to the small woman named Heidi with a thick German accent currently crouching on the ground in front of her with a thick Sharpie marker.
"I circle problem areas."
At Ivy's recommendation, Janey had booked herself a Saturday appointment at FroZen, a new clinic on the Upper East Side that promised to freeze away your excess fat through cryotherapy. Straight out of a science fiction novel, Janey paid two hundred dollars to stand naked for four minutes in a booth cooled to −10 degrees Fahrenheit.
Technicians in crisp white uniforms strapped electrodes to

Janey's bare chest to monitor her heart rate from a very professional-looking control room.

Ivy assured her that cryo had been popular in Europe for a couple of decades, operating in standalone clinics and a few high-end hotels. One two-minute session might burn as much as 600 calories. It was like being in the Arctic, without the polar bears or Al Gore. When your temperature dropped below freezing your body went into fight or flight—it literally thought it was dying. If it sounds like torture, it is. The upside of assuming you're about to freeze to death? You produce body heat faster and burn more calories than the best cardio workouts, even indoor rowing.

Janey tried to make small talk while Heidi crouched down in a mannish squat to get a closer look at Janey's naked stomach and thighs. "You have such a lovely accent," Janey complimented her, hoping the praise would cause her to go easy with that marker. "Are you from Berlin? I absolutely love it there. I run a wedding dress company and a couple of years ago we opened a shop in Berlin. I told my partner that it was the one city besides New York that I could see myself living in permanently." The felt tip tickled Janey's hips where Heidi looped large ovals around the back part of her waist.

Heidi made a circle around Janey's belly button and two more right underneath her butt cheeks. "You have nice calves," the woman informed her.

"Thank you." Janey assumed that was the proper response. "What makes you want to freeze people for a living?"

Heidi considered the question in a way that made Janey think no one had ever asked it before. "It pays better than working in a bar and I watched a lot of *Star Trek* as a child."

Once Janey's naked skin was properly marked, Heidi smacked her on the ass and into the cryo tank. The walls were made of perfectly clean and clear Plexiglas so that the pixie could see in and Janey could see out, watching Heidi as she wrote on her little clipboard and then barked into a microphone.

"Run. Now you run."

No one told Janey she would have to run in this meat locker.

"Get your knees higher. Up high." The German demonstrated with a high march that made her near-translucent pigtails swing in opposite directions.

Each individual muscle in Janey's body began cramping from the cold. The pain crept first into her big toe and then along her calves and up into her thighs. She could hardly lift a foot, much less jog in place. The corners of her mouth even refused to turn upward.

"I can't," Janey yelled back, the words floating from her lips as white condensation. She could feel tears involuntarily form at her eyes, catching on and then freezing her eyelashes.

She began to panic and the panic led her to scream: "LET ME OUT!"

Heidi held up two fingers to indicate that Janey needed to stay in the booth for two more minutes. She'd certainly die before then if she didn't try to escape this brutal contraption. She had no choice but to begin pounding on the Plexiglas, begging to be set free. It did her no good. The door was locked until a perfectly calibrated timer counted down all 120 of the seconds left to force her cellular function into distress. Heidi merely turned her head so that she could no longer see Janey suffer. Two minutes later she swiveled back around, her bright red lips pulled over her gums in an overly enthusiastic grin.

"*Ist es nicht wunderbar?* Doesn't it feel amazing?" The pixie clapped her hands as Janey, weak and exhausted, finally escaped the pod, her teeth chattering, cheeks slick with frost, hair hardened into a helmet of ice. She opened her mouth to speak but her vocal cords were still chilled. She merely shook her head, took the proffered cashmere bathrobe from one of Heidi's assistants, and curled it around her like a blanket. Heidi pulled Janey in for a hug.

"*Sie sind besonder,*" Heidi said. "That means 'I think you are very special.'" With that compliment, Heidi turned on the toes of her gleaming white sneakers and went off to refrigerate her next client.

. . .

Janey was still shivering when she met CJ at the Horse Feather for brunch later that morning. She wrapped her oversized black scarf around her shoulders and tried to keep her teeth from chattering.

"Ethical question for you?" CJ proposed over her meal of one egg white, three tablespoons of plain Greek yogurt, and a glass of skim milk.

"Yes. It's wrong to eat food that's just one color," Janey said, raising an eyebrow. "What happened to clay?"

"It was giving me indigestion," CJ said defensively. "I'm on the white diet. You can only eat foods that are white. It makes sense if you think about it. But that's not what I was about to ask you." The restaurant was more crowded than usual today after it had been mentioned on a blog ranking the top organic/locavore/artisanal dining establishments south of Fourteenth Street. The Horse Feather came in number one in this incredibly narrow and yet apparently quite competitive category. Looking over CJ's shoulder, Janey watched the harried hostess trying to arrange the overflow into an orderly line out the front door.

"Shoot." Janey was pleased with herself for ordering a quinoa breakfast scramble and even more pleased with herself for pronouncing it properly as "keen-wa" and not "quin-oh-ah," as she had the handful of times she'd said it out loud in the past. "But before you do let me state my opinion that food should have color and smell and taste wonderful." As if on command, a waiter slid by their table with six plates of identical avocado toast in a bold emerald color balancing precariously on his tray.

CJ ignored Janey's last statement. "Is it wrong to Facetune my kids before I put them on Instagram?"

Janey almost choked on her latte.

"Why would you need to Facetune the twins?"

"You don't think Tate is getting a little chubby?"

"No. Your son is adorable."

"Just a little paunchy," CJ insisted.

"I think photoshopping your sons will give them a lifelong complex that will turn them into sociopaths like Beau. So yes. I think it is wrong to Facetune your kids or otherwise do anything to tell them there is anything wrong with their little bodies." CJ's eyes fluttered. She was clearly hurt and convinced she'd revealed herself to be a subpar mother, so Janey added, "But the upside is that you'll look even thinner in pictures next to your paunchy son. Now that's a win!" She held her hand up for a high five.

Janey had worried more than once that CJ was going to make her boys manorexic with the way she wore her own body image on her sleeve, but Steven was good at keeping them grounded. No one liked meat and potatoes more than CJ's husband. While he usually laughed with his wife about her various diets and elixirs, he wasn't above laughing at her. The last time they threw a dinner party at their apartment, CJ insisted on the Paperless Post that everyone bring his or her own protein. Steven went out to the GNC around the corner and brought home the largest jug of Muscle Milk protein powder he could find, helpfully offering to mix it into everyone's paleo casseroles.

Now it was CJ's turn to roll her eyes. "It is too easy to feel like a bad mom on a daily basis. If I don't fuck 'em up this way, I'll find a whole new way to fuck 'em up tomorrow. I've been reading this new book by a French feminist that says American moms are way too clingy. She thinks we ought to ignore our kids more."

Janey was startled by the beep of her phone. Since putting on her out-of-office message, her emails had slowly dwindled to a mere trickle as her contacts realized she was unavailable.

"Oooo," she said out loud without realizing it.

"What?" CJ asked.

"Oh. Nothing. I mean. Well." Janey was embarrassed. "I didn't tell you about this shaman I met the other day, did I?" She knew full well that she had not told CJ anything about Stella or about The Workout.

"No. No, Janey Sweet. You did not tell me about the *shaman* you happened to meet the other day." CJ became momentarily distracted by a small man riding one of those hoverboard scooters, the ones with two wheels that seemed to move of their own volition, past their table.

"Is that Justin Bieber?" she asked as two elephant-sized bodyguards rushed to keep pace with their charge.

Janey shrugged and laughed as she began to describe her chance meeting with Stella in the Wandering Juice, sharing matcha with her and then getting an invite to The Workout.

"It was so strange," Janey said. "Stella, the shaman, brought me to a class with her, and the woman leading it, Sara Strong, she actually began crying. And I'm not talking about a couple of alligator tears. She wailed like a baby under serious duress."

CJ looked cross. "I can't believe you didn't tell me you went to The Workout. With Sara Strong! Did you meet her?"

"I did. She seemed nice. I didn't even think about it until right this second."

"She seemed nice? Sara Strong is a fitness god. The Workout is like the most coveted workout in all of New York City. The coolest moms at school go. They all talk about it like they've just been invited to the *Vanity Fair* Oscar party. I can't believe you and your new shaman didn't bring me with you."

"She's not *my* shaman first of all, and it wasn't my invite to give."

CJ pouted and slurped a spoonful of yogurt into her mouth. "Tell me more about the shaman. Stella? Is she covered in bad Sanskrit tattoos?"

"No. At least not that I could see. I don't know what to say about her. I've never met anyone like her. She's incredible. Humble and real. Nothing at all the way I pictured a guru-y person to be."

"Isn't that nice." Janey could tell CJ was still miffed at not having gotten a Workout invite. To alleviate the tension, Janey began to read the email out loud to her friend.

"Maybe you could come to this with me? She's inviting me to an achuma ceremony."

"What's that?" CJ asked, interest spreading across her broad face.

Janey shrugged. "This is what it says: 'We use all the techniques I have absorbed through my world travels to rapidly dissolve stress and come to a place of sustainable inner zen. You will be introduced to something I believe is the great healer of the twenty-first century, the achuma cactus, a healing cactus that has been used by shamans for more than twenty thousand years.' Wait a minute . . . have humans been able to do that for twenty thousand years? That seems like a stretch. Did humans speak twenty thousand years ago?" Janey was baffled by this description.

"Keep going," CJ insisted.

"'The mescaline-based cactus assimilates into your system throughout a nightlong ceremony, which shall take place underneath the full moon. I am the intermediary between you and the cactus.' So I guess it is like peyote?" Janey expected CJ to know more about this kind of thing.

"I don't know. I've never actually tried peyote or ayahuasca. I wanted to when we were on our honeymoon in Tulum a thousand years ago but we couldn't score any. Let's go!"

"Can I get you ladies more coffee?" Janey looked up to see the same handsome waiter who recounted the life story of the turkey just a couple weeks back when she'd come to the Horse Feather with Beau.

"Two more lattes, please," Janey replied.

"Wonderful." He lowered his voice. "And I am so sorry I didn't ask you this before. We were superbusy and crazy this morning, but what milk can I put in your latte? Do you want whole? No, of course not. Ick! Skim, soy, almond, coconut, or camel?"

"Excuse me? Camo?"

"No, camel milk. It's so, so yummy yum. Completely lactose free, you know. Homogenized just like goat milk, but with like double the nutrients."

And for fun, and because she knew she could, Janey smiled up at him.

"Where were these camels raised?"

He didn't miss a beat. "Staten Island. There's a new hormone-free grass-fed camel range out in Richmond County."

"Of course there is. I think I'll have soy."

"Is camel milk white?" CJ inquired.

"More taupe," he explained with complete confidence.

"Okay, then I should probably stick with skim."

"Of course. I'll get those two lattes right away."

Without knowing why, Janey craned her neck to look at the door. Then it made sense. She'd always been able to sense Beau's presence when he walked into a room. There he was. She watched him as he removed his jacket, doing what he always did, dropping it three inches shy of the coat check desk so that the poor girl had to dive over the counter to catch it before it hit the floor. He did this to ensure all eyes would be on him as he walked to his (their) regular table in the corner.

Janey fidgeted nervously with her ponytail, finally pulling it out to let her hair cascade down her back.

Janey watched as a beautiful young woman joined Beau at the table and slithered like a malnourished python into the seat Janey often occupied. She squinted to focus harder as their waiter lingered next to the girl.

Was that their intern?

"Did you know he'd be here?" CJ asked.

"He's always here. We are always here. Together. It's not a big deal." She didn't want to admit she was eager to see him, to share space with him. That it made her stomach churn and delighted her at the same time.

CJ knew she was lying and ignored it, changed the subject to last night's episode of *The Bachelor*.

A few minutes later, the waiter returned bearing their lattes and an absurdly small pitcher.

"I brought you some camel milk on the side so you can give it a sip. I think you'll love it. They sell this in Whole Foods for eighteen dollars a bottle!"

Milk was milk and Janey was far from squeamish, but something about drinking anything from a camel made her queasier than Beau sitting just twenty feet away from them. Her foot began to tap involuntarily on the smooth wood floor beneath the table, her knee rattling the container of taupe liquid in front of her.

"Thanks so much," she said with barely mustered enthusiasm.

"Want to hear a funny story?" the waiter asked.

"Always."

"I was just over at Beau Von B.'s table. He just got here. Did you see him come in? And he was sitting with a woman and I totally thought she was you. That you'd like switched tables! Same long black hair and well last time I saw you the two of you were here together. So I brought your latte over to that table. Except then she turned around and it was somebody completely different. Much younger." He was too young to know that what he just said was insulting.

"And did you happen to catch who it was?" Janey asked.

"Beau just introduced her as his muse. It was so cool."

Now Janey truly felt ill. She grasped the edge of the table until her knuckles were white. Her muscles tensed as if they were preparing to help her sprint out of the restaurant. She looked at her plate of quinoa and eggs and tried to imagine how Beau would look at her plate of quinoa and eggs.

"Sweetie. Are you okay?" CJ said with alarm.

She wasn't okay. None of it was okay.

"Can I get you anything else?" the waiter continued cheerily.

"No," Janey managed through gritted teeth. "We're good.

Thanks again for the camel milk." The waiter nodded, pleased to have introduced the wonders of camel milk to a stranger.

As soon as he was out of earshot CJ reached across the table to pat Janey's hand. "That waiter is a moron. You know that. Beau might not have even said that and if he did . . . well . . . we know Beau is a moron."

Janey wanted to pick up the little white ceramic pitcher of camel milk, walk across the room, tap that Beau on his bony shoulder, and toss the milk in his face. Would she have felt like this if Michael cheated on her? Probably not. But Beau? That was a different story. The intern *was* beautiful. Their similarities stopped at the long dark hair. Her face resembled a young Sophia Loren, exotic and comforting at the same time. Janey racked her brain for what she knew about the girl. She was definitely smart, fresh out of FIT, where she double majored in fabric styling and entrepreneurship. Janey could tell she'd been flattered by Beau's attention from the moment she walked into their studio. When Beau's light shone on you, it made you feel like you could stare directly into the sun without being burned. When it shifted away things felt very, very cold.

"Let's get out of here," CJ said, pulling her purse onto her shoulder and signaling to the waiter for the check. "Let's go buy something obscenely expensive and charge it to your corporate card."

What would happen if she did go over there? She began running it over and over in her head, the scenarios a little different each time. Maybe he would surprise her. Stand up, embrace her. Laugh when she told him the story about the waiter thinking this waifish child was his new muse.

"My muse?" she imagined him saying. "Janey-boo. You and I just had a tiff. No one but you will ever be my muse."

Then the second scenario: "Janey? Is that you? I hardly even recognized you. You look so much older. Did you gain even more weight? I'm sorry, boo! But don't you worry about coming back to work. I found a whole new you!"

Her mind raced with the rational and the irrational. Why had

Beau really put her on hiatus? What were his actual intentions? Was this bigger than her superficial weight gain? Janey pushed the gravelly quinoa around on her plate, feeling her stomach rumble.

"Janey. Janey. Snap out of it." CJ was desperate to distract her from Beau's presence.

"Janey, I'm going to drink the camel milk. Look at me. Look at me. You can't stop me now. I am going for this. Drinking the camel milk." She was really doing it. CJ tipped the milk up to her lips just to make Janey snap out of her shame spiral. As soon as the warm milk touched her lips she made a face like she'd just been given warm blood to drink.

Janey couldn't help but genuinely smile. "Wow. Are you vying for best girlfriend of the year award?"

CJ stood and picked up Janey's purse and slung it over her own shoulder.

"Oh, I get that on an annual basis. They just give it to me now; I don't even need to be nominated. It's not that bad. A little saltier than I prefer, but not bad at all."

She grabbed Janey's hand and pulled her out of the seat and toward the door. "Let's go to Staten Island and expense the whole damn camel. We'll make a fortune bottling their salty milk and never have to work again. We can name her Beau."

Janey glanced one last time over her shoulder and saw Beau staring directly at her. What did she expect him to do? Look away? Look ashamed? He did neither. He raised his hand and wiggled his three middle fingers, daintily waving as if nothing were wrong at all, his lips slowly moving into a cruel smile. And even though his smile pierced her like a dagger right in her side, she managed her own toothy smile right back before she whipped her head around to hide a fat tear rolling down her cheek.

CHAPTER EIGHT

To: SoarBarre Staff
From: Management

Good morning, bitches!

We have exciting news! Demand is surging faster than ever!
We just couldn't be more grateful that people are embracing
SoarBarre. To keep pace we will be raising the price of a
single walk-in Soar by five dollars to sixty dollars apiece. Our
members know they are paying for a premium luxury cardio
experience and we want them to continue to feel this way.
Let us know if you hear of any concerns. Don't forget—our
mission is no less than to change people's lives. You can't put
a price on that.

Let's take a moment to give a shout out to our rock star
instructor Ivy, whose latest column in Self magazine, "Torture
Now, Laugh Later," was the number-one story on their website
all week. We are so grateful for you, Ivy.

*And please remember to call Kimberly at reception by her full
name. Just a gentle reminder that she came into her wholeness
and shed the Kim recently. Namaste, bitch!*

With so much gratitude,
Ally and Lemon

vy thumbed through the rest of her emails while standing in
the kitchen waiting for her Magic Bullet to finish mixing up her
morning protein shake. She must have been making a face when
she read the note from Ally and Lemon because Kelli looked across
the butcher block island at her with an amused smile.

"I wish I'd known you before SoarBarre," she said teasingly.

Ivy glanced up from her phone and managed a smile for her
still fairly new girlfriend. "I wish you had too. But if it weren't for
SoarBarre we wouldn't have met, and who knows what the fuck you
would have thought of the old me. You might not have liked me at
all. I was a completely different person back then."

Without saying a word, Kelli grabbed a large glass container with
a sticky note that said SWEAR JAR from above the fridge and held it
out to Ivy, causing her to fish a twenty out of her wallet and place it
into the already crammed container.

Ivy hoped that wasn't true. She hoped Kelli would have liked her
even more when she was a sweet and serene ballet dancer, but she
didn't say it out loud. Instead, she bit her lip. "I've gotta run . . . but
I'll see you in my afternoon Soar Renegade class."

Kelli nodded as she began packing colored pencils into her brown
leather satchel to head off to teach her own classes at the exclusive
City and Country private school downtown.

"Of course! I wouldn't miss it."

"Great! You're on my list of VVIPs," Ivy said.

"Well I would certainly hope so," Kelli replied in a singsong and sashayed out for her day filled with coloring, listening circles, and nap time.

Ivy reread the email from the SoarBarre management team as she sipped her morning shake—a mixture of whey protein, two cloves of garlic, a raw egg, kefir, mustard greens, collard greens, spinach, and turmeric.

She knew she had no say in the matter, but the classes were already absurdly expensive. Five dollars didn't mean much to most of her clients, but she couldn't help but feel they were committing highway robbery. As she swirled the vile mixture around in her glass, daring herself to keep drinking, another email from Ally and Lemon (they almost always emailed as a pair) appeared in her inbox asking her to "pop" into their office before her morning class.

Ally and Lemon, SoarBarre's cofounders, had met ten years earlier through a shared personal trainer. They were both new moms with a passion for exercise and getting rid of their mummy tummies, and they immediately clicked over a hatred for compostable diapers and the fact that they disliked all of the gyms in New York City.

During a single lunch, on the back of a napkin, they developed the concept for SoarBarre, the most intense indoor workout you could do in just an hour. Lemon had gotten a windfall from a recent divorce, and Ally was so over her job running the New York City office of a small but highly regarded independent film company owned by an obsessive tyrant. With Lemon's money and Ally's Hollywood connections they opened their first studio in Tribeca. In the last year alone SoarBarre had opened locations in twelve new cities and grown its revenue from $42 million to $160 million.

.   .   .

Ivy wasn't there for the first eight years of Soar, and she hadn't known Ally and Lemon before they began working together. Still, she couldn't help but think, as she sat in front of the two women at their double desk in their sprawling office above the Tribeca studio, that they'd begun to morph into each other. They both wore the same perfectly tailored black blazers over bright yellow SoarBarre T-shirts and custom-made boot-cut Betabrand "yoga to boardroom pants." Their perfectly tweezed, never waxed, eyebrows arched in exactly the same spot.

"Thanks for coming in," Lemon said, as Ivy settled herself into an armchair that appeared to be constructed from concrete, just as Ally simultaneously praised her on her last class: "It was so fucking intense. I actually thought I was going to die. It was so perfect. We're so grateful to have you here."

"So grateful," Lemon added. Some days it seemed like Ally and Lemon were holding a secret contest to see who could use more iterations of "grateful" and "gratitude" in a single day.

"Thanks." Ivy smiled and crossed her legs, bouncing one foot nervously up and down. The two women both leaned across the desk.

"We have a mission for you," Lemon said. This was a recent phenomenon, Lemon speaking as though she were M in a James Bond movie. Ivy simultaneously thought it was ridiculous and got a small thrill out of it.

"Have you heard about The Workout?"

"Which workout?" Ivy began to rumble off the names of the SoarBarre customized workout classes: "Survivor, Renegade, Rebel, Insurgent, Iconoclast?"

"No, no." Ally shook her head. "*The Workout,* being taught by Sara Strong. She's Kate Wells's former trainer. She started these new workouts. They pop up in different locations in the city. We've been hearing the clients talking about them. Apparently they're invite only, very hush-hush. Some of our regulars are saying it's the best workout they've ever had. Which is a problem for us." Ally and Lemon exchanged a meaningful look.

"It is?" Ivy asked.

Ally continued. "Because of course our goal is to be the best workout anyone has ever had."

"Right, right."

Ally sat up straighter. "This is a revolution. We're fighting for no less than the hearts and minds of our citizens."

Ivy tried to stifle a laugh as she let her boss continue.

"We need to learn more about this Workout. We need to know what we're dealing with. Is it a real competitor? Is it something we should be seriously worried about?"

"Well, this is the first time I'm hearing about it. I've heard Sara Strong's name. Stupid fucking name if you ask me," Ivy said and then remembered she was addressing a woman named Lemon. "But I didn't know she was doing an actual class. What do you need me to do?"

"Some surveillance," Lemon said, unfazed by Ivy's comment about the oddity of the name. If your name was Lemon, you'd long ago have convinced yourself that it was socially acceptable and not strange at all. "Ask around, try to snag yourself an invite, take some notes, figure out exactly what we're dealing with. We'd just be so grateful if you could find out anything at all."

Ivy felt a tingling sensation creep up her spine. This *was* exciting. She'd start by taking some of her regulars out after class to grab a broth. She'd start asking the right questions. It wouldn't be long before she got herself an invite to this Workout. Her clients loved little more than currying favor with her. She'd have this locked up by the end of the week.

"Give me a week," she said. "I'm on it."

〜

www.wikipedia.com/Echinopsis_lageniformis

Echinopsis lageniformis (syn. *Trichocereus bridgesii*),
Bolivian torch cactus, is a fast-growing columnar cactus
from the high deserts of Bolivia. Among the indigenous populations of Bolivia, it is sometimes called achuma or wachuma,
although these names are also applied to related species such
as *Echinopsis pachanoi* which are also used for their psychedelic effects . . . The plant contains a number of psychoactive
alkaloids, in particular the well-studied chemical mescaline,
which it may contain at levels higher than those of the San
Pedro cactus . . . As with related species, it seems to have a
long shamanic tradition of use throughout its native habitat.

There had been a flurry of text messages back and forth
between CJ and Janey about what exactly a person was supposed to wear to a shaman's house for a twenty-thousand-
year-old cactus ceremony. CJ, who considered this a big night out
without her children and husband, thought it would be nice to
get dressed up. "Heels and sexy tops?" she wrote. Janey thought

it seemed like an occasion for nice but not flashy workout clothes. Janey looped Ivy into the mix after her cousin asked her to have dinner the night of the ceremony. Janey secured her an invite to come with them instead. At the last minute Ivy texted them the definitive wardrobe answer: *Pajamas. Comfy pajamas. I did ayahuasca with some Peruvians at Coachella. Trust.*

Janey was enjoying this motley new girl gang of hers. It'd been years since she'd spent this much time with CJ, who had been, rightfully, busy with her young family. And she and Ivy just hadn't had the opportunity to be close because of their age difference, a chasm that didn't seem nearly as large as it had when Ivy was a teenager.

"How much does a shaman make?" CJ nudged Janey as they stood in front of the double oak doors of Stella's Park Slope brownstone on a tree-lined street in the pricey neighborhood. "Like in a year. What do you think the annual salary of a shaman might be?"

Janey gave a low whistle. "It looks like this one is doing all right for herself." She'd pictured Stella in a funky and adventurous community. Bed Stuy, maybe? Maybe somewhere in Queens. She'd never have thought the shaman had a brownstone in this homogenized Brooklyn enclave where all the young dads wore the same Warby Parkers and zipped around on vintage skateboards and the moms wore a uniform of distressed denim skirts with French striped T-shirts and espadrille sandals from Rag & Bone (with the label removed, naturally). No one wore makeup, but their haircuts cost more than four hundred dollars. Organic food co-ops (don't call them grocery stores) sold misshapen bananas for triple the price of the chain stores. "Down-to-earth" celebrities regularly leaked their co-op shifts to the Page Six gossip column.

From the outside, Stella's house looked like another nineteenth-century townhouse, apart from the front door, which was painted a loud pink and covered in purple Hindi characters.

"You know, I met two new shamans this week," CJ said, tugging on the bottom of her black silk Stella McCartney pajama top as it bunched around her hips. "They were at school drop-off. Bored mommies turned shamans. It's becoming a thing. Remember five years ago when everyone became a handbag designer? Shaman is the new handbag designer."

The three women were greeted at the door by one of Stella's assistants (*A shaman in training?* Janey wondered) who delivered a warm smile as she handed each woman a small slip of paper that said her name, Moon Child, and explained that part of her training this month involved not speaking a single word and living in complete silence. She bowed her head of red ringlets to them.

They tentatively bowed back. "What do you want to bet she's from Jersey and her name is Tiffany?" CJ speculated, grabbing Ivy's can of electrolyte-infused H2BROC and taking a pinched sip.

Inside the floorboards were painted a shiny ebony, covered with beautiful Moroccan poufs and Turkish rugs that Janey knew didn't come from ABC Carpet & Home but likely the actual Morocco and Turkey. A light smell of bergamot incense wafted through the room. The walls were empty except for one large gold antique mirror over the white brick fireplace.

There were maybe ten other people in the room, and as far as Janey could tell none of them were, at least at first glance, the kind of people she thought would be drinking a tea made of psychedelic cactus on a Tuesday night. Stella was nowhere to be found, but the room buzzed about her.

"She's just simply the most magical person I've ever met," one plump woman wearing a purple caftan said to a man, a tall silver fox with a day-old beard. He was wearing a three-piece suit, clearly cut by Savile Row's finest tailors, with a perfect white square peeking out of his left breast pocket. He reminded Janey of Sean Connery, thirty years ago. She watched as he carefully removed his leather brogues and tried to stifle a laugh when she noticed he was wearing sock garters.

He smiled back at the woman in an interested way that made Janey wonder if the two of them were on a date—and not just any date, but a first date. It was an odd choice to be sure, but maybe it beat awkward drinks at the Waverly.

Ivy wandered over to a low wooden coffee table and grabbed a book off of a high stack. The cover was a deep royal blue and featured a blond woman Janey quickly recognized as Stella sitting on top of a mountain and gazing off into the distant clouds and the ruins of Machu Picchu below.

Ivy read the title off the cover. "*From Shame to Shaman.* Seriously?"

"Shhhhhh!" Janey shushed her cousin as the three women gathered to read the book flap silently to themselves.

> This memoir by renowned shaman Stella Bard takes the reader on a journey that proves our darkest moments are the source of our greatest light. She was a world-famous supermodel with a treacherous heroin habit when she fell in love with a shaman in the Peruvian Amazon.
>
> She left her love in the jungle but found herself in the process. She kicked her drug habit, returned home to New York City, got married, divorced and married again, had two daughters, and obtained her PhD in homeopathic healing.
>
> From extracting joy and light out of every day to healing wounds inflicted in this lifetime and before, Hart's insights are filled with warmth, compassion, and wisdom that bring awareness to every cell of your spiritual being.

"Jesus Christ, she's the most interesting woman on the planet," Ivy said. "I mean WOW."

"I think Lena Dunham is the most interesting woman on the planet," a melodious voice said behind them. They turned to see Stella grinning with amusement. She was dressed simply, in a pair of torn baggy jeans that fell off her slender hips and a white button-down shirt, unbuttoned to reveal a pair of blue crystals hanging from a gold chain between her small breasts. "My publishers did a very good job of making my story seem as salacious as possible. But, at the end of the day, I let them do it. They told me it would sell more books. I believe the more people who read my message, the better for the world." She shrugged. "In the end everyone wins. But please feel free to take a copy home if you'd like, that's why they're here. Come on up to the roof. We're about to get started."

"It's below freezing out. Is she crazy?" CJ said to Janey once she thought Stella was out of earshot.

Without pausing in her tracks, Stella answered the question as if it had been asked directly of her.

"It's a heated geodesic dome. It's balmier up there than it is in Rio." She then paused and stepped back for a second, pulling Janey close to her and whispering in her ear. "I have news. I think I can get you into The Workout retreat in St. Lucia if you really want to go. I spent all last night talking to Sara about you on the phone."

"Really?" Janey said. She hadn't had a real interest in going away on some fitness vacation in the Caribbean until Stella had told her she *couldn't* go away on some fitness vacation in the Caribbean.

"Let's talk after the ceremony."

Janey turned to find her cousin leaning in toward them, definitely eavesdropping.

"Hey Iv."

"Whatcha talking about?"

"Oh, just this retreat a client of Stella's is doing. This woman called Sara Strong. You might know her. She is, was, Kate Wells's personal trainer. I went to her workout the other day."

"Yeah, I've heard of her," Ivy said. "I want to hear everything!"

Before they could talk more, they needed to fall into single file to walk up a narrow winding staircase from the townhouse's third floor to the roof.

"How did they get this up here?" CJ asked.

"They must have built it from scratch," Janey responded in awe.

The braided staircase had opened into a giant glass sphere composed of a network of smaller triangles. The glass was so clean and so clear you could see the few stars available to the naked eye through the New York City smog. Heat lamps ringed the outer edges of the dome and a large fire pit dominated the center of the space, with a small opening up top to let the smoke waft up and out. Overstuffed white goose-down cushions were neatly placed in a circle on top of the softest grass Janey had ever felt.

Stella clapped her hands.

"Sit, everyone. Get comfy. We're going to be on this journey for a while. I hope everyone made sure to eat before coming. It is best to begin the ceremony satisfied. If you're hungry, let one of our spiritual assistants know and he or she can bring you a spoon of coconut butter."

Everyone began settling down onto the ground. Janey, Ivy, and CJ staked out three cushions next to one another with Janey sitting in the middle. The silver fox had removed his suit coat and vest and rolled up the sleeves of his white dress shirt to reveal seriously muscular and tanned forearms. Janey tried to catch if he was wearing a wedding ring, but the candlelight made it impossible to make out any small details.

Prior to their journey across the East River Janey had done an extensive search of every possible side effect and reaction one could have to psychedelic cacti. They included, in no particular order, nausea, disorientation, hallucination, headache, dehydration, a sense of disembodiment, mood swings, and intense emotions. Some people claimed they discovered who they were in their past lives, and others were certain they'd been given a message from friends and family beyond the grave. Janey was determined about one thing: she wouldn't spend the night crying about Beau.

Stella's spiritual assistants began pouring glasses of sparkling water and passing them around the circle.

"Remember to stay hydrated. We'll begin in a few minutes. Take a few sips of the water and just pull in a few breaths. It's so special we're all here together tonight for the new moon solar eclipse. New moons and solar eclipses both represent new beginnings. The effect of their power on the earth is simple scientific fact. When we see a new moon coincide with a solar eclipse the earth experiences bigger tides, increased volcanic activity, and extreme weather. Now imagine what is happening within your own body. It's wild stuff! This particular eclipse is at eighteen degrees Pisces with both Mercury and Neptune in the realm, which means we will see a wealth of love, compassion, and understanding emerge during this ceremony."

Janey knew she was a Virgo, but she never remembered anyone else's sign. Michael used to get hurt that she always forgot he was an Aquarius. Anytime anyone began talking about star signs, Janey tuned out. She paid attention again once Stella described exactly what would happen during the achuma ceremony.

"Now, I think almost all of you are first-timers when it comes to the healing ceremony we're about to do, so I want to tell you a little bit about what's going to happen tonight. Achuma is the greatest sacred plant teacher and healer that we know of. In the wild this plant can reach more than twenty feet in height. This is not a mescaline experience, although some of you will experience the psychedelic effects of the cactus."

Janey shifted nervously on her cushion.

"Depending on your emotional state, this process can be chaotic or tranquil. But rest assured we are here to hold your hand. Literally! My spiritual guides will be here to actually hold your hand if you need it, and I don't want you to be shy. Some people feel as though they're dreaming even though they're awake. You may want to lie down, you may want to take a walk. I invite you to wander all over the house. Touch what you want, eat what you want, but the only rule is that you stay inside. You may see colors differently. You may get to see the energy of things. My clients often remember things they had long, long forgotten. Ultimately our goal is to heal the wounds of the past so you can live fully in the present. Now. Does anyone have any questions?"

Silver Fox raised his hand, a gesture Janey found adorable, and asked the question she'd been wanting to ask. "About how long does it last?" he said in a posh British accent that made him sound like Lord Grantham from *Downton Abbey*. CJ nudged Janey's thigh. Janey pinched her back to show that yes, she had noticed this very handsome man.

"Great question, Hugh. Achuma lasts much longer than some of the other traditional medicines, often as long as nine hours. In a few moments we will all drink our tea together and from there it will take about thirty minutes to feel the effects."

"Thank you, Stella. And thank you for the invitation to come on this journey," Hugh said with a polite smile, clearly satisfied with her answer.

The spiritual assistants emerged from the shadows of the dome with trays of large blue soup bowls with handles on either side. They proceeded to place the heavy china in front of each person, including Stella. Janey looked into it to find a bizarre concoction of brown sludge with the distinctive smell of burnt soil and mushrooms. Janey was surprised to see that Stella was partaking of the liquid. She'd assumed that someone would need to remain the grown-up in this room. And as if she'd read her mind, Stella looked up from her own bowl and smiled directly at Janey. "In this ceremony, I will be going on the journey with you. It's of the utmost importance that the guide is on the same spiritual plane as the students. Now we drink. Don't sip and don't chug, but find a healthy balance between the two and let the medicine slide down your throat. You may be tempted to hold your nose but resist. The sense of smell is so, so important to this journey."

Janey had never heard the word "journey" uttered so many times.

"Lift your cups, close your eyes, and let the medicine do its work." Janey lifted the bowl to her mouth with both hands holding on to the handles. It was warm but not hot. She did as Stella instructed, closed her eyes and let the liquid slide into her mouth, ignoring the smell, disregarding the somewhat chunky consistency.

With her bowl nearly drained, Janey felt her gag reflex kick in and made a small sound. Within seconds she felt hands on her shoulders, gently massaging the muscles around her shoulder blades and neck. She knew without turning around that it was Stella, who then leaned down and placed a necklace with a fine chain tenderly around Janey's neck.

"Let's keep our eyes closed, everyone." Stella was back to the middle of the circle. "And take a series of deep clearing breaths to let our digestive systems begin to do their work."

Janey stretched her legs out and played with pointing and flexing her naked toes, enjoying the sensation of her thighs and calves sinking into the grass, waiting for the show to begin. She felt the same urgent anticipation she'd felt as a teenager when she smoked a joint with Beau and went to go see a Pink Floyd show at the Charleston planetarium.

Time became flexible from then on, and Janey couldn't grasp what was happening in any sequential order. Her eyes grew heavy and felt like they were closed for an hour, but it could have been thirty seconds. She stroked the soft grass, then moved her fingers to her face to smell the dirt on them.

After what could have been a week, Stella cleared her throat.

"Let us now call on the moon goddess, Diana, to guide us on our individual paths tonight. We cannot see her—the new moon means she's hiding from us—but we can certainly feel her power, and as the eclipse draws nearer she will reveal herself."

When Janey opened her eyes she noticed that a metal bucket had been placed in front of her. She had just a few seconds to wonder why it was there before she understood. Her body began convulsing and retching as she vomited into the bin. She couldn't look into the bucket without getting ill again, but it felt as if the things coming out of her body were not things she had actually eaten. All around her, everyone was doing the same thing. And though throwing up was one of Janey's least favorite things, she didn't feel self-conscious about doing it in a room full of strangers.

Once everyone was finished, Stella began again. Janey had noticed the shaman hadn't vomited, or if she had, she'd left the room to do it in private.

"Roll onto your sides. Lie in the fetal position until you feel ready to stand. Feel your flow, wander around, feel your bodies. Feel your neighbors' bodies."

Janey rose to her feet and took a moment to steady herself, throwing her arm in front of her to regain her balance. She didn't feel intoxicated, rather the exact opposite: all of her senses were heightened instead of dulled. She must have had her eyes closed longer than everyone else. Ivy was already lying belly down on the ground, topless, while two spiritual assistants took turns gently smacking her back with wooden sticks. Janey put one foot in front of the other and made her way to the spiral staircase, holding tight to the railing the whole way down.

On the third floor she found CJ standing in front of a floor-length mirror twirling like a ballerina and laughing hysterically. Janey watched as she bent into a demi-plié and bowed to herself, straightened and smiled coyly, almost flirtatiously, to her reflection.

Janey continued down another floor. All of a sudden she felt wretched and lonely and empty and miserable. She sank to the floor and began to pick at her biceps. It felt as if ants were crawling all over her arms.

The entire room began to expand and then contract. Expand and contract. The walls began to hum, at first a low vibration and then an entire chorus. "You're fired, Janey. Fired Janey. Fired Janey."

In seconds, two spiritual assistants were on her. One pulled her into his lap and began running his fingers through her hair. Was he French-braiding it? No one had French-braided her hair since she was little, but she used to love it when Miss Lorna ran her long slender fingers through her thick hair, separating it into sections and then weaving them back together. And then it felt like it *was* her mother braiding her hair and Janey relaxed into her soft belly, let all of her anxiety and tension from the past month melt into

Miss Lorna's substantial frame. Love and forgiveness and kindness and acceptance swept through her body. She heard Lorna's voice whisper in her ear: "Honey, what do you want to be when you grow up?"

She responded, "I don't know, Mama. I want to be happy."

Janey may have sat there for an hour before she felt loose and light enough to continue her explorations. Four of the others had gotten into Stella's mask and drum collection and were wearing elaborate tribal masks over their faces. The crew of them, which Janey now realized involved Ivy, beat dramatically on thigh-high calfskin drums. She waltzed back up the staircase and paused in front of the mirror where CJ had channeled her inner child. Janey sat down cross-legged and stared at her reflection. She saw herself as she must have looked at age ten with the French braid in her hair. She smiled at herself.

You're so pretty, she thought. And then another person was sitting next to her in her reflection. It was Beau. Little Beau, not grown-up Beau, and he was smiling mischievously at her.

His lips didn't move, but she heard his voice in her head.

Let's steal Miss Lorna's car and drive to the beach.

I need you to give me a hundred dollars. You can't ask questions, just give it to me.

You know you aren't as perfect as you think, Janey Sweet. Sometimes I think you're downright ugly.

They kept coming, the insults and entreaties to break her parents' rules, to break the law, to give him things, and when she said no he made her feel as bad as a person could be made to feel. These were all things Beau had said or done. Janey just hadn't thought about them in a long time. She'd always been good at only remembering the good things. But now she saw Beau for what he

LUCY SYKES AND JO PIAZZA

really was, not a tortured artist, a near orphan who needed her and depended on her, but as a bully.

Hadn't it been Beau who convinced her working in the family business would be a death sentence? He'd made fun of Sweet Chocolate their entire lives, joking about how they just made fat people fatter. He made Janey feel that returning home to work at the company just wasn't an option. It had broken her dad's heart when she told him she was going to New York to work with Beau instead of home to Charleston after graduate school.

Tears began to stream down her cheeks, but she didn't feel any more pain, rather a sense of relief.

Slowly, she found her way back to the roof. The silver fox was the only one left upstairs, but Janey felt no apprehension about approaching this stranger. He smiled broadly at her and beckoned her to come closer. She sat down in front of him, their knees touching. Without speaking a word they stared into each other's eyes. His were a deep and sincere blue. He reached out and grasped both of her hands. She examined a mole on his left cheek in the shape of a very tiny pineapple. Janey could feel calluses on his hands, harder and rougher on the left than on the right and surprising on such a dapper man. His high narrow cheekbones were slightly tanned, and there was a small dimple in his chin. He wore a chunky silver vintage Rolex on his left wrist, and now Janey could clearly see that he was not wearing a wedding ring but had a thin line of white where one might be.

He stared at her just as intensely, but she didn't feel in the least self-conscious. Not once did she fidget to fix her hair or suck in her stomach. She felt an intense acceptance of herself and her body.

They stayed like that until Stella reappeared. She'd changed out of her jeans and into a flowing gossamer white dress. You'd have no idea the group of them were on a rooftop in Brooklyn. They could have been on a mountaintop in the Andes or on a beach in Brazil. The rest of the folks filed in behind the shaman and returned to new places around the circle. Janey kept the silver fox's hand in hers. It felt strong.

Stella sat and began speaking.

"You've all gone through a process of soul retrieval. The medicine has helped to cleanse you of your negative thought patterns and unblock all of the good energy throughout each of your cells. You've taken steps to heal yourself and now you will be rewarded. Lie down, each of you lie down and look toward the heavens."

Janey reluctantly let go of the silver fox's hand and lay her head back into the downy cushion behind her. The sky had previously been moonless, but all of a sudden there was a violent outline of bright light shining around a perfect orb of darkness.

"Now is the time for healing and transforming past wounds. You are going to leave here a completely different human being. Let the light sink into each of you. Let the new you emerge from your cocoon."

CHAPTER TEN

～

Janey hardly remembered the ride home from Stella's place. She knew it had been dawn when she sandwiched between CJ and Ivy in the back of an Uber that one of the spiritual assistants had called for them. Their driver was an overweight Polynesian woman with a withering lei hanging from the rearview mirror. There wasn't much talking, just some giggling as the three women held hands and smiled at one another. When she got home she picked up Boo Radley and kissed him on the snout. Unused to this kind of affection from Janey, the dachshund promptly hid in the closet. She brushed her teeth, washed her face, and left her hair in the braid. When she finally lay down she passed out for the entire day, not waking again until the sun was coming up twenty-four hours later. She expected a headache to greet her when she opened her eyes, perhaps some queasiness and anxiety, the basic symptoms of a hangover, but was surprised to learn she felt amazing.

Sunlight rushed in from her east-facing windows. Maybe she should order breakfast in bed. Was there a service that would bring food over and place it neatly on a tray in a perfectly Instagram-able shape along with fresh flowers and the *New York Times*? There must be. And if it didn't exist maybe Janey should start it. She'd call it Bliss&Bed. She giggled to herself. What a wonderful idea! She reached over to her night table to grab her phone to make a note and quickly examined her new emails. One from CJ: *I FEEL FUCK-ING AMAZING. WANT TO COME OVER FOR BREAKFAST. I THINK I MAY START TAKING BALLET LESSONS.* And another from Ivy: "I'm so happy we're spending so much time together. You're a beautiful human being inside and out." She didn't curse once.

And then an email from someone named Hugh Albermarle.

Dear Janey,

I hope you don't think this too presumptuous but I asked Stella for your email address this morning and she said you might be pleased to hear from me. We held hands last night. It was wonderful. Want to continue it over dinner?

Hugh

Silver Fox! He'd clearly woken up much earlier than Janey had. Was he asking her on a date? This *clearly* sounded like a date. Hugh was the second man to ask her on a date in as many weeks. After exchanging a couple of flirty one-liner emails over several days, she'd agreed to have dinner with the juice guy that very evening. She smiled, and perhaps due to her newfound new moon clarity, immediately responded without thinking about it too much.

Dear Hugh,

Not presumptuous at all. I'd love to continue some hand-holding over dinner. Name somewhere delicious.

Janey

Boo Radley always sensed when the doorbell was about to ring, and Janey saw him slink out from the closet and grow agitated.

"Who's here, Boo?" she asked the straggly dachshund. She really should take him in for a haircut. Miss Lorna had Boo groomed at least once a week, which was probably another reason the animal despised Janey. She forced him to have a bad hair day every day.

And, like clockwork, the doorbell buzzed. Janey hit the intercom to see who it could be.

"Hi. This is Alex from Sprig with your breakfast delivery."

At first she wondered if she'd somehow conjured Bliss&Bed just by thinking about it. Stella would be so proud. But then she remembered that CJ had promised to find her the very best, the freshest, the most organic and the healthiest daily food delivery service.

Janey opened the door to find a model-handsome college-aged boy dressed as a farmer in light denim overalls and a plaid hunting coat.

"Hi Janey," he said as though they'd met hundreds of times before. "Can I come in?"

"Sure." Janey moved aside to let Alex past her as Boo Radley watched skeptically from the corner.

Alex smiled at him. "Great wire-haired wiener. My grandma had one. Want to show me where your kitchen is?" CJ had explained to her Sprig sent employees, apparently very good-looking ones, to your home to prepare meals for you in your kitchen. Janey hadn't even bothered to look at the bill for her one-month subscription.

"Whooooo hooooooo. Now this is what I like to call kitchen porn. You need to be on Apartment Therapy, mama!" Alex said, placing several reusable bags on the countertop in her kitchen.

Janey smiled. There wasn't a trace of her parents' cozy southern kitchen here. She'd always been a fan of midcentury chic, and the kitchen was the perfect example of the aesthetic, with its pristine white walls, clean lines, and blond wood.

Alex set up, unpacking small brown boxes and unscrewing the top from a large orange thermos.

"Grab a mug. I have some amazing detoxing ginger tea for you.

I'll pour a cup and get your breakfast together and leave you to enjoy it. Today we have gluten-free granola with coconut yogurt and goji berries. We have this tea and a little bit of baobab juice.

"And for lunch I'm leaving you with this super yummy Super Superfood salad with kale, cabbage, avocado, sunflower seeds, blueberries, and a clove of minced garlic. You've got your vitamins A, B, C, E, and K all in one place, plus your carotenoids, flavonoids, selenium, iron, copper, and fiber. We are talking out-of-this-world immune system boosting and anti-inflammatory properties. You'll feel like a million."

Janey couldn't stop smiling at him.

"Is this your full-time job?" she asked with genuine curiosity. "Or are you in college? NYU?"

"I am in school. Thanks for asking. I'm finishing up my degree in integrative medicine at the Holistic Healing Health Institute, HHHI—have you heard of it?"

"I haven't." Janey took a blissful sip of her tea.

"It's in Bed Stuy. Great place. Check out the website. I'm finishing my thesis on whether or not the coregasm can replace a sexual orgasm."

"What's a coregasm?"

Alex began mixing together the ingredients for her Super Superfood salad. "It's when a woman, and sometimes a few lucky men, are able to achieve orgasm through core body work alone. It's way more common than people think."

"I'd love to read that," Janey said, popping a tart red goji berry into her mouth.

"I'll let you know when I'm finished," he said brightly. "Now, I won't be the one delivering dinner tonight. It will be one of my associates, but you should make sure to download our app so you can send us any preferences and adjust your delivery times."

"I sure will, Alex. I actually have a date tonight." Was she really telling this stranger this? "With the guy from the juice shop." Why couldn't she stop talking? "So I don't think I'll need dinner. Can you cancel for me? Thanks so much for breakfast. And good luck with the orgasms."

It took less than three minutes to devour the entire breakfast from Sprig. Janey moved over to her Eames armchair to finish the rest of the tea, folding her lower body into a nest and wrapping herself in a cashmere blanket. She reached up to touch her braid as she stared out the window. God, she missed her mother. Janey missed Reginald too, but she ached for Lorna, felt the loss so acutely in her bones every single day.

Boo Radley looked up at her as she wiped a tear away.

"I'm sorry she gave you such a silly name, Boo," Janey said, reaching to scoop him onto her lap as he tried to wiggle away. "She loved you so much, though. Lorna thought Boo was the best character in that whole damn book." She did. She always said, "That Boo is real and that's what matters in life, Janey. He's the best of them all. No pretension. Just goodness." Her mother had been just goodness, and Janey hadn't appreciated it enough when she was alive. She'd been so obsessed for so long with pleasing Beau. Why had she done that?

Lorna loved Beau too. It was always so clear she felt sorry for the little boy and wanted to set right all the wrongs forced on him by his parents. But she'd been wary of him too.

"That boy only cares about that boy," her mother had told her more than once.

. . .

Janey dressed carefully for her date with this juice guy. She couldn't for the life of her remember his name (his email was actually Juice Dude@gmail.com), and she would need to try to figure it out before she slept with him. She still wasn't sure she *would* sleep with him, but she wasn't opposed to it. And if it happened then it happened. She was a grown woman. And she wasn't having any coregasms, at least not yet. She could never remember exactly what constituted her core anyway.

She selected a pair of dark jeans and a light grey cashmere V-neck sweater that showed just the right amount of cleavage, adding her favorite bohemian black felt hat for good measure and her Chanel boots, feeling sexier than she'd felt in a long time.

Juice Guy had offered to pick her up at her apartment (chivalry wasn't dead!), but even though he'd already seen her topless, she'd watched too many marathons of *Law & Order: SVU* to agree to have him come to her home. She'd told him she'd meet him down at the Wandering Juice and they could head out from there. By the time seven p.m. rolled around she was absolutely starving. The Super Superfood salad wasn't half bad, but it had done nothing to fill her up, and her stomach had been growling since an hour after she'd finished eating it. She'd unfortunately cleared the apartment of all other food, which CJ had promised her was the only way the food delivery services actually worked in your favor. Otherwise they were just delivering you bonus food, and as CJ liked to say, "Bonus food just makes your bum big."

She hoped they'd be going somewhere to eat right in the neighborhood. Janey knew of a yummy vegan Thai place right on Eighth Avenue that could be his style, but she'd already decided that she would let him select the restaurant. She was sick of making decisions for men. She wanted to be fawned over for once, to have someone else do the thinking. She wondered if that was antifeminist and decided that she didn't care.

Juice Guy was sitting down at one of his long picnic tables like a customer when she walked into the snug space. The guinea fowl chirped loudly at her arrival and that same girl, the one with the plant tattoos, was talking to the birds in hushed tones.

He rose right away and enveloped her in a hug. Janey breathed in his unfamiliar scent, something smoky and raw mixed with a sweetness like oranges. He kissed her on the cheek and squeezed her hip ever so slightly. Janey was keenly aware that he'd already seen her topless.

"The guinea fowl are up in arms today."

"Why?" Janey asked, smiling. "Thanksgiving isn't for almost a year. It seems they're living the life right now. Badgers can't even get in here to get them."

Juice Guy laughed. "One of them just stopped laying eggs earlier this week, and it's thrown the others into a tizzy."

"Menopause," Janey said, raising an eyebrow and quickly thinking that forty-year-old women shouldn't say the word "menopause" out loud.

"Maybe. We're trying to figure it out. I'll keep you updated on whether she lays." His eyes were kind, wide and a little droopy like a Labrador retriever's. Everything that came out of this man's mouth sounded vaguely sexual and Janey liked it. A lot.

"So, where are you taking me?"

"It's a surprise." He winked at her. Janey marveled at how tall he was. She hadn't noticed it when he was standing behind the counter, but he was several inches above six feet. She felt small, and at five foot nine she never felt particularly petite around men.

"Bye, Jacob. I'll see you in the morning," Fern Tattoos said distractedly, reaching one hand into the guinea fowl pen. "And bye, Lainey."

I don't know your name either, Janey thought. Jacob. That was his name. Janey filed it away, replacing "Juice Guy" in her mental file for him.

He immediately grabbed her hand as he led her out the door. Hand-holding twice in twenty-four hours. Ivy was wrong; dating was easy. Maybe dating when you were a little bit older *was* simpler. You knew what you wanted. There was less bullshit. And Janey, at forty, didn't feel any pressure to get married again right away or have kids. She found she was excited just to enjoy herself. She liked the way he ran one of his fingers over the top of her knuckles. Now, at a time when she thought she had zero interest in romance, she had two potential suitors.

"Well, I'm starving. Come on, at least give me a hint where we're going."

"Do you really want to know?"

"I do!"

"Well, you seemed like an adventurous girl so I thought you might be into dumpster diving."

CHAPTER ELEVEN

Y ou're funny." Janey shot Jacob her most winning smile and pushed a lock of dark hair out of his eyes. "So there's this great vegan Thai place I know right around the corner. It's never crowded. We can just walk in."

He grabbed both of her hands. "I'm serious. Do you realize how much food gets wasted in this city on a nightly basis? It's gross. I had an eye on you in yoga. You've got a spark, Janey Sweet. I know you're going to love this."

"See, it's not that I think I won't love it," Janey tried to explain cautiously, not wanting this date to end before it even began. *Was this worse than Iranian George Clooney asking if she wanted to do cocaine?* "I'm not dressed for it. These boots." She gestured down, realizing that her vintage motorcycle boots *did* look beat-up enough to frolic in a trash bin. "They weren't made for divin'. And I'm really not wearing the right top . . . cashmere absorbs smells like you wouldn't believe."

"Yeah . . . well . . ." As he seemed to consider changing his mind, an adorable look of realization crossed his face.

"I have a sweatshirt for you. A Wandering Juice sweatshirt. One hundred percent organic hemp." Without another word he disappeared back into the juice shop, emerging a minute later with, as promised, an avocado green Wandering Juice hoodie, which he handed to her along with a North Face backpack.

He really *was* handsome and she really hadn't had a date in a long time. Janey sighed.

"So where's this dumpster?"

"Come on." Jacob beckoned to her, hailing a taxi for the two of them outside the shop. They sat thigh to thigh in the back of the car, trading small talk about nothing important—what they'd been up to for the past few days, what they both loved about Philadelphia. Jacob expressed a real interest in the fact that she'd attended an achuma ceremony. After the taxi dropped them off at the corner of Second Avenue, her date disappeared around the corner of the Whole Foods on Houston Street. Janey's heart began to pound with the knowledge that they were about to do something she assumed was illegal and she knew would be gross. But doing anything with this absurdly tall twenty-something single dad could just be the most fun she'd had all year, so she pulled her juice hoodie over her ears and followed after him behind the brightly lit mecca of organic food.

A chain-link fence guarded the massive grocery store, secured by a simple padlock. Jacob interlocked his fingers and indicated to Janey that she could place her foot into his hands for a boost.

"Just climb over," he encouraged her.

Her mantra for the evening had become "Don't think. Just do. Don't think."

Because if she thought too hard she'd go home and pour herself a neat bourbon with a twist and curl up with a book. She placed the heel of her boot into his hands and raised her arms as high as she could above her head, hoisting herself up and over the fence, feeling stronger now than she had a month ago, when she could hardly complete a push-up.

Jacob appeared to leap the fence in one swift movement and was soon standing next to her on the other side.

"Fuck, you're hot," he said and pulled her hips close to his. "I promise you it's less disgusting than you think it's gonna be."

Behind the building were two large dumpsters, a family of tabby cats, and two doors clearly marked EMPLOYEES ONLY.

"What if someone comes out?" Janey asked, eyeing those doors.

"They won't." Jacob smiled mischievously. "They have a schedule and I just happen to know it. Look, it's company policy for these big chain stores to throw things out way before they need to. But there's always an employee who's on our side, who thinks that corporate policy is a wasteful pile of shit. So they post the schedules on FreeCycle.org. That way you know when it's safe to dive. Come on. We've got half an hour. I'm actually surprised we're the only ones here."

He went silent for a second and stretched down to touch his toes. "I was teasing you before. It's your first time. I'm not gonna make you climb into the dumpster . . . unless you really want to."

Janey smiled and shook her head.

"No worries. Okay. I'm going in and I'll toss to you. Once we fill the backpacks we'll get out of here. Sound good?"

"Let's do it," Janey said.

And in another swift motion, Jacob was up and over the lip of the dumpster. Janey looked nervously out onto the street, certain that everyone walking past them knew she was committing a crime. But life seemed to go on as usual, as herds of young men and women descended on the now wildly hip and expensive neighborhood for a night of seventeen-dollar martinis. Before she knew it, Janey had her hands filled with avocados, bananas, and onions.

"Anything with a thick skin is completely safe." Jacob's voice echoed on the metal edges of the can. "I know guys who go for the grapes and apples, but that's a little too hard-core for me." He tossed her a container of waffle mix, a cylinder of cinnamon with a slight crack in it, three cardboard boxes of gluten-free pasta, likely tossed because their packaging was slightly damaged. There was a whole chicken, still wrapped in plastic, two loaves of ciabatta, and hunks of Brie, cheddar, and blue cheese.

"Today is the sell-by date on these guys. But they still have a few more days in them."

Within twenty minutes, as promised, both of their backpacks were filled and Jacob bounced on his toes in front of her.

"Are you ready for the second part of the evening?"

"This wasn't it?" Janey said coyly. "There's more?"

"I don't want to be presumptuous, but I was hoping you'd come home with me and let me cook for you with all our spoils."

"Where's home?"

"Not far. Orchard Street. I'm gonna cook you a feast tonight, baby girl."

Janey couldn't explain why she found him even sexier now than she had at the start of the date. "Lead the way."

As they walked, hand in hand, through the Lower East Side, Jacob occasionally reached into his backpack to take out a banana, a hunk of cheese, or a loaf of bread to give to someone who appeared to be down on his luck, sitting on a heap of cardboard and garbage bags in the small alleyways between the former tenement buildings.

"You're like Robin Hood," Janey said with genuine appreciation as he handed a carton of muffins to a bearded man sitting in a doorway with his pit bull. "Except instead of stealing from the landed gentry you're pilfering from corporate America."

Jacob puffed out his chest. "You can call me Sir Robin, milady. In fact, you can call me whatever you wish . . . as long as you call me." His nerdy humor reminded her of Michael, but in a good way. He laughed at his own cheesy joke.

Jacob lived in a tidy two-bedroom walk-up above Russ & Daughters Cafe. The furniture was a step above Ikea but still standard bachelor fare, a black leather couch, bookshelves filled with college required reading and science fiction, and a fish tank. In the corner was the most immense dollhouse Janey had ever seen.

"You have a daughter, right? Where is she tonight?" Janey kneeled down in front of the massive toy to see that it had been mostly carved by hand, with furniture from various found materials: bar stools with bottle caps for the tops and individual-sized cereal boxes for beds. The kitchen floors were all made from pieces of wooden wine crates, and the tiles in the kitchen were smoothed over sea glass. It was beautiful.

"Did you make this?" Janey yelled into the kitchen, where Jacob was unpacking their spoils.

"What?" He peeked his head around the corner. "I did. Yeah. I made it for Sunny. She's with her mom tonight. Allison, her mom, is an actress, a stage actress, for Broadway shows that move around the country. So Sunny's with me most of the time, but when Allison's in town I want them to spend as much time together as they can, so she's there. I think the best thing you can do as a father is show you care about the kid's mother."

"Were you married?" Janey stood and walked into the kitchen, passing a framed school portrait of a little girl with wild black hair and Jacob's puppy-dog eyes. She took the large goblet of wine Jacob held out to her.

"I hope you like red. This is a 2011 from Mendoza in Argentina. I bought a case when I was there last summer. No, we weren't married, and Sunny was not exactly what you'd call planned. We'd just been dating six months and I thought she was on the pill. She wasn't. So it goes. The kid's still the best thing that's ever happened to me, no regrets. Sunny was so tiny when she was born. She was two months early. Allison hardly gained any weight for the pregnancy. Try making an out-of-work actress eat. It's harder than sleeping in when you have a toddler. I was so relieved the day they took Sunny out of the incubator that I proposed to Allison. Got down on one knee right there in the hospital."

"What'd she say?"

"Thankfully, no."

"You didn't want to marry her?"

"I didn't. But I don't think I want to marry anyone. Marriage is bullshit in my opinion. Who needs a piece of paper?"

Janey disagreed, but she didn't say it out loud. Even though her own marriage hadn't worked, she loved the concept of marriage, of pledging your commitment to another person, of having one best friend in a harsh world. It just had to be the right person.

"How old is Sunny?" The wine was good and it helped Janey shed her doubts about the rest of the meal.

"She's four and a half going on twenty-seven. I built that doll-house for her last birthday, and I have no idea how to top it except maybe a ride on a rocket ship. If you have any suggestions, let me know."

"I have no experience with little girls, or kids for that matter," Janey said, savoring another sip of the dry red.

"But you were one once. Right?" Jacob handed her a peeler and a sack of russet potatoes. "Or you just came out of the packaging like this. A fully formed beautiful adult woman?"

"I *was* a little girl," Janey laughed. "It was a long time ago. And I don't know if I did all the normal little girl things." She thought of Beau and how the two of them had tried so hard to act like adults. *Stop it!* she warned herself. *You are having dinner with an incredibly sexy, mature, interesting man who seems to like all of the things he knows about you so far. Do not think about Beau.* "So, do I get to know what we're making tonight or is that a surprise too?"

"You're helping me cook! I'm a modern man." Jacob delivered a comical curtsy. "I believe in equality in all things, including the kitchen. I thought we'd have some crispy potatoes with a garlic aioli and then for the main course a coq au vin, all ingredients courtesy of tonight's adventure, save for the au vin. What do you think?"

"I'll withhold my judgment about any food that came from a dumpster. I don't know why I assumed you'd be a vegetarian."

"Ehhhh. I like to think of myself as a flexitarian. It means I avoid meat except for when it's delicious . . . and humanely raised. That's different from a freegan, who only eats meat he finds on the ground or in the trash. You'll be so impressed with this dinner you'll want to open a dumpster-only restaurant with me."

"We can call it Dumped; the *Times* will love it." Janey enjoyed his youthful exuberance about everything. "So is this your go-to first date? Do you take all the girls to the alley of Whole Foods and then lure them back to your kitchen?" Janey regretted them the moment the words left her mouth. A wounded look crossed Jacob's handsome features.

"You're the first date I've had in a while," he said quietly. "Being a full-time dad doesn't make it easy to pick up chicks." He smiled. "There was something special about you. I noticed it the first time you came into the shop."

Janey felt like a creep for letting her assumptions get the best of her. She'd seen this handsome man and assumed all was well and good in his world and she was one in a string of ladies. She of all people should know that appearances were deceiving and everyone was dealing with his or her own shit.

"I'm sorry." She put her hand on his, noticing that he bit his fingernails. "So how long have you been working in the juice shop?"

His easy smile returned. "Since I opened it. The shop's mine. I don't just work there."

Janey tried not to look so surprised and knew this time he was choosing his words in order to keep her off guard as he sliced the chicken into thin cutlets and immersed them in a bowl of red wine. "I came out of Penn with no idea what I wanted to do. So like half my class I went into Consulting with a capital C. I worked eighty-hour weeks traveling to places like Tulsa to tell big bosses at companies that had been around since before I was born that they needed to downsize in order to stay competitive. I had no idea what I was talking about, but they paid my company five hundred dollars an hour for my supposed expertise. Then the market crashed, I got laid off with a six-month severance package. Everyone told me to get another job, another big job. But I ignored them. I backpacked around South America for three months, got healthy again. I had lived on Doritos, Big Macs, and Thai delivery for those five years out of college. I got into juice and used my last bonus to open Wandering. That's my life story in a nutshell."

He threw his arms over his head to simulate being in some kind of nutshell.

"And how's it going? Business?"

"It's good. My rent's still low, but things could get touchy if they raise it later this summer, which they definitely could. There's one thing, though."

"What?"

"Have you heard of broth?" Jacob said, wincing a little.

"Like soup?"

"Like soup with nothing in it. Just broth. Just vegetable stock or chicken stock or beef stock. Just broth."

"Yeah. Broth. I think my friend CJ was on an all-broth diet once. Right after her all-yogurt diet. But before the all-cauliflower diet."

"It's a thing now. A new wellness trend on all the blogs. Anyway, some guys opened a broth place across the street from Wandering. They're calling it BRO-th." Jacob turned the word into two syllables, "bro" and the "th" sound. "Their shtick is that juice isn't manly enough, so broth is the right diet for guys, for bros. It's so stupid. But it gets me mad."

Janey thought back to the irritation she felt when David's Bridal ripped off one of B's early designs. Everyone kept telling her that imitation was the highest form of flattery, but she still stewed over it more than ten years later.

"That sucks. Does that mean you *lower* your prices?"

Jacob shook his head. "Just the opposite. Our investors said we need to raise them to stay competitive. Our customers are crazy enough to believe that the more expensive something is, the better it is for you."

"Oh that's so true," Janey exclaimed. "The sad truth you learn working in the wedding dress business is brides want to pay a fortune for their wedding dress. If you try to lower the price they think it's less luxurious."

Janey had a wild hair of an idea, but she didn't want him to think she was telling him he was running his business all wrong. But when it came to business and making money, Janey had never been very good at keeping her ideas to herself.

"Do you need an actual store? Is it like a coffee shop where people linger and buy a lot of things, or could you operate out of a juice truck that could move anywhere? Then you wouldn't have to deal with BRO-th anymore and you could probably save a ton of money on rent if they raise the price."

Janey searched Jacob's face for any sign she'd offended him, but he just stared past her for a second and then met her eyes. He'd been pondering the concept.

"It's a great idea. It would take a capital investment. But it's something cool to keep in the back of my mind. We could do it even if we kept the store. It would be easier and probably more lucrative than opening another location."

She couldn't believe her wineglass was already empty. Thankfully, so was Jacob's, which meant she didn't feel bad pouring herself another, even though she rarely had more than two glasses of wine at a time anymore, and this glass was so large it definitely held two normal glasses. She gestured to his goblet with the head of the bottle. He nodded.

As she poured, Janey began to tell him the story of B to change the subject. "I started the company right after business school with my best friend. I ran it. He designed dresses and I sold them. And that went great for a long time. And a couple of months ago I decided to take some time off." She felt so stupid saying it like that, but the truth was too absurd to explain to a near stranger.

"A single woman running a wedding dress company?" He raised one eyebrow, and Janey realized it was his polite and lazy way of asking whether she'd been married.

"I got divorced last year. No kids," she said. "We'd been friends since college and we outgrew each other. So that's me in a nut-shell," Janey said, throwing her own arms over her head. "Divorced and unemployed and forty." Shit. She hadn't meant to say "forty." It just came out. But she had said both "divorced" and "unemployed." The two of those were worse. Right? "I feel like one of those Life-time movies or a nineties network sitcom with Calista Flockhart."

"Come on. I've got you beat. Fell for the struggling actress, got her pregnant. Scruffy hipster single dad. I wear a lot of flannel shirts. They make sitcoms about guys like *me*."

"I'd watch that show."

"Would you now?" He stepped closer, moved her wineglass out of the way, and leaned in close. God, he was sexy. And funny. And smart. And now that she knew his name she had absolutely no problem sleeping with him tonight if that's what ended up happening after dinner. The wine must've been kicking in because she was ready to head back to his bedroom before dinner even began.

"I would. I might not watch it in real time, but I'd binge-watch it later." She looked up at him and parted her lips just a touch, hoping he was about to kiss her.

"Your heart rate is higher than average."

"What was that?" Jacob pulled back. "Did you say something?"

Janey blushed and grasped her wrist. "No. It was this watch. I guess it's not a watch. This FitThing. It tells you how many steps you walk and your heart rate and a slew of other uninteresting sta-tistics about your body. It was a gift from a friend, and I don't know how to use it."

Jacob turned her arm over and unclasped the device.

"Oh, right. Sunny's mom has one. She's obsessed with hitting, I think, fifteen thousand steps a day. Last time she was in town she dropped Sunny off at nine and then circled the block like a hundred times just to hit her goal. Give me your phone. I'll see if I can fix it."

Janey reached into her purse, disappointed that the possibility of a kiss was lost for the time being. As she surrendered the phone she noticed a new text from Stella.

"Hold on a sec. Let me just check this."

Workout tomorrow? 6 am?? We'll talk St. Lucia. Hope your week is beautiful!! ☺

She'd never make a six a.m. class if she stayed here tonight. Not that it was an option just yet, but before her FitWhatever had gone and spoiled the moment, things were going well. Jacob came up behind her, placing his hands on her hips.

"Everything okay? Your heart rate back to normal?" She turned to look at him. She liked watching him smile.

"Everything's good. A friend just wants me to meet her early in the morning for a workout thing."

"How early?"

"Six."

He whistled. "That's early. I don't want to be forward." He blushed and walked away from her, busying himself on the other side of the kitchen to chop shallots. "But I was hoping you might stay over. Nothing has to happen. Don't think I'm that kind of guy. I don't get much time on my own. I like spending time with you. I spend most of my free time at home making funny faces, pointing at things, and explaining to Sunny why her mom is gone all the time. It's nice to be with a grown-up."

Janey glanced down at her phone and then at her outfit. What did she have to lose by being honest?

"Do you have any grey sweatpants I could borrow?"

CHAPTER TWELVE

The Wall Street Journal

COFFEE POOPED OUT OF BRAZILIAN BIRD
SELLING BIG IN STATES
By Henderson Cole

Using an experimental form of biodynamic farming, a rare and endangered pheasant has produced the priciest and healthiest coffee beans in the world.

The Jacu bird, an odd-looking animal native to the Mata Atlântica rain forests of northern Brazil, were once an invasive species to the coffee plantations in the region. Now local farmers have figured out how to capitalize on the former pest.

Brazilian farmers are harvesting coffee beans ingested, digested, and then released by the Jacu. Yes, the Jacu bird actually excretes this coffee before it is sold at a premium price point.

And buyers are shelling out the big bucks for this biodynamic organic wonder, $4,000 per 60-kilo bag, four times the normal price . . .

Thi is time Janey knew exactly where she was going when she arrived at the Pearl Street building for The Workout. She buzzed herself in like a pro, made her way to the top floor, and procured her own cup of tea. The drink, warm and sweet, was exactly what she needed to alleviate the headache of a red wine hangover and fatigue from three hours of sleep. Her eyes opened wider. She stood taller. They should sell this at Starbucks. Maybe she should mention that to Sara Strong. And speaking of Sara Strong, there she was.

"Good morning, Janey. I feel so blessed that you joined us again."

"Hi. Morning. Thanks for having me. This tea is so good." Janey finished it and turned around for more. Sara put a light touch on her arm.

"You shouldn't have more than one before we get started."

"Okay. It's just so yummy. You could bottle this."

"That's the plan." Sara smiled wryly. "We're negotiating a deal with some local vendors right now. Stella told me you're a business genius. I'd love your advice. Maybe we can talk sometime." Janey still couldn't place her accent. It moved around the globe with every sentence. Was it South African now?

"I'd love to help."

"Great. I'll have one of the ladies reach out and we'll set something up." Janey assumed "one of the ladies" meant "assistant." It was uncouth to say "assistant" anymore. Sara punctuated their conversation with a nod and walked confidently to the other side of the room. Janey had never seen anyone with greater efficiency of stride.

Janey ignored her admonition and reached behind her to have another tea. She found both a second cup of the hot liquid and Stella when she turned around.

"Darling girl! Is there a new trend in oversized fitwear no one has told me about." Stella's eyes danced with merriment. Janey looked down at the grey sweatpants that were at least three sizes too large for her and tied into a triple knot at the waist. At least they were the right color. She was trying.

"I didn't stay at home last night," Janey whispered.

Stella responded with a wide grin. "Good. That's exactly what you needed. So happy for you. You look adorable. Let's start a new trend of giant pants, you and I. We'll have them on *Man Repeller* by Friday. I saw you talking to Sara. Did she mention St. Lucia?"

"No. She did mention her new tea business."

"She's negotiating with Organic Boulevard—the owner is a huge Workout fan—but things are stalled. Something about approvals from the FDA or something. I don't know. But your brilliant mind would be much appreciated, I'm sure. Strange she didn't mention the retreat. You're all set, though. Last week of March. I'll have the details sent to you this afternoon. I'll be flying there straight from Morocco. Shaman conference. We can meet up at the airport and drive together from there if you'd like."

"Great," Janey said. She wanted more tea.

The Workout was the same as before. Each movement made her feel more energized. It was easy to see why The Workout was so addictive. All evidence of a hangover disappeared. Janey felt strong and sexy and powerful. She wasn't even taken aback this time when Sara sat on the floor and wailed like a baby. She joined in, screeching like a newborn tasting air for the very first time.

As she prepared to leave at the end of class, Janey saw Stella and Sara huddled in a corner. Was Sara sneaking furtive glances over at her? Could they be talking about her? Maybe Sara really didn't want Janey to come to her private beach getaway. The high of the class was wearing off and a dull ache returning to the center of her forehead. Janey wished they could start all over again.

"Janey Sweet? Is that you?"

Janey stopped wondering about Sara and Stella and turned to see a tall thin woman of indeterminate age with bright red glasses.

"Hey, Audrey." She'd known Audrey McKay for years. Audrey was the best crisis PR consultant in Hollywood. A hundred years ago when Hugh Grant got caught getting a blow job from Divine Brown, it was Audrey who put him on *Letterman*. She turned Kim Kardashian's sex tape into a billion-dollar empire. Janey and Audrey became acquainted when a particular client of Audrey's needed a couture wedding gown to wear down the aisle that would hide the fact she was seven months pregnant with someone else's baby.

The women exchanged the obligatory air kiss.

"Don't you fucking love it here?" Audrey dropped the word "fuck" as adjective, adverb, and verb. It reminded Janey of Ivy, and she made a mental note to try to catch up with her cousin later that afternoon. "I fucking love this class. I feel like I've run a marathon and done a Master Cleanse on top of a colonic. I'm exhausted now, though. Don't you miss the days when we all just did liposuction and didn't have to work out? I've been coming here for three months and I've lost twenty pounds. Twenty pounds at my age is like a hundred. How are you? Why didn't you call me after the doughnut situation? I heard all about what happened. Beau has some balls on him, doesn't he? Or does he? I never could tell. I would have gotten you half that company and on *Oprah!*"

"It was a bruffin," Janey murmured under her breath as she moved toward the elevator, Audrey glued to her side.

"I still own half the company. I'm just taking some time off, Audrey. But thanks so much for your concern. But what about you? Tell me which Hollywood star's love child you're hiding this week."

Audrey began pecking away at her phone. "Celebrities don't need publicists anymore. They have Snapchat. I do have a huge client here in New York City. Can you keep a secret?"

Janey pushed the button for the first floor. "Better than you."

Audrey took the ribbing in stride. "Fine. I'll tell you. I'm working for Swiss Chard."

The name didn't ring a bell for Janey, but then keeping track of all the new young Disney stars turned pop stars and bisexual models turned Golden Globe–winning actresses was a full-time job.

"Is that the little rapper boy? The one with the clubfoot and the lisp the tweeny girls are crazy for?"

Now it was Audrey's turn to laugh. "No, no, that's Maxwell Rutebegah. I'm working with the Swiss Chard Farmer's Council of America. I'm representing the plant. The wonderful, sustainably grown vegetable that's so high in iron you'll never get a bruise again. The world's perfect superfood that time has forgotten. The leafy green that will kick kale's ever-loving ass."

"You're doing crisis PR for a vegetable?"

"Of course I am. Chard's in crisis. For the past three years kale has been having its moment. Everyone orders the kale now. Did you even know about kale before 2012? Of course you didn't. Kale was something eaten by Birkenstock-wearing hippies out in Petaluma who do alot of crystal healing between growing their own pot, sprouting their own grains, and naming their children after constellations. But then kale went and hired Tom Cruise's publicist, and now kale is all the rage. The chard folks are livid. They want a piece of the pie."

"So what exactly do you do for Swiss Chard?"

"What *don't* I do? I'm really just getting started. We need to get chard booked on all the top cooking shows, *Top Chef, Foodie Diva, The Chew, MasterChef, Iron Chef, World's Greatest Chef.* Last week I met with each and every associate producer. They're the ones who do the grocery shopping, you know, and I told them, 'You have a recipe for kale? Try chard instead.' And then I gave them all-access passes to Bonnaroo. I've already gone on the offensive against kale. You'll see some serious investigations in the coming weeks about how kale might not be as good for you as you think. It can actually cause toxins to build up in your brain. Do you know how terrible that is for pregnant women? I have a doctor who says it might actually cause autism, but you didn't hear that from me. And did you know that the majority of kale is farmed using child labor?"

Janey shook her head.

"You'll know it soon. *Nightline,* Sunday night. We're getting celebrity influencers on board to start talking about how much they love Swiss Chard. Fingers crossed we've got Caitlyn Jenner. Everyone just loves Caitlyn these days. Then the athletes Serena and Venus of course. They aren't cheap, but man can they sell. I had a meeting with Natalie Portman's people. You know how vegan she is." Audrey rolled her eyes at the word "vegan." "But she wouldn't sign anything unless we promised to lobby to make all chard GMO free. Christ, we don't have that kind of money. Hollywood is a steal compared to buying votes in D.C."

They'd reached the street, and Audrey's black car appeared to be double-parked right outside the door.

A light went on behind Audrey's bright blue contact lenses.

"Have you tried chard?"

"Probably, but you know all green vegetables just look like salad to me."

"Hmmmm . . . maybe once you lose the weight and get the job back, you give an interview to *New York* magazine crediting Swiss Chard with your reinvention? Can I give you a ride back uptown?"

There were no free rides with Audrey. Janey fibbed.

"I have an appointment down here."

"Okay honey. Well, call me. We have money. Gotta go. Getting Beyoncé to work chard into her next women-empowering super ballad. Do you know what she did for sales of lemonade?"

Audrey, coupled with the lack of sleep and the crash from her endorphin high, had Janey ready to curl into an exhausted ball. Her dog walker had visited Boo Radley this morning, so she had nothing to do but get home and fall right into bed, but as she raised her hand to hail a taxi she heard Stella behind her.

"Janey! I thought I'd missed you. Breakfast?"

"Sure. Somewhere close, though."

"I know just the place."

Stella grabbed her hand and led Janey down a tiny side street and into a doorway that didn't look at all like a commercial business, but inside it was one of the coziest coffee shops Janey had ever seen, all whitewashed walls and long wooden tables with giant benches covered in overstuffed cushions.

"I love this," Janey said.

"Just opened. Another one of my clients. Former stockbroker, walked by here every single day. When she burnt out, she burnt out huge. Quit onstage ringing the NASDAQ bell with those guys from Google, the two who started it. I took her away with me to Tibet for three whole months. Then she decided what Wall Street needed was a little oasis of calm. Thousands of people work down here and there was nothing but a few Lebanese delis with three-day-old falafel and sad salad bars. So she opened this. The coffee's phenomenal. Have you heard of the Jacu bird? He processes the coffee beans in his intestines before they are harvested. It sounds gross but it's the best damn coffee you'll have in your entire life."

"I went dumpster diving last night," Janey said, which seemed the logical response to ordering coffee pooped out of a Brazilian pheasant.

"Of course you did. You beautiful little minx. The French have this wonderful saying, *'Je suis bien dans ma peau.'* It means 'I feel well in my skin.' You are just looking so well in your skin! It pleases me!" Stella paused. "I want to hear all about it. And on that subject I need to tell you all about Hugh Albermarle. Did I tell you he was an earl? He was very smitten by you. I see nothing wrong with you exercising all of your options right now."

Of course. Janey had almost forgotten, in the haze of wine, coq au vin, and the best sex she'd had since college, about emailing with the silver fox.

"Of course. Hugh Albermarle. He emailed me."

"I know," Stella said, her eyes twinkling. "And you definitely need to go out with him. He's a gem. I'm not saying the owner of those wonderful paunchy sweatpants is not a gem as well, but you'll enjoy spending time with Hugh and, besides, now is the time for you to be spending as much time with as many different men as possible."

Everything made sense in Stella's instructive voice.

"So, Hugh will never tell you this himself. He's so humble, but I've known him for years so I can brag for him. He's one of the most successful M and A bankers in all of New York City. He's just the nicest guy. I have no idea how his wife of twenty years could leave him. And with two teenagers. She's off in Europe somewhere. Hugh brought the kids back from boarding school, enrolled them in Spence. He's practically royalty back in the U.K., but he'd never tell you that either. He's sweet and wonderful and the two of you are both in a time of transition, which is such a magical time. So I knew you had to connect. You'll see him?"

Janey nodded as the barista called Stella's name to pick up their coffees. When she lifted the lid, Janey sniffed the shadowy liquid, not sure what to expect, but it smelled like regular dark roast. She took a tentative sip.

"I emailed him back. We're going to have dinner. My second date this week."

Stella threw her head back and laughed.

"That's because you've found your light. You're not hiding behind your job anymore. You're learning to love you. You're coming into your wholeness." Janey thought about Kim turned Kimberly at reception back at SoarBarre.

Stella leaned into the wooden table and grabbed both of Janey's hands. "I think you were so painfully unhappy before. You're healing now."

Janey didn't want to talk about her pain. "Tell me more about St. Lucia."

"It's going to be the best week of your life. Eight days of fitness, spiritual guidance, ayurvedic cooking in the most beautiful setting in the world. Sara limits the retreat to fifteen women, so it's very, very exclusive and very hands-on. The utmost in luxury."

"What's it cost?"

Stella paused. "Fifteen thousand dollars, all inclusive."

"I shouldn't have asked."

"But it's worth every penny. You know I don't care about what anyone weighs, but you'll lose fifteen pounds in that week alone."

"It's a lot of money, Stella."

"I know. But think of it as an investment in your future. In future you."

For the first time since meeting her, Janey felt uncomfortable around Stella.

Janey sipped at her ten-dollar coffee. "I'll let you know by the end of the week."

⌒

CHAPTER THIRTEEN

C an you ride a miniature horse?" Ivy gazed skeptically over at the petite Appaloosa tethered to a fence post beneath a heated tent in CJ's equally undersized backyard. "Is it legal?"

"I don't think they're like ponies," Janey replied, feeling her heart go out to the alarmed small animal who had been rented as a prop for the twins' fifth birthday party. The women attempted to scavenge something edible from the peanut-, gluten-, and sugar-free party buffet that made Janey long for the old staples of children's birthday parties like pizza, chicken fingers, and ice cream. "I'm not sure you're actually supposed to be riding them. They're just for pictures. But what do I know?"

Miniature horses were just the latest fad in kid birthday party entertainment, following behind the illustrious line of magicians, trapeze artists, *Frozen* re-enactors, and hypnotists. The horses didn't come by themselves. They were a part of a mobile petting zoo and menagerie of baby animals, including a lamb, a half-dozen chicks, a tiny goat, two piglets, and some bunnies. Janey had been at every one of the twins' birthday parties since they were born for the same reason CJ came to each and every B runway show. Janey had no interest in children and CJ had even less in wedding dresses, but showing up was what friends, the real kinds of friends, did. Every year CJ began planning the twins' birthday party at least six months in advance in an attempt to outdo her across-the-street neighbor, Estelle Landry, whose twin girls also had a March birthday and whose toddler fetes were regularly featured in Page Six.

Most of CJ's mom friends were nice enough to Janey, but she still had a nagging feeling they thought less of her because she didn't have kids of her own. The United States was slowly evolving into a place where it was okay for a grown professional woman to say she didn't want children, that she was happier not producing offspring. But the small talk surrounding the life choices of thirty-something to forty-something women inevitably raised the subject of procreation. For the first couple of birthday parties the mom friends asked her when she and Michael were planning to get pregnant. Then they must have decided something was wrong, that they couldn't get pregnant, because without prompting they began offering up acupuncturists and IVF specialists and asking her pointed questions about her vaginal mucus. Now that her husband was out of the picture they clearly didn't know what to say to her. Plenty of them had failed marriages under their belts, some of them had two. But to be divorced, over forty, without kids—that made Janey something different altogether. Who knows, maybe bringing Ivy to this year's event was the right choice. The mommies could finally think they had her figured out. She was clearly a lesbian. A hot cougar lesbian.

CJ's imposing figure cut through the crowd, throwing her arms up in surrender.

"The bartender just got here. He's setting up. But there's vodka in the freezer and fresh pressed Green juice, Red juice, and Orange juice, all courtesy of the Wandering Juice." CJ nudged Janey with a wink. "So make yourselves an organic cocktail. It'll take the edge off."

"I'll make the drinks," Ivy said, rising to reveal her toned midriff in a yellow SoarBarre microtank with bright gold letters. "Everyone here is a potential client," she'd reminded Janey when her cousin gave the questionable outfit a double-take. "My body is my best advertisement."

Ivy pulled a bottle of artisanal organic vodka from CJ's icebox. "So, have you been to one of Sara Strong's classes again? I'd love to go with you sometime. Can I be *your* VVIP?"

"Yeah. Next week? It's great. It's actually weird how much I like it and how good it makes you feel. While you're working out you don't even want to die. And they have this crazy retreat to St. Lucia coming up." Janey stopped herself from saying any more. It was strange that she felt so protective about The Workout.

The scrum of just-arrived four- and five-year-olds beelined for the mini horse, as Steven desperately tried to inflate a bouncy castle in the only remaining space left in the backyard.

Stepping into CJ and Steven's townhouse was like wandering onto a Bollywood set. When they moved in, CJ had the downstairs walls painted dark red and adorned them with framed vintage saris dating back to before the British Raj. They'd knocked down most of the interior walls, and the large living room spilled into the kitchen, which in turn opened into the backyard garden. Delicious incense burned in each corner.

CJ's mom and aunt, both in bright blue embroidered salwar kameez with gold bangles lining their arms, bustled around the kitchen, commenting on how dreadfully skinny CJ's American friends were.

Ivy pulled glasses down from a shelf. "Seriously, who exactly is getting rich off this mason jar bubble? Do you think we could invest?" She held up one of the old-timey jars before turning her attention back to Janey. "St. Lucia?"

"Apparently the place is owned by some crazy socialite interior designer and her venture capitalist husband. Some famous director helped them finance it. Maybe Martin Scorsese?" It was Martin Scorsese. She'd overheard Sara talking about it one day after the class. She called him Marty.

"Sounds amazing. When are we going?" Janey hadn't seen Ivy this eager in a long time.

"Oh, shoot. I don't think I can bring anyone."

Ivy laughed. "I meant to the class, not St. Lucia." A quick sense of relief washed over her. She took a sip of her Green juice and vodka and wished it had a splash of tonic.

"Tuesday morning? Six a.m.?"

"Okay. Text me the addy and I'll meet you there. Anything I need to know before we go?"

"Well, it's strange. You're only supposed to wear all grey. I thought it was totally weird the first time I went, but now I can see that the monochrome actually has a calming effect on your brain."

"A calming effect on your brain?" Ivy laughed. "Who the fuck are you?" One of the mommies gave her a horrified look and clasped her hands over her kindergartener's ears.

"Ugh. Sorry," Ivy said uneasily before adding in a lower register: "Like you don't curse at home or watch *Game of Thrones*? Don't look at me like that." She turned back to Janey. "Anyway. A calming effect? You're turning into one of them."

"One of who?" Janey asked.

"One of those people who talks about journeys and mantras and life force. You've drunk the Kool-Aid."

I drank the bird poop, Janey thought to herself and struggled to find the right response for Ivy.

"You work at SoarBarre."

"Yeah? So what? I don't *believe* in SoarBarre. I let them pay me. I still believe what I've always believed about weight loss. You want to lose weight and feel healthy and strong? Eat less, move more. No one needs me screaming at her."

"Then you should open your own exercise studio," Janey said, with all seriousness.

Ivy didn't want to admit out loud she'd considered doing just that, hundreds of times, but she was scared she'd fail and then end up as a giant nobody and have to go back home and live in Charleston where her parents would insist she marry a nice boy and make babies like the ones who were currently torturing a small animal not five yards away. "Anyway. Whatever. I was kidding. Well, not kidding, but whatever. Tell me about your date with the juice guy."

"Jacob."

"Cute name. Tell me."

"It was great. What kind of details do you want?"

"All of them."

"Me too. I need to hear everything too." Janey turned to see CJ spooning a gooey yellow liquid into her mouth from another mason jar.

"Are you eating butter, CJ?" Janey asked her friend.

"Nope, it's ghee. Clarified butter," CJ corrected her.

"You're on a butter diet?"

"Clarified butter." CJ scooped another dollop into her mouth as she turned to eye the children. "Clarified butter is a thinning fat. It contains a conjugated linoleic acid, which apparently helps you lose really stubborn fat. It mobilizes the other fat cells like a drill sergeant made of fat for your fat cells. It's liquid gold. But you have to make sure to buy the desi cow ghee, which comes from the milk of the hunchbacked Indian cows that have lived a completely stress-free life. It doesn't work as well if it comes from agitated cows. It's next to the olive oil at Whole Foods." CJ grabbed a tin from the counter with a picture of a happy batty-eyed bovine under the name HOLY COW GHEE! "Come on, Janey, spill about the juice guy," CJ whined. "I saw him when I stopped into Wandering Juice this morning." She began describing Jacob for Ivy's benefit. "You can actually see his pecs through his T-shirt. I haven't seen any pecs in fifteen years. Steven has tits now. Breasts. My husband has bigger breasts than I do. I need to hear about hot sex with the juice guy." CJ wasn't even bothering to whisper as Steven finally opened the flap to allow children into the bouncy castle.

"Me three," a very pregnant woman Janey didn't recognize chimed in from across the room. "I haven't had sex in two years."

"You're pregnant," CJ said incredulously.

The woman waved her hand. "I don't even remember it. Come on. Hot juice guy. How hot are we talking? Also, CJ, are these mason jars BPA-free?"

"Hot," CJ said. "And yes, Ella, of course they're BPA-free. Do you think I'd have anything in my house that wasn't BPA-free?"

"Channing Tatum or Chris Pine?"

"Channing Tatum."

"I can work with that. Do you think he'd want to do a photo shoot?" That was an odd response, but no more odd than learning that a pregnant woman outside of the New Testament hadn't had sex in two years.

"Ella runs Vogue.com," CJ explained about the massively expectant brunette, who nodded.

"Hot men get clicks, especially hot men who look like they work with their hands and do things that might involve dirt and wear plaid. Let me know if he'd be interested. Our audience loves a hot modern farmer. Tell us all about the sex!"

The woman's face was so eager Janey worried she'd go into labor if she didn't tell her everything. But it was the mini horse that saved her. He let out a braying shriek of terror as both of CJ's twins tried to climb on top of him at the same time.

"Fuck. I told them *not to ride the mini horse*. I should've gotten the hypnotist." CJ leapt up to calm the beast.

"Let me help," Ivy said, grabbing a bottle of champagne and chasing after her. "I've got this."

The horse reared into the air like a very small bronco ready to charge the prairie. The paunchier of the twins fell to the ground in tears. Janey tore her eyes away from the incident to pour more vodka into her mason jar and saw a familiar face.

"Hello, Janey." It was Anna, head of customer service at B. "How have you been?" she asked coolly.

Janey always liked Anna. She'd hired her away from Bergdorf five years ago when B began getting complaints from customers about their shrinking sizes. Anna had created a system to deftly deflect customer concerns that they would never be able to fit into a B gown. They forged a partnership with concierge trainers and nutritionists who promised to shrink a bride to accommodate the dress. When that didn't work, staff would recommend other wedding dress companies, ones that carried a wider array of sizes. In hindsight Janey was disgusted that this made B even more popular. Headlines at the time read B DRESSES CAN AFFORD TO TURN AWAY CUSTOMERS. Their sales doubled the next year.

But Anna had recently grown frustrated with her job. About six months before the breakfast that imploded Janey's life, Beau had renamed the Customer Service department the Customer Delight department and made Anna the vice president of delight. He changed it on the website and on her business cards. He was convinced that it was the most innovative decision he'd ever made for the company . . . ever. It was the only decision he'd made for the company that year.

"It's not a title," she'd complained. "It's made up and I'll never get another job."

Janey had promised to get it changed back, but she'd been gearing up for two Hollywood weddings and hadn't gotten around to it.

"Anna, I'm so sorry I didn't change that title for you. It was a crazy couple quarters." The woman nodded and looked down at Janey. Anna felt like a stranger now. Wasn't it weird that when you worked with someone every day she began to feel like family? Even when you couldn't stand her there was a sense of intimacy. You knew things about her that her friends didn't. You watched her chew salad with her mouth open at her desk or pick her nose when she thought no one was looking. She irritated you when she typed too loudly or left her coffee mug in the sink without rinsing it, but you let it go in the name of workplace camaraderie. But then you left the job and poof, she was gone. Out of sight, out of mind.

"You don't look fat at all. I can't believe Beau said what he said to you." Anna pointedly stared at Janey's midsection, which was cloaked by a baggy fisherman's sweater she'd obtained during a work trip with Beau to Dublin a few years earlier.

"Thanks, Anna. That's nice of you to say."

"So what's next for you?" Anna looked away for a moment to shout at a little blond girl with an upturned nose and pronounced cheekbones wearing a light blue princess dress. "Honey, honey . . . don't let that piglet lick you on the mouth. Are you kidding me? Okay. No piggy kisses." Ivy waved at the woman and snatched the swine from the child. Anna turned back to Janey.

"I want to strangle whichever mom started this birthday party petting zoo trend. No. You know what? I'll bet it was the gay dads. Those fucking guys." Anna poured herself a mason jar of artisanal vodka, not bothering with the juice. "So Beau has that intern, the one with the spindly legs, taking all his meetings with him, and he's getting weirder by the day. I don't think he's eating food at all. I see him nibbling on pieces of Swiss chard every once in a while, but other than that I haven't seen him put anything in his mouth. It probably wasn't the best time for you to leave."

"For me to leave?" Janey said. She hadn't left. She was told not to come into her office.

"Beau told us you weren't coming back."

Janey let the words linger in the air as her stomach began to clench in anger. Without thinking, Janey got defensive.

"I'm coming back, Anna. I just took some time off."

The woman's expression changed, softened. The anger disappeared and was replaced with something new. Was it pity?

Ivy returned, slightly out of breath, to top off her cocktail.

"Thanks for taking that pig away from my daughter," Anna said gratefully, lifting her empty glass.

"Is that your daughter? With the sparkly dress? She's so cute. She looks like a little Joan Rivers," Ivy said.

"Excuse me?" Anna replied, clearly offended.

"Like a little Joan Rivers with her funny little face," Ivy, who was clearly a little drunk, said without a trace of malice.

"I can't believe you just compared my toddler to Joan Rivers."

"Joan was a great comedienne and outstanding American. Don't speak ill of the dead," Ivy slurred before she bounced from her heels onto her toes and cantered to the bouncy castle.

"Do you know her?" Anna asked. "Are her kids in school with mine?"

"No clue who she is." Janey shook her head. "Your daughter looks like a little Kate Winslet."

"She does, doesn't she." Anna glowed with pride.

"So tell me more about what's happening at B." She owned half that company—well, almost half that company. She *was* going to get it back.

"I'll be back in a few weeks," she pressed on. "Beau, as usual, doesn't know what the hell he's talking about." Janey had the beginnings of a plan. "In the meantime, how about you keeping me updated on what's happening at B? Between us, of course. I want to be ready to hit the ground running the day I get back, and I don't want to play catch-up. I've just been working on this top-secret new line . . . in Shanghai." Janey finally felt like her old self again.

Anna appeared relieved and confused at once. When it came to choosing sides, it was clear she wasn't on Beau's. The woman would help her out.

"I'll tell you anything you need to know. I'm the vice president of delight, remember? Let me know how I can delight you."

CHAPTER FOURTEEN

~

Vice.com

**THE PERFECT MEDITATION APP FOR PEOPLE
WHO ARE REAL AS F*CK!**

Meditation isn't just about chanting and breathing. It's really about building a healthier relationship with how you really feel. And sometimes what we really feel is "F*ck my life." Am I right? Few things feel better than dropping the F bomb every once in a while. Just ask Kanye. Welcome to the F*ck My Life Meditation app, guided meditations with a sprinkling of profanity that express how we really feel about Tuesdays. The standard meditation instructs the listener to "breathe in strength; breathe out crap. With each breath, feel your body saying, 'I'm letting this shit go.'" Talks you off the ledge every fucking time.

T he notebook on Ivy's lap was pink and announced in gold cursive on the cover "Leave a Little Kindness Wherever You Go." Kelli bought it for her at the Columbus, Ohio, airport when she visited her parents last month, and since then

Ivy brought the thing with her to group therapy to take notes in the hopes it would cure her newfound anger at the world.

Group therapy (they used to call it consciousness-raising) was all the rage back in the seventies when like-minded housewives got together to talk about divorcing their husbands and getting pixie cuts in the name of second-wave feminism. Dr. Ron Goldblatt brought it back so angry millennials could figure out what was making all of them so angry. He had, in fact, just signed a six-figure book deal with Random House based off his irate twenty-something clients. It was called *Pissed,* and they already anticipated a *Times* best seller.

This particular group, handpicked by Ron, was a special breed— all of them working in the health and wellness industry. While they all had jobs that ostensibly should make them feel better, something about what they did made all of them feel worse.

There was the budding yoga instructor whose boss, the poster woman for zen on the Upper East Side, kept telling her she was fat.

Ivy and that girl, Summer, got on right away when Ivy shared her own story about being accepted to the New York City Dance Academy out of high school. Her acceptance letter said, in plain language, "We would be pleased if you would lose twenty pounds by the commencement of fall semester." At first it hadn't bothered her. It was important for female dancers to be under a certain weight, otherwise they were difficult to lift. But the weight didn't melt away that summer, and Ivy went to extremes, eating nothing but lettuce, spending an entire day in the sauna, wrapping her body in plastic garbage bags and running around the block. She'd dropped the twenty by week one of school.

Ivy loved telling this story in group therapy. She'd commanded everyone's attention for the entire hour.

"What happened next?" Summer asked.

"We had weigh-in every week. Most of the time I was okay. But some weeks I was a pound or so over, and the dorm mom would say things like 'Little piglet had too much ice cream this week.' And then I wouldn't eat for the next four days."

"That sounds like every single time I go to work," Summer said quietly. "I can't even count how many times I show up and my boss points to my belly and says, 'Too much of the chunky.'"

There was Seth, the co-founder of BRO-th, who had a serious doughnut addiction and was just sick of being the poster boy for soup. "We started it as a joke in B-school and now we're the BRO-th guys. That's all we are. I didn't get an MBA at Harvard to be the soup dude." There was a massage therapist who'd developed an aversion to touching people in her personal life. "Too much touching all day," she complained. And then they had the CrossFit mogul who really just wanted to be an accountant and the artisanal paleo chef who was a secret vegan.

Ivy fit right in, the angry, angry spin instructor who just wanted to be nice again. This week, Ivy was delighted when Ron started off their session with her.

"Ivy, have you thought about quitting your job?"

"Have you thought about paying my rent?" Ivy snapped before guiltily backtracking. She exhaled and imagined her breath like little wisps of cotton candy. "Of course. I think about quitting my job every day. But I don't have a backup plan. I'm not qualified to do anything but this. I was a ballerina. There aren't many companies out there looking for classically trained ballerinas. I don't even have a résumé." Ivy rolled her eyes and sighed low and long. "And I don't know what I want to do when I grow up."

Ron raised an eyebrow. "You don't feel like a grown-up?"

"Come on, Ron. No one in New York is a grown-up."

The other members of the group nodded in solidarity.

"You can stay a kid here forever," Ivy continued. "I don't hate all parts of my job. I like that they pay me a lot of money. I hate that I have to yell at people. I like that I get to work out for work. That's nice. I wish we didn't charge so much money for the classes. I feel guilty even though I know our clients are real rich. But I wish people didn't think fitness needed to be so expensive. That's not fair. It's like only real rich people can be thin. Is that right?"

Summer chimed in. "And then thin isn't even good enough. Thin is only the beginning."

"Girls. No cross-talk," Ron admonished. "What would you do if you didn't have to worry about money, Ivy?"

Ivy picked at her cuticles. "Like Janey?"

"Your cousin Janey? You know we try not to use names in here."

"Yeah, my cousin Janey. My cousin who doesn't have to worry about money, like at *all*!" Ivy loved Janey. She really did. But sometimes it was hard not to resent the fact that her cousin was so nonchalant with her millions and millions of dollars. She acted all ashamed of the Sweet family's chocolate money, acting like B was the only thing that mattered. But Janey could go home and work at Sweet and be the most important woman executive in South Carolina anytime she wanted. Where was the shame in that? People liked chocolate. Not people in New York, unless of course it was 95 percent dark, cultivated from fair trade cacao, and grown by a tribe that used clicks instead of words to communicate. But owning a whole chocolate company was nothing to be ashamed of. It wasn't like the family business was porta-potties. "Janey acts like losing her job is the worst thing that's ever happened to her when she could move home and run Sweet Chocolate, which happens to be a Fortune 500 company, but she's too stuck up to do that." Saying these things out loud made Ivy hate herself even more. But that's how she felt, and you were supposed to be honest in therapy.

"What would you do if you had Janey's money?" Ron prodded. Ivy didn't have to think about it. She knew what she would do. She'd start her very own class—a ballet boot-camp fitness workout. It would have the stretching and elongation of the muscles from ballet and enough cardio to burn calories. It wouldn't take much money. She wanted to teach outside and charge people ten dollars, which almost anyone could afford for a good workout. But that wasn't going to pay her rent. Ultimately she needed this bonus from her bosses at SoarBarre. That might give her the kind of security she needed to do something on her own.

She shrugged at Ron's question and began to doodle dancers in her pink notebook. "I want to start my own business. And I might have the chance. But I need Janey to cooperate with me, and I don't think she will."

"Why does Janey need to be involved? Are you asking her to invest in your business?" Ivy gave Ron a horrified look. Family didn't lend family money. It caused rifts, problems that haunted subsequent generations. She'd never just flat-out ask Janey for money, even though she knew she could spare it.

"The owners of SoarBarre offered me some money. Kind of a bonus, see? They're all scared of this new class people are doing. It's called The Workout and it's super secret and now all the rich ladies who spent all their time at SoarBarre are going there. So Ally and Lemon want to know more about it. They want to shut it down. And they asked me if I could help them. So I'm like their private detective."

"Where does Janey fit into all this?" Summer asked, genuinely interested.

"She's like friends with the owner of it. She's going to an island with her on a retreat and she has the super secret invite. So I asked her to bring me along to a Workout and she said she would, but at the last minute she texted me last night and canceled. That's one of the reasons I'm so pissed off today. Isn't that the shit? It sucks, right? And I need this money from Ally and Lemon. If they really give it to me maybe I could quit and do something new, and I think that's what would make me happy. But then Janey had to go and ruin it all!"

· · ·

Ivy had told Ally and Lemon yesterday that she'd be going to a Workout today, and now she had to make up a story about what it was like. She couldn't tell them she didn't go. She'd already told them what she knew, starting with the fact that Sara Strong made everyone in The Workout wear grey. That was weird enough, but it made both Ally and Lemon pause for a second.

"We could institute a uniform policy," Lemon said.

Ally chimed in. "Do you think people want to wear uniforms? We can give them uniforms." Then they went all hive mind, acting for a moment as though Ivy weren't even there. Yellow tanks and shorts, they decided. Everyone would wear yellow. And they could sell the uniforms for $150 a pop.

And then Ivy told them about St. Lucia, embellishing it to make it seem as if she knew more than she did. By the end of their conversation she had them convinced she knew everything about this luxurious Workout retreat, so much so that Lemon told her SoarBarre would buy her a plane ticket to go spy on it. They were going to fly her to the Caribbean. She'd never even left the country except for that one time Janey's mom and dad brought the whole extended family to Mexico for Lorna's fiftieth birthday party. But now Janey was acting all cagey about everything. And if she kept this up then Ivy wouldn't get the bonus and she could even lose her job, because her bosses had already bought her a really expensive plane ticket.

"Maybe I can help," Summer said. "I do yoga for Kate Wells."

Ron's eyebrows knit together with consternation. "That's a side-bar, ladies. Take it outside of the circle. Now we have about five more minutes left. Does anyone want to talk about anything else?"

Seth, the BRO-th guy, tentatively raised his hand.

"I hate soup."

CHAPTER FIFTEEN

J aney was distracted by what Anna told her at the twins' birthday party. Beau didn't just want her to take some time off. He
was lying about her to the entire company.

She'd also gotten seven emails from Anna since that birthday
party. Her daughter, the one who did resemble Joan Rivers, came
down with what Anna was referring to as the swine flu, so Anna had
been working from home. She'd been forwarding Janey two months
of memos from Beau, each of them more erratic than the last. Now
Janey needed to figure out exactly what to do with them.

There was a memo sent the afternoon of the doomsday breakfast
that informed her coworkers Janey was "taking a lovely vacation to
Sweden for the next two weeks." It explicitly instructed the staff not
to "bother her" since she was "dealing with her own personal issues."

What the fuck, Janey thought.

From there Beau concocted even more elaborate stories for her.
She'd fallen love with a Swedish furniture designer and decided to
stay even longer. According to Beau, Janey was learning Swedish
and taking to life in Stockholm. Again, the staff were instructed to
avoid contacting her.

A final email from Beau claimed that Janey would no longer be
involved in the day-to-day workings of the company and that all

business decisions would be made by him personally with the help of a to-be-named board of directors. It was becoming clear that Beau never cared about her weight, not really. He wanted the company all for himself and he was willing to humiliate her to get it.

She began leaving voicemails for the Sweet family attorney, but she worried that the absurdity of the situation made her seem ridiculous, so she tried to keep them as vague as possible until she could actually speak to him. What Beau was doing had to be illegal. But she had no idea what laws he was breaking. He had something up his sleeve.

She was so preoccupied with figuring out what was going on that she nearly forgot all about her date with Hugh Albermarle. He had tickets to the opening night of the New York City Ballet, a presumptuous first date but one Janey couldn't possibly refuse. Maybe Stella had advised him he had to do something spectacular to woo her from her juice date.

Never in her life had Janey juggled more than one guy at a time. It was hard enough keeping track of one, his likes and his dislikes, his friends, his jobs, whether he had a crazy mother or an overbearing father. CJ had become an expert at it, and when she was hooking up with a handful of guys all at once back in her twenties, Janey once asked her how she managed to keep track.

"Excel," CJ told her very matter-of-factly. "I keep a spreadsheet of all the information. Basic stuff. How many siblings, what restaurants they take me to, whether they like to go down on me or not."

Janey hadn't even been on a date with Hugh Albermarle yet, and she didn't know how she'd keep things straight. For the past three weeks she'd been texting with Jacob nearly nonstop (even though half those texts were in emoji), and she had even missed this morning's Workout because Allison was back in town and had taken Sunny out to Fire Island. She felt awful canceling on Ivy, but the opportunity to spend the morning in bed with Jacob was more appealing than curling into the fetal position and crying with Sara Strong.

The sex with Jacob *was* phenomenal. He was attentive and kind and had so much energy, which Janey chalked up to the fact that juice really was the natural Viagra. Thinking about Viagra made her think again about Hugh Albermarle, who was at least thirty years older than Jacob. She'd never had sex with someone that much older than she was. What would his body be like? Would his skin be all loose and droopy? She would've canceled if the setup hadn't been made by Stella. She didn't want to hurt the shaman's feelings, especially not before they set off for eight days in St. Lucia together. Janey tried to conjure memories of the hand-holding with Hugh and the excitement she felt after the cactus ceremony, but all she could think of was how hot Jacob looked with his shirt off.

. . .

She'd been wearing jeans and sometimes yoga pants to her recent dates with Jacob. For visiting the ballet with Hugh, she carefully scoured the contents of her closet, looking at dresses she'd almost forgotten she owned. No matter what the scale said, she was feeling thin and toned, the way you do right after your period ends and you haven't eaten salty things for a couple of days. Janey finally found what she was looking for all the way in the back of the closet. She zipped the dress out of the plastic cover and was enveloped in a tumble of black fabric. Lorna was the only other person who'd ever worn this Giorgio Sant'Angelo, and that was before Janey was born. She could almost smell her mother's lavender perfume as she pulled it over her head, allowing the material to wind and flutter with attitude around her curves. She paired it with an Elsa Peretti gold cuff, and as she slipped into her simple black ballet flats she was surprised to notice that her stomach now had a bit of a flutter in anticipation of the date.

Janey went to Lincoln Center all the time for Fashion Week but hadn't been to the ballet since Ivy's accident, and she'd never even heard of this particular piece, *La Sylphide*.

There was an intimate reception in the lobby prior to the performance where Janey had agreed to meet the silver fox, but when she arrived he was nowhere to be found. She helped herself to a glass of sparkling water and politely refused a champagne (too many calories) and a petite lettuce cup filled with puréed vegetables.

"Silly little things, those lettuce cups," she heard a posh British voice say behind her. "But I think the mayor passed a law saying appetizers can no longer be served on toast in New York City. I'm so sorry, my dear. I promise to feed you as soon as this is all over. In fact, we can leave and I'll feed you now if you like." His blue eyes twinkled mischievously.

"I'll survive." Now Janey remembered why she'd said yes to this date in the first place. No man had ever looked so comfortable in a tuxedo. She imagined he had a whole section of his closet dedicated to nothing but tuxedos, vests, cummerbunds, and Italian shoes. "I do miss toast, and not toast with avocado, but real toast with real butter and real jam." She let her southern accent seep into her voice when she mentioned butter. She didn't add that she hadn't eaten any of those things in two months.

"I knew we'd get along splendidly. My people aren't known for their food, but I invested in a new gastropub not too far from here where the chef does wonderful, wonderful things with proper toast and bone marrow. We'll go when we've had our fill of culture. Just say when. We can leave absolutely anytime."

They were interrupted by a savagely tall and slender teenager wearing a long tulle tutu over a sleek black leotard.

"Can we ask you to say a few words, Your Excellency?"

Hugh smiled out of the corner of his mouth.

"You can call me Hugh, Natasha. I keep telling you that, but I think you like saying 'Your Excellency.' Does it make you feel like we're on *Downton Abbey*?"

Natasha blushed. The assistant was brand-new at this, and trying to be polite. Janey smiled at her and answered on her behalf.

"It makes *me* feel like I'm on *Downton Abbey*. I think I'll start calling him 'Your Excellency' too." Janey winked at Natasha.

"If you like." Hugh shrugged. "I'll call you Madame CEO. So what should I say to this crowd of ballet fans? I never know what to do in these situations. The truth is I donated a certain sum to the new wing of this place because my daughter decided she wants to be a ballerina and my soon-to-be-ex-wife made us patrons. Don't get me wrong. I love the arts, but no one here knows who the bloody hell I am."

Janey thought back to all the times she'd found herself in a similar situation, fancy dinners for FIT alums, CFDA galas, once a political fund-raiser for a state senator. Most of the time they'd invited Beau to speak, but he rarely showed up at those things unless he knew he'd be photographed for the *Times* Styles section.

"Just make a toast," Janey said with confidence. "No one wants to hear a speech. You have a damn sexy British accent. Raise your glass to the dancers and the good-looking people here in this room who made tonight possible. You'll make everyone feel like a million bucks and get them into their seats that much quicker."

"You're a genius." Hugh's compliment made her feel like she'd aced the most important exam of her life. He was good.

Someone dimmed the lights, and Hugh clinked his glass. His toast was much wittier than the one she'd suggested, and the entire room fell in love with him, women and straight men alike. Without her having to ask he strode assuredly to the bar and picked up a glass of champagne for her and a neat whiskey for himself.

"I think I'd like one of what you're having." She smiled. "That's what sweet southern belles like to drink. None of these bubbles." For the second time in less than ten minutes she could tell she impressed the silver fox.

"Will you marry me?"

"Your divorce doesn't sound final yet." Janey had no idea if she'd be so confident on a date if she hadn't already been practicing with

Jacob. Shit! Did she really just think of Jacob as practice? And just this morning she couldn't imagine going out with anyone but him. The truth was, any man would pale in Hugh Albermarle's shadow, even sweet, sexy Jacob.

He took her ribbing in stride. "And who knows how long it'll take? Probably longer than usual since she refuses to come back from Europe."

Janey softened. "I'm sorry. I shouldn't joke. I'm going through my own divorce and it's awful. Simply awful. Even if you want it to be over, nothing is worse than legally ending a marriage." As the words came out of her mouth she thought about how much worse legally ending her business partnership with Beau might be. *Stop it,* she thought. *Do not do this tonight. Not when you're on a date with this wonderful-seeming man.*

"Thank you for that. For understanding." Hugh guided her to a private box with two plush velvet seats. "I'm only just starting to date again. Stella told me not to say that, but what's the point in pretending? I have no idea what I'm doing."

Janey settled into her seat and gazed down at the stage. My god. This was the way to see the ballet. It felt like a private performance for the two of them. "I like that you're not pretending. It's all new to me too. The honesty is refreshing, to tell you the truth. But we didn't come here to talk about divorce all night. What do we know about *La Sylphide*? I haven't been to the ballet in ages, even though my cousin, Ivy, was a ballerina with this company."

"We know a lot. I strangely know a lot. It's a tragic story." Anything in Hugh's perfect accent could sound like a tragic story if he wanted it to. Janey hoped they wouldn't turn down the house lights before he finished telling it. She loved watching his hands move as he talked. "It's one of the world's oldest classic ballets and utterly heartbreaking. Probably a terrible ballet to bring you to on a first date, and I do apologize. It takes place in Scotland, which may be one of the reasons I'm so partial to it, on the night before a big wedding. A young Scotsman is lured away from his wife-to-be by a beautiful winged spirit. He leaves his wife on their wedding day, nasty chap, but when he catches the spirit, or the sylph as they call her, she withers and dies, so he loses both women in one swoop."

"That's a terrible story. I'm depressed and the ballet hasn't even begun."

"I know. I should have lied to you and told you it was about a princess who loses her shoe."

"Too late now."

"We can leave at intermission." He had reached over to grasp her hand the moment they sat down and now clasped it between those long elegant fingers, gently stroking the top of it as if they'd been to dozens of Scottish ballets together and this was their regular private booth.

"Did your wife, sorry, your ex-wife, enjoy the ballet?" Jancy couldn't help but wonder if he was merely re-creating a comfortable pastime.

"Hated it. We never came. She preferred polo . . . and not just the ponies," he added as a dry aside.

Janey didn't know why this put her at ease, but it did.

They didn't leave at intermission, and they didn't get up to mingle either. Hugh swiftly exited their balcony and returned with two more Tullamores, neat.

Before either of them knew it, the performance was over and they were standing near Lincoln Center's magnificent fountain. It was a sight Janey never tired of, the fountain lit from within at night, spouting golden streams several stories into the air.

"This feels like quite the New York moment, doesn't it?" Hugh placed his large hands on her shoulders to make sure she was warm. She allowed her body to melt backward into his broad chest.

"It really does." Janey turned to face him. He was shorter than Jacob but less wiry, much stronger, more of a man. "Tell me more about this toast with the, what did you say? Bone marrow?" She could indulge a little tonight. She deserved it.

"It's close. My driver's out front."

When they arrived Janey recognized the name of the restaurant from a rave review on *Grub Street,* but she pretended not to have heard of it just yet. This neighborhood south of Lincoln Center, northern Hell's Kitchen, was becoming the new place for trendy restaurants. But this place was unmarked, not even a sign outside.

Janey glanced at the menu as they settled into a comfortable corner booth. She'd been limiting herself to a thousand calories a day. This menu, of course, listed the number of calories in each dish. Almost every menu in New York City, even at the fancy restaurants, did that these days. Janey often wondered if it would be better if menu items came with both a calorie count and commentary. Three hundred calories for your kale salad—Congratulations on your self-control. One thousand calories for your French fries— Are you sure you want to do this? Three thousand calories for that burger smothered in cheese and bacon—You're screwed.

Janey slid the menu across the table and let Hugh do the ordering. She'd be mindful of her portions. Hugh was a man who loved to eat. She didn't want to be one of those women who just ordered a side salad. She wasn't one of those women!

Hugh had an encyclopedic knowledge of New York City restaurants and could list almost every one he'd been to and what he'd eaten there. They discussed nothing but their favorite meals for their first hour at the restaurant.

She was thoroughly engaged in everything he was saying, only occasionally allowing her mind to wander. What caused his marriage to end? Had the wife been the first to cheat? Had he? Had they married too young? How long ago had he taken off his wedding ring? She'd stopped wearing hers a week after Michael left. Did he want to get married again?

He wasn't only knowledgeable about New York. Hugh Albermarle was the British Indiana Jones. In the past five years alone he'd summited Everest, trekked the Lut Desert in Iran, cage-dived off the coast of South Africa, scrambled across the Wadi Rum in the footsteps of Lawrence of Arabia, and gone dogsledding in Finland.

Over several more whiskeys and a double order of the bone marrow toast and other plates of food, which kept arriving at the table even though Janey never saw Hugh order a thing, she learned his entire life story, starting with Cambridge and ending here as a managing director at Credit Suisse.

"I have my own division. It's interesting. To me, at least. It's how I found Stella, actually. Ever since health and wellness became the newest form of conspicuous consumption, we've been trying to make financial bets on the industry. About fifteen years ago our analysts predicted yoga was going to become the go-to exercise for Americans. At the time, yoga was not exactly a household word. It was practiced by tie-dye-wearing hippies who needed something to do once the Grateful Dead stopped touring. But we predicted it could be the perfect American exercise, a class where they make you lie down in the end and tell you you're a goddess."

For a second Janey considered telling him about Free the Nipple, but decided it wasn't the right moment to talk about her breasts, and she remembered that was where Jacob asked her on a proper date.

"So we invested in Lululemon and Gaiam and high-end gyms like Equinox. We backed the first farm-to-table food chains and farm-to-face beauty lines. Have you heard of Skinny in a Bottle?"

Everyone knew about Skinny in a Bottle. It was sold at checkout counters right next to the 13-Hour Energy drinks. Janey had no idea what it was made of. Some kinds of vitamins and minerals they claimed sped up your metabolism.

Hugh continued. "I met the Skinny in a Bottle creator when she was a new mom selling juice out of her garage. We turned her little holistic business into every woman's fantasy in a bottle. Now we have Skinny in a Bottle, Youth in a Bottle, Happiness in a Bottle, Hate Your Husband Less in a Bottle. Kidding about that one. I took her public for two billion dollars over the summer."

Janey was impressed, not just with Hugh's business acumen, but by how much he seemed to truly enjoy his job. Hugh seemed to adore talking about the ins and outs of the companies he funded. "Am I boring you?" Hugh asked politely.

"Just the opposite." Janey ran her finger along the rim of her glass and smiled. "I miss talking business." Out of the corner of her eye she saw a man making a fuss on the other side of the room, waving his hands manically in the air, gesticulating with a glass of clear liquid. Of course Beau was here. Wasn't Hell's Kitchen the hot new gayborhood? Why couldn't they have divided the city into his and hers quadrants? She never ran into Michael. It hadn't happened once since their separation began. In hindsight that was likely a tribute to the fact that the two of them never really liked visiting the same places. But Janey and Beau liked all the same places. The alcohol had a warming effect on her and made her feel a little silly. Janey told Hugh to pause for a moment and signaled the waiter to come over to their table.

"What's the fattiest thing on this menu?" Janey asked, scanning the piece of paper.

"Well, ma'am, we serve actual fat, pork lard, rendered and clarified of course, but we smother our crispy fries in it. I'd say that's about as fatty as fatty things tend to come."

"That's perfect. Could you send two servings of that to the loud gentleman at the table in the back? You can tell him Janey sent it over. And maybe a bowl of the brownie sundae, with extra chocolate sauce. And we'll have one of those here as well." Janey smiled at Hugh. "It's an inside joke with a friend."

Hugh didn't completely understand what she'd just done, but he had that twinkle back in his eye.

"Speaking of fat, there's something else too. The pendulum is starting to swing a bit in the other direction. I'm starting to think about it."

"What's that?"

"The good kind of fat!"

"The good kind of fat?"

"Women have been depriving themselves for so long. I'm taking a look at the simple healthy indulgence. I'm making bets on olive oils, butters, cheese, and dark chocolate."

"Oh, I can tell you some things about chocolate, Hugh."

"Can I order you another drink?"

She didn't want this evening with this beautiful and brilliant man to end.

"As long as you split this sundae with me."

CHAPTER SIXTEEN

Y ou don't find it a little politically insensitive?" Janey asked
CJ as the two women ascended from the L train to Williamsburg. "Something about it feels icky to me."

CJ, still dragging her SoarBarre foot uselessly behind her,
shrugged.

"I'm Indian and it doesn't bother me."

"I'm part Irish, and a boot-camp class claiming IRA members as
founders might make me uncomfortable."

The day before, they'd signed up for the latest SweatGood pass
craze, Tamil Tiger Boot Camp, a military-style cardio and weight-
training class led by former members of the militant separatist
movement from Sri Lanka.

"Blast your metabolism with this mix of mental conditioning and
physical training as you allow our highly trained military operatives
to take your fitness to the next level," read the class description.

"No one would take a class led by members of the IRA anyway,"
CJ explained. "Who wants to work out with a bunch of pasty old
white guys who drink beer all day? The Tigers were fierce. And
don't you think we're doing a service to these people? They're refu-
gees and visitors to our country. We're helping them live the American Dream."

As usual, it was useless to argue with CJ about fitness or geopolitics. She grabbed her friend's elbow to steady her as they stepped onto the curb, narrowly avoiding collision with a trim, determined woman power-walking a double stroller. The studio door was just a few down from where they were standing, and Janey could see a line forming outside on the sidewalk for the next class. As they approached, she spied a familiar vehicle, a bright blue Tesla with vanity plates reading SPRSTAR, idling at the end of the street.

"Shit! Beau's here." Janey paused and squeezed CJ's arm. "Fugh! I can't with him right now."

"How do you know?" CJ squinted to make out the car. They'd had a big laugh when Beau shelled out a ridiculous amount of money for the custom-designed vehicle last year because he had a crush on the Tesla founder, Elon Musk.

"There it is! The car of the future. Ugh. You don't think he's here for this class, do you?" CJ steered Janey away from the line.

"I can't think of any other reason he'd be in Brooklyn," Janey said. "Beau doesn't leave Manhattan unless he's boarding a plane."

CJ straightened to her full five feet two inches. "Then we confront him. You were going to have to run into him sometime."

"I already did." Janey told CJ how she'd sent Beau lard fries during her date with Hugh, causing her friend to erupt with laughter.

"I didn't think you had that in you. That's probably why he's here. He has to work off a whole week's calories after you sent him a bowl of fat. Let's do this, mama. You don't have to talk to him. I can call him a motherfucker, but you don't have to say a word. And afterward maybe one of the Tigers could tie him to a chair and inflict some torture on the little bitch."

She turned to CJ. "How do I look?"

"Gorgeous," CJ said simply. "Stunning. The best you've ever looked."

Janey glanced over her shoulder at the growing line. As far as she could tell, Beau wasn't already standing in it, and no one had emerged from the car. Wasn't it like him to let everyone else queue and cut in front at the very last second?

"Can we at least wait for everyone to go in so we don't run into him?" Janey pleaded. "We can duck into this shop for a minute." She pointed to the windows of the clothing store behind her, a place that sold children's clothes made exclusively from baby alpaca wool. "I'll buy something for the twins." She grabbed CJ's arm and pulled her into the warm little store that smelled faintly of wet goat. The door gave a little chime as they entered, but the bored salesgirl behind the counter didn't even bother looking up from her iPhone.

CJ fingered the soft sweaters and mittens tied together with a string. "These won't fit the twins. They're getting bigger by the day. I don't know if I should stop feeding them or what."

Janey pinched her friend's arm.

"I'm kidding," she said. "I'm trying to get them to be more active. Steven thinks they're fine the way they are. 'They're boys,' he says. 'They're supposed to be a little beefy. We have little football players on our hands.'"

Janey hardly heard what CJ was saying. "The line's moving. Beau's getting out of the car."

The petite salesgirl with a conspicuous unibrow finally decided she should be cordial. "Can I show you the spring line? We just got these in from Peru." She picked up a pair of furry child-sized leg warmers. "All of our wool is fair trade, and the sweaters are knit by a co-op of former prostitutes in Lima."

"I'll take two of these little hats. I'm all about supporting former sex workers," CJ said, picking up a red beanie and an orange one. "Their heads are a completely normal size."

Janey watched as Beau bounced from the backseat of the Tesla, holding the hand of someone behind him in the car and dragging her onto the sidewalk. It was the girl. That beautiful intern. His new muse. Her replacement. She felt the early symptoms of a panic attack, tingling fingers and a gnawing tightness in the back of her throat. It hadn't bothered her that her ex had gotten a new woman pregnant, but seeing her former business partner and best friend, her *gay* former business partner and best friend, bringing this giggly little girl to a boot-camp class was enough to reduce her to tears.

CJ handed the salesgirl her credit card and came over to sling her arm around Janey's waist. "You're better than he is. You know that. Let's go. Don't let him cheat you out of burning like a thousand calories with some reformed terrorists. We took the subway here, for god's sake. We're working out with that militia."

They were the last to walk into the class and forced to stand in the back of the large warehouse, a former sugar refinery that retained a faint scent of burnt confectioner's powder. Over the next five minutes, two Sri Lankan men in full combat fatigues and with precise British accents carefully explained the plan for the next hour. They would be divided into teams and made to compete against one another in various obstacle courses constructed throughout the old warehouse, which included tasks such as lugging boulders across the room, building stockades with thirty-pound sandbags, dismantling them and rebuilding them on the opposite side of the room, crawling on their stomachs underneath a maze of barbed wire, and scaling a two-story wall.

Beau was practically joined at the hip with his leggy new gal pal. The pair of them wore matching Rick Owens sweatpants and oversized hoodies with the words BE A UNICORN emblazoned on the front. On his head, Beau wore a rainbow-striped headband. They kept poking each other in their slim sides and giggling in each other's ears. He usually despised public physical fitness. His trainer came to work out with him in his apartment where no one else could witness it. This new girl must have made him come.

"We could go over and say hi. Don't you think it's weird for the two of you to avoid each other? You didn't get a divorce," CJ said with her trademark practicality about all things that didn't have to do with her weight or the size of her children's pants.

But it wasn't that simple at all. This was like the worst divorce of all time, one Janey hadn't initiated, hadn't wanted. When she looked at Beau with this new girl she felt cheated out of the life she thought she should have. It didn't make any sense. He was a gay man and she was a straight woman. Theirs wasn't a love story, and yet the pain of the split was as real as if they had been married for twenty years. She kept thinking back to an interview she'd seen ages ago between David Frost and Truman Capote where Truman had argued that true friendship was so much more intimate and deeper than love. At the time Janey hadn't thought much of it. She'd just been researching something about *Breakfast at Tiffany's* for the launch of a dress called the Audrey, but now the quote echoed in her mind.

The Tamil Tigers were wildly polite for former members of one of the world's most dangerous armies, sprinkling their instructions with the words "please" and "thank you" and "if you would be so kind." They conducted a lengthy roll call of all thirty guests, forcing the group to hold a steady plank position the entire time. Next up they were told to divide into teams at the start of various obstacles around the room.

"If you could please assemble your four-person team at one of the stations then we shall begin the first drill," the taller of the Tigers said into a megaphone. Janey and CJ grabbed each other's hands, the way you did when partnering up on field trips in grade school, and smiled at a pair of similarly aged women standing nearby. The Tigers took the competition seriously, giving each team a color— theirs was pink—and lighting up a giant scoreboard on the back wall. Each team received five points if all four members finished a particular obstacle course before the other team. Despite being one of the older teams in the room, the pink team was weirdly good at walking across a slack line and climbing an agility ladder. Janey looked over at Beau's team and saw him struggling to stand on a balance beam while carrying a cement block. What did he think about this place? About the Tigers? They'd spent the better part of their entire lives talking about everything, critiquing the world, cataloging everyone else's dysfunctions. Did the silence between them feel as deafening to Beau as it did to Janey? Would he laugh if she made a joke about all of the hipsters in the room pretending to guard Sri Lanka's democracy by carrying organic burlap sandbags?

With the hour ticking down to the class's final minutes, the pink team was in the lead and poised to face the yellow team in one final obstacle. Janey could hear Beau's high-pitched giggle before she turned to face him. She knew her hair was a mess. She'd caught her ponytail on a length of barbed wire during the last drill and she was drenched in sweat.

"Hey there, Janey-boo," she heard him say, realizing then that he'd known she was there the entire time. He lowered his voice an octave. "Hello, Chakori." Beau despised CJ, had always looked at her as competition for Janey's love, and refused to call her by anything but her given name.

Janey forced herself to smile. "Hi, Beau."

"It's good to see you taking care of yourself," he said in a condescending voice. "I didn't know you were back in the States."

Of course with his new officemate next to him, Beau would maintain the charade of her leaving the company, of her fleeing to Europe on a whim.

"You little shit," CJ spat at him before Janey had the chance to correct Beau's lie. The Tigers ordered them to line up. This particular course involved carrying a large sandbag through a pit of mud, climbing a wall made of ropes, leaping off onto a trampoline over a trench filled with fire, belly-crawling under dangling live wires, and then conquering a set of monkey bars.

It was the playground from hell, which meant it was the worst kind of hell for Beau, a little boy who couldn't play sports and sat on the sidelines of the schoolyard for thirteen years. Sure, grown-up Beau was strong and he was scrappy, but Janey was intent on winning this race. Beau was the last in his line, and so Janey hung back.

As CJ sprinted ahead of the leggy muse, Janey turned to Beau.

"You know damn well where I've been. How dare you poison our employees against me!" She could feel the hairs on her arms rise as she reprimanded him, and it felt good. To his credit, Beau flinched at her words.

"You're looking a little less jiggly right now." He reached over and grabbed Janey's waist and pinched her love handles. "Still have a ways to go."

She saw her teammate dive beneath the barbed wire, which was Janey's cue to take off. With Beau close behind her, Janey heaved the sandbag up and over her head with barely a grunt, lifting her knees high to slog through the muck. At the other side she threw the bag on the ground in front of Beau, causing him to stumble and fall facedown into the gloop.

"YASSSSSSS!" she heard CJ scream. Even her FitWand was excited for her. "You've reached peak heart rate. You are burning an optimal level of calories," it announced. "You are a good human."

Janey turned to see Beau fume as he wiped the sludge from his face, taking off a palm-sized swipe of concealer with it. She was halfway up the rope wall when she felt a hand clasp her ankle and realized Beau was trying to pull her off. She kicked down at him, ignoring whistles from the Tigers admonishing them. All eyes in the grimy warehouse were on them. This race brought out Janey's basest instincts. She finally wiggled free from his slippery grip, taking great pleasure when her heel grazed his expensive new nose. She summoned all her arm strength to heave her body over the top of the wall and onto the trampoline below. She could see CJ standing at the finish line holding her phone in front of her taking a video. Next to her, Beau's muse nervously chewed on a perfectly manicured finger. Janey could feel him gaining on her when she emerged from beneath the live wires. She stretched her arms to begin the monkey bars. Beau hated monkey bars. She remembered sitting with him at recess while he mocked the other children who organized races to see who could cross the bars the quickest.

"They call them monkey bars because they're for stupid, brainless monkeys, Janey," he'd say to her, and she'd nod, because she wanted him to think she was also too smart to do something so silly.

Not now. Now she wanted him to see how much better she was at this than he was, how much stronger and faster she could be. In the middle of the metal contraption Janey knew she had him beat. She threw her legs up over the bar and hung upside-down to face him as he dangled from the first rung. She smiled, flipped back right side up, and continued, crossing the finish line and bringing home more of a victory than the Tigers would ever know. Her teammates greeted her with high-fives, and CJ wrapped her arms around her waist. She'd already gathered Janey's coat and purse and began moving her toward the exit as Beau dangled helplessly from the metal bars.

"You're so fierce. You're a fierce, fierce warrior queen and don't you forget it," she said. "Now let's shower and find a bar where we can consume some empty calories and celebrate how fierce you are."

‎ ✦ ‎

www.elle.com

HOW HOLLYWOOD'S FAVORITE BLOGGER EATS EVERY DAY

She's an Academy Award–winning actress, ridiculously successful blogger, skin-care guru, and a mom to two of Hollywood's most adorable kids. And did we mention her killer bod? Kate Wells's daily diet is filled with things you've never even heard of, but you'll be dying to try.

By Maxima Moore

When juggling busy careers and lives, it's not always easy to find the time to hit the gym or prepare a healthy meal. For inspiration we're asking influential women in a variety of industries to share a typical day of eats and fitness to see how they balance a healthy lifestyle with their jam-packed schedules. Today we're lucky enough to talk to our favorite A-lister Kate Wells about the magical superfoods that keep her going.

6:00 A.M. I wake up according to my body's circadian rhythm, but always before the sun rises. I'm the first in my household to get out of bed, so I cherish the moments of peace before the place turns into a zoo. I begin the day with ten minutes of Kundalini yoga and then treat myself to Moon Juice's Beauty Milk, which is chock-full of tocotrienols, which boost muscles and regenerate tissues to promote cellular functions that make the skin really glow.

7:00 A.M. With the kids awake I become a full-time mommy and I need extra energy. I have a warm chi drink filled with 25 grams of Parsley Health's Rebuild protein and two liposomal vitamin-B complex packets, which is a better energy boost than two espressos. I also take two scoops of probiotics. A healthy gut is a happy gut.

9:00 A.M. Once the kids are off to school I indulge in an alkalizing green juice to balance my moods. I promise you it's even better than therapy. And a lot cheaper.

NOON-ISH. For lunch I make a super seaweed salad (raw and enzyme rich!) with sprouted brown rice proteins, daikon, maca, and cilantro with a raw tahini Dijon-based mustard. If I need a protein boost I'll add a poached egg.

3:00 P.M. If I'm hungry midday I'll binge on a banana, mango, and bee pollen paste. So decadent!

7:00 P.M. A couple of times a week I let myself indulge in whatever the hell I want to eat. If you keep your diet too strict you'll never stick to a healthy plan. If I'm cooking for friends (like Mario, Jay & B, or Cameron) I'll prepare something like a yummy squid ink pasta. I learned the recipe at a tiny bistro in Taormina, Sicily. But if it's just the kids and me then I prepare simple chicken or fish tacos with a side of grilled kale and an avocado and papaya salad—it's like summer on a plate! The taco shells are made from Kernza, a perennial wheatgrass known for its carbon-capturing root system.

11:00 P.M. I finish the day with what I like to call sex bark and spirit truffles. The sex bark is a natural aphrodisiac made from heirloom dark cacao and a ho-shou-wu herb tonic used by ancient scholars to improve the sex drive . . . every little bit helps, right, ladies? I then give myself an extra treat of spirit truffles made of dark chocolate, spirit dust, and hemp seeds. The spirit dust activates the pineal gland and the hemp seeds nourish the brain and stimulate the subconscious to make for incredibly vivid dreams and the deepest sleep you'll ever have.

vy was taken aback when Kate Wells answered the door herself and smiled at them sweetly, wrapping Summer in a hug and delivering three kisses, Dutch style, on her cheeks.

"Hello darling. I'm so happy you came by. Is this the wonderful trainer you were telling me about?" Kate turned her attention to Ivy and took one of her hands in both of hers. "I'm Kate."

Ivy stopped herself from saying "I know." She still wasn't sure how she was supposed to behave in front of celebrities. SoarBarre had plenty of famous guests, and she always erred on the side of treating them like anyone else. She once screamed at Meryl Streep in the front row that she was a lazy goddamned bitch. She felt terrible afterward and chugged a bottle of wine alone that night while watching *Mamma Mia!* Kate was prettier in person than she was on-screen and in magazines, softer, with the most perfect skin Ivy had ever seen on a human. It looked as though it were lit from within.

"Hey. I'm Ivy," she said, maybe a little too loudly.

Ivy tried to look as though she wasn't looking around the classic old townhouse. She knew from a Google search that *Vogue* had done a massive makeover of the space a few years back for a photo shoot. They'd painted everything lilac, even the banisters, stairs, and floors. From the entryway, Ivy could see into the sitting room. It was a crowded space with massive sapphire velvet sofas and a rather magnificent white piano. It felt more like the waiting room at Tracie Martyn than an actual home.

"Come in. Come in. The place is a mess. I just got the kids off to school. We launched the new vagina skin-care line this month so I've been working nonstop. This new line of products will be a hurdle. People don't think about skin when they think about their vaginas. There are pores down there just like the rest of your body, and it's important to keep everything tight and healthy."

She looked over her shoulder at Ivy. "Summer told me a little about you. Instructor at SoarBarre? Former ballerina? How cool is that? I haven't been to the ballet in ages, but I was obsessed when I was a little girl. We went to the *Nutcracker* every single year and I just enrolled Dusty in a class."

"I've been at SoarBarre for a couple years, but I'm thinking of starting my own thing." Ivy wasn't sure why she said that. "I do some training on the side, though. I miss ballet," she added. "Let me know if Dusty likes it. I'm happy to come over and show her a few things." She was sure people offered to come help Kate Wells with things all the time.

"She'd love that. It's the sixth new thing she's tried this year after archery, horseback riding, synchronized swimming, the harp, and Frisbee golf. I'm hoping this one sticks. What can I get you ladies to drink? Sparkling water? Juice? Wine? Is it too early for wine? Probably. But we have some if you'd like. I'll have a tea. Does that sound good? I make this yummy hibiscus tea with lemon. Apparently it's the perfect thing to drink when you have your period. I call it my uterus tea." Ivy and Summer nodded together and laughed at the concept of uterus tea from a woman who had just developed a skin-care line for vaginas. "Let's go sit in the library. Mariana will bring it in for us."

Kate Wells's library was an actual library, two stories tall with floor-to-ceiling shelves of books, arranged by color and size, making the shelves appear to undulate like sine curves. Large teak ladders climbed all the way to the ceiling. The furniture was comfy and cozy, two overstuffed white couches with tight square leopard-print pillows and dark leather Moroccan ottomans. The fireplace had clearly been blocked years ago, and Kate had placed her one and only Oscar on a brick inside of it. Well-curated art hung on the walls. Ivy thought she spied a Bacon and maybe a Rothko. She allowed herself to sink into one of the couches.

"You're looking at me funny . . . like I'm a unicorn," Kate said pleasantly from the chair opposite Ivy.

"It's just that . . ." She didn't know how to put it into words exactly.

Kate raised an eyebrow. "I'm more normal than you thought I'd be?"

Ivy exhaled. "Normal" wasn't the right word.

"You're so much nicer than I thought you'd be."

Kate let out a laugh that was deep and low. It was a movie star laugh, the kind you read about in the openings of lady magazine profiles, the ones where the stars always rush in to meet the journalist fashionably late with an intimate kiss on the cheek before ordering French fries. It was the kind of laugh the person could replicate on command. "Thank you! The press spins everything I do out of proportion. I swear, I'm not the freak they make me out to be. Take, for example, all those stories that I work out six hours every day. You know how that happened?"

Ivy and Summer both shook their heads. An incredibly small Filipino woman walked in with a large tray of their teas, a bowl full of a thick yellow oil, and a small glass cube with agitated specks fluttering inside it.

"I was giving an interview to *Vogue* to promote a movie, a bad movie I might add, that one where I was the telepathic superhero who could control the weather, and they asked me how much I exercised that day," Kate went on. "Just that one day. And I stopped to think about it for a minute. I'd just given birth to Dusty, so I was up all night because she had terrible colic. The only way she'd go back to bed would be to put her in the stroller and walk around the block. So that was three hours a night of power walking and jogging. I rode my bike to the set in Brooklyn every day, which was another hour each way, and then I'd do an hour of Pilates or yoga. So six hours." Kate paused and took a long sip of her tea. She knew how to play an audience. "And the journalist wrote, 'Kate Wells keeps fit by training for six hours every single day.' Well that was true and it wasn't true. And every article about me since has talked about me working out six hours a day. I don't bother to correct anyone anymore. No one wants their movie stars to be normal."

Kate picked up the glass cube from where Mariana had left it and opened the lid, extracting what looked like a small fuzzy bumblebee. She calmly placed the bee on her willowy arm and winced.

Did it just sting her?

"You *do* write a blog where you talk about how much you love two hundred and fifty–dollar cashmere T-shirts and activated cashews. And you include things like spirit dust in your recipes. It's not like you can buy spirit dust at Trader Joe's. I've tried," Ivy replied practically. Shit. Maybe she shouldn't have said that.

"Who doesn't love cashmere T-shirts?" Kate made a fake offended face as she grabbed a pair of tweezers and plucked the bee off her skin, putting it back into its box. "And spirit dust is just crushed turmeric. You *can* buy that at Trader Joe's. I'm just willing to try all of it, even the weird stuff. No one would read the blog if I just wrote, 'Eat less sugar and get off your ass and you'll lose weight.'"

"*Yes!*" Ivy exclaimed, wanting to fist-bump the pretty actress. "Move more, eat less!"

Kate calmly pulled a second bee from the box, pulled up her T-shirt, and placed it on her taut belly.

"Are those bees stinging you?"

"Of course," Kate said. "It hurts less than getting a tattoo and more than acupuncture. But it's so worth it. Reduces inflammation and injects you with natural collagen and biotin. Mother Earth's Botox!" Kate plucked the second bee off her body by the wing, brought it close to her lips, and mouthed "Namaste."

Ivy changed the subject. "Summer said you're looking for a new trainer, or someone to work out with? I can do six hours a day."

The joke fell on deaf ears. Kate sipped her tea and waved her pretty unpolished fingernails in the air. "Of course not. I'd love someone to do high-impact cardio and weights with me three times a week."

Ivy made a note in her pink notepad. "Okay. I specialize in high impact. I've been working on a great new cardio workout that's like ballet with weights. Are you working with anyone else right now?" She didn't want to just come right out and ask Kate why she'd stopped using Sara Strong as her personal trainer.

"Not right now. I worked with the same trainer for a long time, but we ended up having very different opinions about what was actually healthy." A cloud passed over Kate's sunny face. "I'm in the market for someone new."

Ivy knew better than anyone that personal trainers really were the new therapists. She had clients tell her things they wouldn't have dreamed of telling anyone else. She'd recently trained a corporate attorney who admitted to Ivy and only to Ivy that Caitlyn Jenner inspired him to begin transitioning to become a woman. For years he'd been raiding his wife's closet when she went out of town on business. Now that she had passed away he was finally doing something about it. And he needed her help to get rid of his back fat. He hated how his chubby back looked in Agent Provocateur corsets. Sweating together created an intense closeness. She had no doubt Kate would open up about Sara Strong within a session or two.

"When do you want to get started? I teach at SoarBarre in the morning and the late afternoon, but I'm free in the middle of the day."

"Let's do Friday? I have a good feeling about this, Ivy. Can I get anyone a uterus tea or mustard oil for the road?"

CHAPTER EIGHTEEN

There was one hour of the day when sunlight streamed directly into the front windows of the Wandering Juice. The rest of the time it dodged and weaved behind other, grander buildings downtown, but Janey found herself in that glorious patch of March sun as she sipped a Red and plotted the final logistics of her St. Lucia trip. Who would watch Boo Radley and water the plants? How long did her food delivery subscription need to be put on hold? Should she Airbnb her apartment? How did she sign up for Airbnb anyway, and how could she make sure she wasn't renting her place out to a bachelor party in town from Tampa? Or a Hungarian producer shooting Internet porn? She had a friend who rented her Hamptons beach shack for a month last summer only to learn it became the backdrop for more than one hundred lesbian pornos. It was her husband who pointed it out, which led to other issues.

She'd stopped into the juice shop with the intent of saying good-bye to Jacob, and he invited her to go to a human bowling alley with him in Brooklyn that night. Apparently the pins were people and the ball was made of pleather. Why did anyone want to do that? Since it was her last night in town she'd been hoping Hugh would ring her and ask her for a drink. Of course, she could also ring him. But she didn't.

She was also thinking about her chance run-in with Beau. She wanted to text him. The knowledge that he'd been planning to oust her from the company they built together depressed her terribly. But, at the same time, maybe this was the exit strategy she needed.

She raised a hand to her forehead to shield the light as she looked across the narrow street at the growing line outside of BRO-th. It *was* now all the rage for both gay and straight men from their twenties to fifties, all of them lined up in their wool skullcaps and grey peacoats for pig, beef, and chicken BRO-th.

She took a break and distracted herself with a few moments on Instagram, scrolling through CJ's pictures of the boys visiting the Bronx Zoo over the weekend. She was definitely Facetuning. The twins looked positively anorexic with exotic parrots perched on their teensy heads.

Wow. Sara Strong had more than 250K Instagram followers. How was that even possible? Janey scrolled the trainer's feed. It was mostly nonsensical inspirational sayings like "Don't let anyone treat you like a yellow Starburst. You are a pink Starburst" and "Blessings come in as many shapes and sizes as a rock on the beach." All of them were tagged with #Fitspo, #Strong, #Sweat, #Fit4Life, #ObstaclesMeanNothing. Another post just said, "You. Exactly the way you are. I love you." The caption on the bottom read, "To all my sisters out there in the world, I love you more than all the depths of all the universes. Be your own being. Be my being. Be all the beings." Janey wasn't certain the sentences were written in English, but they made her feel lighter, happier. They didn't need to make sense. Maybe everything made too much sense. God, now she was *thinking* in Sara Strong's aphorisms. Janey found it interesting that you rarely saw Sara's face in any of these photographs. She was always shot from behind, typically gazing off toward some fuzzy beautiful horizon or with her hands forming a victorious V over her head.

The girl at the next table noticed Janey before Janey noticed her. She could feel her eyes glancing up to stare at her every couple of minutes. Finally, Janey looked over the top of her computer to see who it was. Long legs, wide-set cat eyes, shiny dark hair, no makeup needed. It was none other than Beau's new muse peering shyly in her direction. They made eye contact and she gave Janey a tentative smile and wave before gliding toward her table.

"Ms. Sweet?" she said politely when she approached. Janey stiffened.

"I'm Alizza. From B. I was at that awful boot camp with Beau. The one with the terrorists." The girl stretched her long elegant left hand toward Janey, a slight sliver of an emerald-cut diamond set in simple rose gold on the ring finger. Out of the corner of her eye Janey could see Jacob peering out from behind the counter. She wouldn't have blamed him for giving this girl the once-over. All the young women at B were stunning. Beau surrounded himself with an army of beautiful women, each one taller and younger and thinner than the next.

"I don't want to bother you," the girl said shyly. "I just thought I should introduce myself. You've always been such a huge inspiration for me. I was disappointed we didn't get to work together when I was at B."

"You're not with B anymore?" Janey said quizzically.

"Beau fired me yesterday." Janey looked over to the table she'd been sitting at and noticed it was covered in pieces of sketch paper filled with designs.

"I just saw the two of you together last week. You looked like peas in a pod," Janey said, hoping to keep the bitterness out of her voice. To her credit, Alizza looked slightly ashamed.

"You know how Beau is. He loves you one minute and can't stand you the next. I think he kept me around because he was missing you." Now the girl had Janey's attention.

"What's that you're working on?" Janey nodded to the pieces of paper littering Alizza's table.

"Oh, it's nothing."

Janey craned her neck to get a better look. "It definitely looks like something. Can I see?"

The girl's face flushed. "They're terrible. When I showed them to Beau he was disgusted. Completely disgusted. I think it's why he let me go." She reluctantly handed Janey the pieces of paper. "Maybe I overstepped my bounds. He just seemed so interested in everything I was doing. I thought I was being helpful."

The girl's sketches were simple—bridal dresses with long sheaths with low backs, strapless mermaid gowns, nothing fancy, but sophisticated and definitely beautiful.

"What didn't he like about these? You have a good eye." Janey looked at the sketches and saw the spark of something.

The girl sat, crossed and then uncrossed her long legs in front of her.

"I suggested that we do something simple, an exclusive B line for J.Crew. These designs are all easy to replicate and I found a factory in Minnesota that was completely owned and operated by women who said they could produce them affordably. I love B. I would love to wear a B wedding dress." She blushed again. "But I can't afford it. I live with four roommates and my fiancé is a guitarist. So I suggested to Beau that women my age might be interested in a more affordable line. We could still do the incredible couture work and higher-end dresses, but this could be a new market for us."

Janey felt a twinge of regret for writing this girl off. What kind of girl boss was she? How dare she judge a pretty girl by her shiny hair alone.

Alizza continued. "But Beau looked at me as though I said something horrible, like I'd suggested we start making black wedding dresses."

Janey laughed. "You know, Beau did once suggest we make black wedding dresses, for divorcées. He went so far as to get samples made. I still have them at home in the spare closet."

Janey had long seen a need for them to expand B out of the

ridiculously high-end market and into something more afford-able. They had all the celebrity clients and the industry cred. They wouldn't damage the brand if they made a more affordable line. Everyone was doing it. Vera Wang worked with Kohl's for god's sake. But every time she'd mentioned it, Beau lost his mind. Why had she allowed herself to run her business based on his temper tantrums for so long?

"Do you know your production costs?" Janey asked. "Per unit?"

Alizza rattled figures off the top of her head. "A hundred dollars for labor, two-fifty for fair-trade textiles from Bangladesh, twenty-five dollars for shipping. I figure we can sell for between eight hundred and a thousand dollars per unit."

Janey nodded. That was definitely the ballpark for places like J.Crew and BHLDN, and these dresses had a style and a flair unlike other off-the-rack wedding dresses. She had a spark of inspiration. With costs so low and the right technology you could theoretically create cost-effective couture, letting a bride design her own wed-ding dress piecemeal on an app. What if a bride could pick the fabric, color, and cut of her dress, eliminating the designer from the process entirely? Eliminating the Beau. Now that was something she could work with.

"What do you plan to do now?" Janey asked with genuine curiosity.

"I don't know." The girl shook her head and looked ready to burst into tears. "Beau told me he'd make sure no one else in the indus-try hired me. I thought of applying for a job with BHLDN or Stone Fox. I love affordable luxury and I love wedding dresses. I loved working for B. I wanted to stay there forever."

Janey found herself wishing she could pet the girl's hair in a soothing maternal way, like Lorna had done for her.

"You can't stay in one place forever." Oh, wow. Janey realized she was saying the words to herself as much as the girl. "You're tal-ented. I can introduce you to Molly at Stone Fox, and if she offers you a job you take it. If not, then let's talk more in April?"

Alizza nodded. "I'm so happy I ran into you. I was hoping I'd see you. Can I admit something creepy?"

Janey nodded slowly.

"I follow you on Instagram and I saw you take pictures here so I thought I might see you here one of these days if I just kept coming in." She looked over her shoulder and shot a winning smile at Jacob. "The juice is the best too."

"That's the creepiest thing I've ever heard." Janey laughed. "And smart. Very smart. We'll talk soon. Okay?"

CHAPTER NINETEEN

A late-season snowstorm assaulted New York the night before Janey was supposed to fly to The Workout retreat. It was the kind of snow that went from fluffy cotton to brown slush, converting avenues to swamps and testing the patience of tried-and-true New Yorkers, who prided themselves on their ability to weather all extremes.

Thank god she was getting out of here.

Janey treated herself by using the B frequent flier points to upgrade to first class for the flight from New York to St. Lucia, transforming the brief flight into a vacation with white linen table-cloths and a constant flow of champagne.

Stella had promised to meet her at the airport, and together the two women would drive the hour or so to the retreat location. She'd received a text from the shaman the night before takeoff: *Ready for some Vitamin Sea? Game. Meet change. #BLESSED.*

There would be at least six hours of workouts a day and two meditation sessions. Strictly organic fruits and vegetables, no fatty food whatsoever. Stella warned her in the nicest way possible that the clientele was very high-end. Of course it was. Who else could afford to pay fifteen thousand dollars for a week of weight loss?

"But they're very nice," Stella said. Stella never had an unkind word to say about anyone. "I think you'll get along with them. It will be fifteen women." Janey did the math. That was nearly a quarter million dollars, and even with expenses deducted, she was certain Sara Strong was pulling in a sizable six-figure payday for eight days of work.

Work. God, she missed work.

It'd been almost three months since her fateful breakfast with Beau at the Horse Feather, and she needed a plan. Janey worked best when she had a strategy and the tools to implement it. The fact that she was a forty-year-old woman with one job on her résumé was not lost on her. She was aware that the depth of her experience might not make up for the lack of breadth and variety. What were her actual skills anyway? She knew how to build a business from the ground up. She was a whiz at global branding and marketing. She was able to manage large and tender egos with aplomb.

In Janey's management classes in B-school they'd created decision trees, elaborate "if this/then that" scenarios. If you increased the number of brick-and-mortar stores of your business, then you might see more customers and increase brand awareness, but you'd also have a large capital expenditure. If you fired all your employees and moved all of your sales onto your website, then you could forgo large capital costs, but a thousand people would be out of a job. Janey had disliked these scenarios because they never assigned any judgment to a particular outcome. Everything was black or white. Life was anything but. She doodled a decision tree of her own on the back page of the *American Way* in-flight magazine, just past the list of newly released movies and artisanal gluten-free snack options that cost twenty dollars.

If she fought Beau for her old job, she'd have to work side-by-side with a business partner she no longer trusted or even liked. If she simply walked away from B she would get a small payout and be forced to watch Beau drive their beautiful business into the ground. There had to be a middle ground, but she didn't know what that looked like yet. Janey accepted another glass of champagne from the flight attendant and let the bubbles do the job of quieting her mind. Alcohol was probably off-limits for the week of wellness, so why not indulge in a second glass? A spacious yawn escaped her lips.

She had said no to the invitation to go hipster bowling with Jacob the night before. On the couple of occasions she met his friends (all of them under the age of thirty), they'd made her feel astonishingly unhip, due mainly to their passion for suspenders and Amish-farmer beards and eclectic choice in hobbies. Instead she texted Hugh to meet her at the new Japanese whiskey bar down the street from her house. He'd written back in less than a minute, telling her he'd cancel a late meeting and come to see her. He was so pleased she'd texted! He used three exclamation marks!!! They had yet another wonderful evening together, talking about his work and hers. She divulged everything she knew about the chocolate industry. Sweet had been a milk chocolate company for so long, packing as much sugar into the product as they could. But she liked what Hugh was saying about good indulgences. Maybe the company should be looking at dark chocolate options and different kinds of treats. They had the market share. Every American kid had grown up on Sweets. Now they could give them something a little healthier.

She put the decision tree away for the time being and flipped open this week's *New York* magazine. The cover line made her smile—"The Good Kind of Fat." Inside was a personal essay from Matilda Singh, one of Hollywood's most popular young actresses. She also happened to write, direct, and star in her very own network sitcom. CJ had long claimed the two were related in some complicated way, but Janey was used to CJ claiming a relation to most famous Indians.

When she first started out in network television, Matilda was on the chubbier side, although the one time Janey met her in person at a Golden Globes party at the Beverly Hilton, she realized it was true that the camera did add at least fifteen pounds.

Matilda was curvy, like CJ, but wore it well and frequently posted Instagram photos of herself in crop tops and short skirts with the hashtags #RealWomenHaveCurves, #NoShameinMyGame, #Sexy Bitch. This essay in *New York* mag was in response to a recent scandal where another magazine, *Blushed,* had Photoshopped Matilda's curves so much that she was virtually unrecognizable. The actress raged on social media about the retouching, and the magazine had been forced to apologize, albeit very carefully. They released their own statement, also via Twitter, explaining that their art department would sometimes excise a stray hair or a pimple and that they were sorry it was not to Ms. Singh's liking. They said nothing about slicing off both of her hips and elongating her legs by several inches. Matilda's writing was clean and concise as she railed against Hollywood's perpetuation of unhealthy body stereotypes. The actress talked about her own fitness regimen and diet, which did include some spin classes and yoga, dark chocolate, leafy greens, mainly Swiss chard (god, Audrey was good), and French fries. She was adamant that she didn't want to live in a world where she couldn't eat French fries.

Me neither, Janey thought. No woman should have to live in a world without French fries. But wasn't that exactly what she'd been doing for the past three months? Hadn't she allowed Beau to try to dictate how she should look, what she should weigh?

Janey leaned back into the seat, closed her eyes, and concentrated on the sound of the plane's wheels thudding down onto the runway as the entire flight erupted into raucous applause. The humidity hit Jane like a tidal wave when she stepped out of the plane and walked down the stairs to the boiling black tarmac. She pulled her hair into a high bun, brushed her bangs out of her face, and hoisted her bag higher onto her shoulder. Janey had limited herself to a single carry-on. Stella promised she didn't need much more than workout clothes, a couple of flowy dresses, and a sweater to ward off an evening chill.

Just past customs, in the arrivals hall, Stella towered at least a foot above the scrum of resort drivers holding their laminated signs for guests and the taxi drivers competing for who could shout the loudest at the tourists. Stella had her own sign that simply read SWEET, a wide smile, and a perfectly knotted Hermès scarf. She wore a white tank top that could have cost a dollar or a hundred dollars and a battered pair of ripped jean shorts. Janey was jostled by a group of sombrero-wearing Pi Kappa Alpha brothers from the University of Alabama. One of them grabbed the soft flesh of her backside before pumping his fist into the air and yelling, "ROLL TIDE!"

"Hellooo!" Stella cut through the cacophony, helpfully grabbed Janey's carry-on, and kissed her lightly on the cheek. "How was the flight? Did you sleep? No worries if you didn't. You can spend the rest of today settling in and lounging. The others don't arrive until tomorrow."

Twenty minutes later the women were in Stella's rental car. "I could only get stick shift, so brace yourself." Stella warily shifted the car into a higher gear. "Tell me about last night's date with the good earl. He texted me. Hugh is smitten with you, Janey Sweet. Very smitten."

Janey couldn't help but smile at the mention of Hugh's name.

"He's wonderful."

"I know, dear girl, and he thinks the same about you. I want to hear everything, but first let's get onto the road. There shouldn't be too much traffic once we're out of town. How much do you love this convertible? We're like Thelma and Louise, except no one will die in the end," Stella said in her low, gravelly voice.

Janey pulled in a breath of fresh island air and fiddled with the radio stations, trying to find something other than American pop from ten years ago. She finally settled on Bob Marley's "No Woman, No Cry," which felt fitting for the occasion and the setting. She took off her sunglasses and closed her eyes. The sun felt nice on her eyelids.

"You're like a whole new person from when I first met you."

Stella smiled. "You're living a life filled with abundance and purpose. You're becoming very wellthy."

Janey had only recently discovered the concept of "wellth." They used it on all of the health and fitness blogs. It meant something along the lines of forgetting about money and embracing wellness as a life path. From what she could gather on Instagram the hash tag #wellth was mainly attached to photographs of very fit people doing headstands in places like Mount Kilimanjaro and Machu Picchu or eating organic gluten-free croissants in a tangle of white sheets in a fancy hotel in Provence.

"So Beau is trying to oust me from my own company. Did I tell you that? He's telling everyone that I quit B and that I'm not coming back."

Stella put a warm hand on her leg. "Oh honey, that's awful. What are you going to do?"

"I don't know. Half the time I'm crazy with rage and I want to sue him for everything he's worth and take the company back. Then sometimes I want to give the whole thing up and try something new. But I don't know what I want to do next. I thought I was supposed to have all this figured out by now."

Stella nodded serenely.

"We're never meant to finish our journey. There's no such thing as 'grown up.' You'll figure it out. Maybe you'll figure it out this week. Try to just relax into this. Don't worry too much about Sara and about the other women. Worry about you. You'll go back home with some clarity."

It took less than a half hour to escape the bumper-to-bumper traffic of downtown and to reach a highway that ran parallel to the turquoise sea. The temperature was comfortable, in the high seventies, and the beach was crowded on this Sunday morning with young women spread out on blankets, reading glossy magazines, teenagers playing Frisbee close to the water's edge, and entire families gathered around grills near the parking lots.

"I could live here," Janey said.

"Why don't you?"

"Why don't I?" Why didn't she? Nothing was keeping her in New York. The questions made her uncomfortable. She changed the subject.

"When is Sara getting in?"

"She's been here for a week. I'm worried about her, to be honest. Her energy is off. You could talk to her, you know. About making a life change. Talk about someone who has reinvented herself. She made a complete transformation in less than a year."

Janey remembered Ivy asking her questions the other night about Sara Strong's backstory.

"What exactly happened with Sara and Kate Wells?" Janey said in a voice she hoped was light and breezy.

Stella didn't seem put off. "I know Sara's side of it. But you never know anything listening to just one side. She said Kate was jealous of her, competitive. The two of them were going to open a studio together but she said Kate wanted total control, demanded to be the sole owner of the company, refused a fifty-fifty split."

Janey nodded. That sounded familiar.

"Sara couldn't take it anymore. She told Kate she didn't want her money and they broke up. Friend breakups are always worse than love breakups. But enough about Sara Strong. I want to talk about Hugh. What do you think of him?" They drove past rolling green hills covered in lush tropical plants. Roosters and street dogs trotted together on the gravel shoulder of the narrow highway.

"He's divine. Everything about him is perfect and wonderful."

"And the juice boy?"

"Also great." Janey stretched her bare toes onto the dashboard, making fuzzy toe prints on the windshield. "They're different. If you'd have told me dating would be so fun I would have gotten divorced years ago."

"But maybe you wouldn't have appreciated it so much then! My first husband was terrible. Emotionally and physically abusive. I don't think I could appreciate having such a wonderful husband now, if I hadn't gone through a very, very bad marriage the first time around."

Janey stayed quiet. It was rare to get private details about Stella's life.

"My first husband was really possessive. He once cut off my hair, right down to the roots, while I slept and burned me in the side with his cigarette. He was a brute and a weak, weak man. I stayed for a year after that. We all have to hit rock bottom in order to appreciate the good bits in life."

Janey reached over to touch Stella's milky white arm. Her thoughts turned to Beau, who was abusive in his own way, and she wondered if this was her rock bottom. If so, she knew she should count herself incredibly lucky.

"No one deserves that. How long were you married?" Janey asked. "The first time?"

"Five years." Stella appeared lost in thought. She was silent for a couple of minutes. "You'll have to meet my new husband when we get back. He's wonderful. You'll like him a lot." The two women lost themselves in quiet for the remaining fifteen minutes of the drive.

Before she knew it they'd arrived at the jungle sanctuary, a small peninsula that jutted into the crystalline waters. "This place is like heaven," Janey said in awe. "We've just driven into the best screen saver of all time."

"Right? You'll love it here."

The retreat occupied most of the property, a giant eight-bedroom house with five freestanding luxury yurts. At fifteen thousand dollars for the week Janey thought she would have gotten her own yurt, but part of the experience, Stella promised her, was sharing space with another one of the women.

Jungle encroached on nearly every corner of the property. Vines crawled like narrow snakes along the façade of the main house, which was built in a delicate French Colonial style, with large white columns and a pale green tiled roof—Palm Beach and Lilly Pulitzer meet *Heart of Darkness*. Janey counted no fewer than eight gardeners clipping already perfectly pruned flowering plants and trees. The manicured lawns were dotted with sculptures of Hindu deities. Ganesha with his large foot balanced on the back of a mouse had been turned into a birdbath. To his left was Parvati, sitting serenely in the lotus pose with a fern growing out of her head, and down the way a fierce Hanuman, the monkey god, had been converted into a free-flowing fountain with water spilling out of his limbs. Inside her yurt, the walls were painted robin's-egg blue and covered over in tiny gold stars; mud cloth tribal tapestries hung from the door. The space's overstuffed couch and poufs were upholstered in Muriel Brandolini floral cottons. "Talk about glamping!" Janey cried.

Each yurt came equipped with a palatial outdoor shower and personal infrared sauna, which Stella explained warmed the organs and internal tissues.

"Does wonders for detoxing, lymphatic issues, and high blood pressure," she explained. "I recommend at least twenty minutes every single morning and fifteen before you go to bed at night."

Two handsome men in crisp white shirts and matching short shorts carried Janey's bag into the yurt for her. "Can we unpack for you, madam?" one of them asked her. She shook her head. The idea of someone rifling through her bag, folding her bras and underwear into perfect triangles unnerved her.

She thought she'd packed light, but turns out she hadn't needed to pack at all. The thatched bamboo wardrobe contained seven identical grey tank tops, four pairs of grey shorts, and three pairs of grey stretch pants.

Janey put her own clothes next to The Workout uniforms and laced up her bright yellow sneakers, assuming they were a violation of the retreat's strict color therapy and deciding she'd risk it. She lathered a sweet-smelling sun cream on her shoulders and face, not bothering to rub it all the way in. The concierge, an obliging local with chocolate-brown eyes and acne-scarred cheeks, informed her there was a sandy path to the beach if she just kept walking north on the property. It felt nice to be walking on something other than pavement for a change.

She heard the yelling before she could see who was making such a scene. Thirty yards away she saw Sara Strong hanging out the second-story window of the main house screaming into a cell phone, waving a cigarette in the air. Without a stitch of makeup on, Janey could clearly see the large dark rings beneath her eyes.

"What do you mean you can't get it through customs? It's tea, for Christ's sake! Tea. You're not even going to try? Well then, don't fucking come. It's herbal. You know that and I know that and there's nothing wrong with bringing it on an airplane. But whatever. If you're going to be such a fucking baby about it then don't bring it and don't come at all. I'll figure something else out." Janey ducked behind a large bougainvillea and watched Sara hang up the phone and scream out the open window.

"Pahhhhhhhhhhhhhhhhhhh!" the woman shrieked and stubbed the end of her cigarette against the windowsill before letting it drop down into a bed of oleander. Knowing she had witnessed something she wasn't supposed to see excited her. Rather than being turned off by the outburst, she finally began to see Sara Strong as an actual human.

But why *couldn't* the herbal tea go through customs?

. . .

Janey woke early the following morning to light streaming in the windows of the yurt and a big-boned blond woman sitting cross-legged on a meditation cushion next to her bed.

"Hi! I'm Suzy!" This woman, draped in at least three layers of next season's Isabel Marant, must be her roommate.

"Don't get up. I was just meditating. Landed an hour ago. I took the first jet out of Teterboro . . . wanted to make the most of the day. You got here last night? Don't you just love it here? Isn't it wild? It's so *Mosquito Coast,* I can't stand it. Of course it's probably not PC to mention mosquitoes these days . . . not with the Zika virus going around and all those poor tiny-headed children. We had a benefit for it a few weeks ago at the public library. So sad. I can't even look at the pictures. What brought you here?"

Pauses didn't exist in Suzy's syntax.

Janey sat up and wiped the sleep out of her eyes. "Do you know Stella?"

"*From Shame to Shaman*. Of course I know her. Love her. I keep telling her I want to work on a documentary about her life. I used to make docs for PBS back when they had money. Now that the kids are in kindergarten I'm jumping back in. Just closed a deal with Vice to shoot north Indian transvestite rhino poachers."

Suzy was attractive in the way that loads of money allowed a woman of a certain age (Janey guessed she was mid-fifties) to remain preserved. She'd never be thin again, if she ever had been thin in the first place, but her muscles were taut and strong. She was meaty, like a waitress in vintage German beer advertisements.

Her roommate stood and began pacing the room, clearly unable to sit still for longer than fifteen seconds. "I love Sara Strong so much. I keep telling her that I will go to any class and any retreat and anything she does anywhere in the entire world. She's a beautiful soul and the things she does for people are just magical. I've lost fifty pounds. That's fifty pounds I've had since my kids were born. I feel such a connection with her. It's like we've been best friends for our entire lives."

Janey wanted to mention that being best friends rarely involved paying the other best friend thousands of dollars but stopped herself when she remembered how many hundreds of thousands of her family's money she'd invested in B in the early years. Some friendships *were* transactional.

"Don't you love this yurt? So much better than actually having to visit Mongolia." Her roommate laughed with a snort.

Suzy seemed nice enough, even if she did talk like a Moonie, but Janey needed caffeine to follow her erratic trains of thought.

"Are they serving coffee in the main house?" She swung her legs over the edge of the bed and was pleased to find a pair of grey Havaianas flip-flops waiting for her.

"Oh no, girlfriend! No coffee for the next week. That's why I got my fix on the plane. They looked at me like I was craaaaaaazy when I ordered two triple espressos, but you do what you need to do!"

"Right. Well, maybe tea?"

Sara Strong's fight on the phone over the herbal tea came rushing back to Janey. It still made no sense to her, and she wondered whether she should mention it to Suzy, but she felt guilty for accidentally eavesdropping on what was very clearly a private conversation.

Suzy jogged in place, jerking her knees higher toward her chest with each iteration. "Or maybe we can find a juice? Do you wanna walk over with me? Have you unpacked? I guess we didn't need to pack much. I still like being prepared."

"I have. I didn't bring much." Janey looked at two leather Louis Vuitton suitcases now sitting empty in the corner of the room. "I'm ready to go. Let's take a wander and see who else is here."

CHAPTER TWENTY

Breakfast for the ReVigor-8 guests was served in a ballroom worthy of an Edith Wharton novella, all grand chandeliers, gold leaf, and crackling with uncomfortable conversation about money and status. By the end of a generous helping of kale scramble (kale, more kale, kale congealed to look like eggs, and more kale), Suzy, of course, knew everything about everyone and was more than happy to be the mistress of introductions.

There was Wendy Lu, lover of diamond-studded toe rings, total tiger mom in the midst of a nasty divorce from her Swiss banker husband. Her best friend was Jessica Seinfeld, and she wouldn't let you forget it. Every other sentence began with, "And then Jessica Seinfeld and I did this . . . ," or "You won't believe the trouble Jessica Seinfeld and I got into in Paris last year," or "I probably shouldn't admit this, but I was the one who gave Jessica Seinfeld her carrot muffin recipe for her last cookbook." She always used Jessica Seinfeld's full name to full effect. Wendy's parents were immigrants from a small soy farming village on the outskirts of Seoul, but now Wendy only traveled by private jet as the lead attorney for David Lynch's Transcendental Meditation foundation. More diamonds dribbled off the fine gold chains layered on her porcelain neck.

Of course Miranda Mills, the formerly plus-sized supermodel, who was now so skinny her grey workout uniform draped off of her like a muumuu, was in attendance. She was flanked on either side by her two mommy friends, the three of them wearing identical Mexican huarache sandals they'd picked up the week before on another wellness retreat in Tulum. Visiting wellness, yoga, and boot-camp retreats could, Janey was learning, be a full-time job.

There was Cosima, whom Janey knew of from CJ. The forty-something education consultant was notorious in mommy circles because she had made a mint helping terrified parents through the byzantine admissions processes in Manhattan's private schools. The higher Cosima's fee, the more likely the admission for even the dullest and slowest of children. Steven, who toughed out his entire childhood in Bronx public schools, had forbidden CJ from hiring someone to get the twins into preschool. But Janey suspected she had slipped Cosima a little something on the side, since the twins' social skills in preschool interviews had needed a little help. Cosima had one daughter born of sperm and egg donation but had never married. Copious Botox and other injectables gave her a perpetually puffy, but never old, appearance. Her eyebrows were perfectly arched—sugared, not plucked—and poised in an arc of everlasting surprise. She arrived at the table in flowing grey pants and bandeau bikini top. Suzy whispered that she had used Cosima to get two of her boys into Dalton. "And then she tried to fuck my husband. Total sex addict," Suzy said under her breath, but not really.

Constance was a well-known television presenter who came to New York from Toronto in 2001, right before the planes struck the Twin Towers. She proved her chops as a news reporter for the local network by camping out at Ground Zero for weeks on end. Shortly afterward she was scooped up by CNN and bounced around the cable news networks before landing a gig on the *Today* show. A red silk turban popped against the sea of sameness, holding back Constance's wonderful Afro. Why she was here, Janey hadn't a clue, since she was six feet of glorious fitness. Her skin was so dewy, so glossy, and smelled so deliciously of a light almond oil that Janey had to be careful not to reach over to touch her.

At the end of the long table sat Svetla and Nadia, a pair of Russian heiresses whom Suzy called the Russkie hookers behind their backs, despite the fact that they were the wealthiest individuals at this table. Janey pegged them both to be in their late twenties. Their father had controlled 20 percent of the motherland's natural gas until he met a suspicious end during a train ride from Minsk to St. Petersburg. According to the authorities he'd fallen from the train just as it crossed over a bridge high above a three-hundred-foot gorge. The pair of girls had identical blond hair extensions, and they were difficult to tell apart except that Nadia's extensions were pulled into a ponytail, revealing an elaborate tattoo of the Kremlin across the majority of her upper back.

Becky was the ultra-athlete. Employee number five at Google, she'd since cashed in and made fitness her full-time job, ultramarathoning in the Alps and competing in Iron Mans in Hawaii, all on a vegan diet.

"I just eat plants. No powders, no supplements, no sugar. People don't believe me, but I have all the energy I need. Sometimes I'll dig them right out of the ground wherever I am," she explained, a hunk of kale stuck between her two front teeth. Where Wendy was dripping in diamonds, Becky was dripping in wearable fitness tech, a FitWand on one wrist, an advanced heart rate tracker on her ankle, a headband that measured her body temperature, the Garmin runner watch, a scarf that quantified her daily sun exposure, and a band across her belly that, she explained, created a 3-D rendering on her phone of which muscles she twitched hardest throughout the day.

There was the owner of this giant plantation, Maizee Vanders, a fifth-generation New Yorker married to a seventh-generation New Yorker, both of whom "worked" in the hazy world of philanthropy, which seemed to involve traveling the globe to check in on their many, many homes. Maizee, who also fancied herself an interior designer, was one of those rich people who liked to cultivate an "I'm just like you" attitude by claiming she did things like shop at flea markets, mop the floors, and change dirty diapers, when you knew she had a staff of at least twenty-three people who were actually doing all of those things. She and her husband, Bryson, had two perfect tow-headed children, and the entire family was frequently photographed for *Town & Country* and *Architectural Digest*.

But when it came down to it, Janey liked Carol the best, an older woman with an odd French accent, short corkscrew curls, and crooked European teeth. Originally from Morocco, she eschewed the retreat-issued clothing and was dressed in mom jeans, a chambray button-down, and yellow Crocs. Her adoring husband bought her the trip as a present for her sixtieth birthday and she seemed quite confused about what exactly was supposed to be happening this week.

"Where are zee eggs and bacon?" she inquired when the hunky waiter, wearing little more than grey skivvies and a leather strap around his chest, handed her the plate of greens. Carol scowled at the purple cauliflower hummus. "Zis is baybee food, no?" She darted her dark eyes furtively around the room, scouting for something that didn't come out of the ground.

Someone should have scooped Cosima's jaw up off the floor as she ogled the waiter's glistening chocolate-colored thighs.

"I wonder if he lives on the property," she said, shoveling a forkful of green into her mouth.

Janey took a bite of the green mash and determined it was indeed baby food, but not the worst thing she'd ever put in her mouth.

"Could I get some Tabasco? Or Tapatio?" Janey asked. Hot sauce made anything better.

Who knew what they'd be serving for lunch? Or if they'd be eating lunch at all.

"What's the Internet password here?" Constance asked. "I know it was written in my room, but my iPad didn't save it."

"SpiritJunkie1234," Maizee replied, an edge of annoyance in her tone that was not in the least bit spiritual.

"Thanks! I'm dying to post some pics to Insta."

All of the women put some kind of device—a phone or a tablet— onto the table. Wendy looked over at Cosima's phone.

"Ewwwww. Aren't you Facetuning before you post that? You have such great legs, but don't you think you should tone your tummy a little before you show it to everyone? That's the best thing about Insta . . . making couture tummies!"

Janey expected Cosima to snap back that the tone of her tummy was none of the other woman's business, but instead she just nodded in agreement.

"You're right." She swiped and tapped and swiped and tapped and then held the screen up for all of the other women to see and approve.

"Is this postworthy?"

Janey looked at the woman's ostrich-leather encased iPhone 8S. Cosima had elongated her shape into something inhuman, stretching her torso out to the length of her legs and eliminating any curve from her hips. The other women made tiny golf claps.

"Super gorg. Love it. Post it. I'll double tap," Wendy said. "Wait. Are we all following one another? Janey, what's your 'gram? I think I have everyone here but you."

"Just JaneySweet. Short and simple."

Wendy tapped her phone and searched for Janey's name. "OHMYGOD. You work for B, don't you? I love those dresses. I wore Vera for my first wedding, but you can bet I'll go B for my second. If I can ever get the son of a bitch to sign the divorce papers. I love the backless gowns and the ones with the cutouts at the waist. I met the designer Beau last month. He's so funny! You must love working with him. He had us in stitches all night. All his little comments. He's such a bitchy queen. I love him."

"What's not to love?" Janey said, feeling her stomach clench.

Wasn't that part of the reason she'd fallen for Beau? He was hilarious and mean and made you feel like you were a part of a very special clique. Except she wasn't part of that clique anymore. "Beau's a talented designer," Janey added. *Be the bigger person. You are the bigger person,* she thought. *Be Michelle Obama. "When they go low, you go high."*

"I love this picture of you here on the beach. Did you take this yesterday? Do you 'tune? Maybe you want to make your butt a little more little? What do you think?"

"Thanks for sharing your opinion," Janey said evenly, biting her lip. *I didn't ask for your opinion,* she thought to herself. Her butt was probably the tiniest it had been in a decade. "But it really isn't a problem for me," she said without meeting the other woman's eyes.

This was a lie.

It amazed her that someone she didn't even know was telling her she had a big bum and that person was also wearing a necklace that said FEMINIST in bright gold letters.

Sara Strong wasn't at breakfast, but her presence remained palpable. All the women, except Carol of course, who murmured something about going to find coffee and read in the hammock, nattered about her in reverent tones.

"She's starting a revolution."

"I've never felt more connected to my inner core."

"She's made me finally love my body."

"Jessica Seinfeld and I were in her very first class. We go at least once a week."

It was Stella, not Sara, who glided into the grand room at the end of breakfast and announced the day's schedule. They'd begin with the morning workout. After that they'd have lunch and discuss the rest of the week with Sara herself. "What I can tell you is that you are in for a real treat, eight whole days of movement and yoga, dance, sweat, sharing meals and dreams, jungle bathing, tea ceremonies, singing songs. We have so many extracurriculars for those of you who need to stay busy. There are workshops on fermenting foods, weaving, dyeing fabrics, and making plant medicines. Remember, it's in our blood and soul to create. I'll be conducting personal workshops to help you discover your spirit animal!" Stella added. "And don't forget. Everyone should start thinking about what she wants to do for the Thursday night talent show."

Janey caught up with Stella as the shaman poured herself a pulpy beet juice into a Waterford crystal champagne glass. "Where's Sara?"

"She's in the studio. I'm not sure what's going on, but she's all amped up. Aggressive. Even for her. I told her to take some time to settle herself before we got started this morning. How'd you sleep?"

"Like a chubby, happy baby," Janey admitted honestly. There were few things better than falling asleep to the rhythmic crescendo of waves pounding the sand. Janey noticed looks of horror pass across the women's faces at the word "chubby," but she ignored it. That was something Lorna had always said when she slept well, and Janey liked the way the words felt coming out of her own mouth.

There was no mention of Kate Wells by any of the women at the table, but while the women wandered together down a sandy path lined with palm trees and ferns the size of Volkswagens to their first class of The Workout, Suzy told Janey that Kate's footprint remained on the retreat. The studio that had been carved out of a former maid's cottage specially for The Workout ReVigor-8 had been styled by Kate in collaboration with Marc Jacobs.

Janey heard "Eye of the Tiger" from the *Rocky* soundtrack blasting from the studio. Inside Sara Strong twirled wildly in tight concentric circles, her arms flailing above her head.

It wasn't until all of them had filed into the room and leaned against the pale blue walls that she finally threw herself on the ground, let out a wail, and lifted her head to acknowledge their presence.

"Hello beauties," she said with a strange smile. As she stood

Janey could see every muscle in her tiny torso move through her thin grey unitard. She slowly walked the periphery of the room, bowing to each of them individually.

Janey didn't know what to do when someone bowed to her. Bowing back felt strange, so she opted for a too-wide smile, an overly ambitious nod, and a thumbs-up. When Sara finished greeting everyone, the music stopped on cue, and the fans began to whir from above, blowing Sara's hair angelically around her face as she walked to the center of the room.

"I love each and every one of you girls so much for coming down here. You have inspired me. Moved me. Blessed me. Like you I still struggle, and this week we will sweat in the struggle together," Sara announced in her high-pitched girly voice with its odd accent. "This morning during my meditation I couldn't get certain thoughts out of my head. I wrote them down so that I could share them with you. When things like this come to me, I know it's the universe asking me to share its wisdom with you. Here is what came to me: I know we are often comparing ourselves to other women who may be younger or more fit than we are. The problem is that every year as we get older we have a larger group to compare ourselves to. Stop comparing. Acknowledge other people's greatness and you will be more powerful and centered. Others will notice and embrace your confidence. There's nothing sexier than someone who is content with herself and trying every single day to be better and improve on her own terms."

Wait a second. Wasn't that exactly what Sara had said the first time Janey came to The Workout? The other women were regulars. They must have heard it before. But no one seemed taken aback. They smiled and clapped. Cosima swiped a tear from her cheek.

Sara paused and raised her hands and her eyes skyward. "This is . . . THE WORKOUT!"

Local men, each more handsome and wearing less clothing than the next, filed in with trays of the signature Workout tea.

How did they get it here? Janey wondered. Each of the women gratefully took her cup and sipped while Sara repeated a series of mantras in Sanskrit.

The next three hours were a blur of wind sprints, squat thrusts, Zumba, something called conscious dance, and ten straight minutes of jumping jacks followed by another ten of jumping rope.

It all ended with a five-minute handstand.

"An inversion is the best way to see your world differently," Sara said. "Sometimes when I'm having one of those awful work dinners and I can't stand talking to another person I go in the bathroom and do a handstand for five minutes and I immediately feel better. Of course I wash my hands before I go back out."

Carol walked out of the studio at the mention of standing on anything other than her feet. They would never see her again. Janey later learned she'd booked herself a room at the Ritz.

Janey, who hadn't done a handstand since fourth-grade gym class, dragged her mat over to the wall for balance, cautiously kicking one leg into the air and then the other.

By the time it was all over, Janey's entire body ached and she was starving. The promise of food was all that motivated her to drag her weary legs back to the lavish open-air dining room. A small terra cotta pot in the shape of a bull sat at each place setting next to a beautifully woven lace napkin. Janey's tummy rumbled, and she realized she could smell herself. She was a sweaty, nasty, hungry mess.

Sara floated into the dining room like a fairy, wearing a fresh pastel grey unitard. "Let us give grace to the earth and the sun and the sea and all of the sources of nourishment we're receiving today. We're so grateful."

The group chanted after her: "We're so grateful."

Janey was just grateful for whatever kind of lovely stew the local chefs had cooked up and put in this little pot.

"Bon appétit!" Sara said, making no move to sit and eat herself, pacing instead, like a hungry tiger in a cage. Janey realized she'd never seen Sara put anything other than tea into her mouth.

Janey carefully removed the top of the pot, checking first to make sure it wasn't too hot.

No. It couldn't be.

Fuuuuuuuuuuuuck!

It was clay.

Janey made eye contact with Stella across the table and mouthed, "No way," exaggerating the consonants.

Stella gave a slight shrug, looking over her shoulder to see if Sara was watching. She was in an animated conversation with one of the waiters. Stella slowly pushed her chair back from the table and beckoned Janey to follow her. No one paid them any mind. The other women were clearly so hungry they could think of little else except shoveling clay into their mouths.

Down a short, dark hallway they left the opulence of the rest of the property and found themselves in the sterile and dilapidated staff quarters. The paint on the walls curled off in plate-sized patches, and water stains formed dark shadows on the ceiling. Once in the kitchen, Stella spoke rapid-fire French to one of the cooks. He looked at Janey with a kind smile and opened the oven to reveal a batch of freshly baked rolls.

Janey drooled from the smell of the fresh bread and didn't care when the roll burned her tongue. It was the sweetest thing that had ever touched her lips, a piece of pure heaven.

"I'm sorry," Stella said. "I promise I wasn't lying when I bragged about the fresh fruits and veggies and organic yummies. Sara is different this time around. And the women are different. They're demanding extreme results. They don't want food here. All of these women could be potential investors in Sara's new gym project, and she's just eager to give them whatever they want."

Janey grabbed a second roll. She'd swallowed the first whole.

"Does Sara smoke?"

"I doubt it. Why?"

"I saw her smoking a cigarette and hanging out the window last night." Janey felt like a tattletale but she was too curious not to ask. "She was so mad. Yelling into her phone. Something about not being able to get the tea across the border."

"Oh yeah. There was some problem. I didn't really understand it, but apparently she needed to buy something local and she was worried it wasn't the same as what she could get in the States, some kind of vitamins maybe for the tea or the smoothies."

Janey grabbed another warm roll and broke it in half, offering one piece to Stella, who crinkled her nose.

"Gluten makes me a bad person. Hey, why don't you take the rest of the day off? It's all optional, you know. Go have a lie in a hammock and stare at the sea. I can even have the guys back here cook you some real food and bring it to you in your room so no one has to know."

"You think it's okay?"

"It's more than okay. I'll tell the others you had sunstroke or something and need a lie down. Don't worry about it. This is your retreat. Take care of yourself."

· · ·

Janey spent a glorious afternoon and evening all by herself, walking the deserted beach. She dove into the waves and let herself float for what felt like an hour, her muscles loosening in the salty water. And as Stella had promised, a delicious dinner of baked red snapper in coconut sauce with sides of roasted broccoli, kale, and cauliflower arrived on a tray in her room, while the other women dined on more clay. She'd finished reading one of the novels she brought with her and stayed up fairly late, but Suzy still hadn't come back to the yurt by the time she fell asleep.

Janey tossed and turned most of the night, dipping in and out of dreams.

One stuck with her. The smell of the clay permeated her nostrils. She was back in high school, in the art studio. Beau spent most of his time there. He ditched other classes to sit in the studio's back room and draw. In the dream Janey was wearing her white dress from the debutante ball, but it was too tight. Much too tight. It felt like the dress was suffocating her. She walked into the art room and found Beau sitting on one of the high stools. It was seventeen-year-old Beau. He looked up at her and smiled sweetly. "Come see what I've made, love." She walked toward him. The room was hot, boiling hot. He reached out to touch her dress, making a dark brown stain with his hands, which she now saw were covered in wet sticky clay. He wasn't drawing. He was sculpting. He was sculpting little figures, little women. "They're you, Janey. I made you," he said. She couldn't speak. She opened her mouth, but no words came. All she could do was watch as he slid the small figures into an oven to bake them. As she stared at him, seventeen-year-old Beau became twenty-year-old Beau and then thirty-year-old Beau and then Beau today. The Beau from the breakfast table who told her she was fat and made her feel unworthy of everything she'd accomplished. She walked over to the oven, her dress getting tighter every second, finally splitting along the seams of her waist. Inside the kiln the clay Janeys dried and cracked and crumbled to dust.

. . .

Janey woke the next morning to a man in a white lab coat standing over Suzy's bed, connecting a needle and a tube to the crook of her roommate's arm.

"Shit, Suzy! Are you okay?" Janey sat straight up, pulling the white sheet to her chin. "Suzy?"

Suzy rolled her head toward her.

"I'm great, honey. Morning IV treatment. Super vitamin B booster, liquid magnesium, vitamins C, D, K, and some other letters I don't remember. Three fat burners and L-carnitine to help use stored fat and build lean muscle." She looked up at the doctor, nurse, or lab technician. "Sweetheart, do you do Botox too? I could use a little update this morning."

Janey slowly eased herself out of bed to pad to the bathroom, careful to give the doctor a wide berth.

"You want one, honey?" Suzy called after her.

"Nah, I'm good. Maybe tomorrow. I'm taking a shower."

Mobile IV treatments and clay. How the hell had she wound up here?

The whole crew of ladies was bright-eyed and perky at breakfast.

"You missed a wild time last night, Janey." Maizee giggled.

"We danced till dawn," Miranda said, high-fiving the blond mommies who sat on her left and right. "These local boys have rhythm. Let me tell you. And the mescal they have here. Ohmigod. It's like the best. No hangover. All natural. Super organic."

Janey was surprised. There was no food at the retreat, but there *was* a late-night disco and artisanal liquor.

Suzy giggled. "And then we went skinny-dipping! Whooooooooooo-oooo!" Suzy had paired a cowgirl hat with her grey Melissa Odabash resort wear this morning.

"Sorry I missed it. I'll try to stay up tonight." Janey had no interest in partying hard while she was here, or really partying hard at all. She couldn't even remember the last time she took a shot. She looked at Stella across the table and raised her eyebrows. Stella just smiled and concentrated on her chia pudding.

The chia seeds were strange little things, and eating them felt like swallowing baby food that tickled as it went down your throat. Janey wondered how everyone was so alert and perky, and then she remembered the man in the white coat at Suzy's bedside. Holy shit. They'd all been given hangover treatments this morning. No one looked the least bit worse for wear. It was true. Money could buy you almost anything, including a hangover-free life if you didn't mind an IV drip in the morning.

"I got a great night's sleep and explored the beach," Janey offered. "It's incredible here. Sand for miles. I didn't see another human being."

"Let's go paddle-boarding this afternoon," Stella piped up. "Anyone's welcome to join. We have Workout in the morning and free time before evening Pilates. Boarding is so good for your core, and it will be blissful to be out on the waves."

"Did you sign up for a massage yet? Or a colonic? We have a guy who does the most profound colonics," Maizee asked. "The massage slots are going quick, and you have to sign up for one with Scott. He does something very, very special at the end." All of the other women at the table giggled.

Janey shook her head. She could use a massage. Every muscle in her body felt as though it had been rolled in shattered glass. "I didn't. How do I sign up?"

"Oh darling, just tell me what time is good for you and I'll arrange it. I arrange everything around here." Maizee sighed. "But you absolutely want Scott. He has magical fingers." There were the sniggers again.

"What does he do?"

"He just makes you feel really, really good," Suzy said. "I had him yesterday afternoon. My husband hasn't made me feel like that in years."

She'd somehow stumbled into an outlandish middle-aged sorority party complete with shots, late-night parties, and happy endings. God help her if she made it the rest of the week.

CHAPTER TWENTY-ONE

~

vy hadn't expected the retreat to be in the middle of the damn jungle. She'd assumed it would be in the tourist zone and there'd be a nice (cheap) Hilton or Radisson nearby, but the Vanderses owned miles of jungle and beach, and the closest place she could find to stay, even though SoarBarre was willing to pay whatever it cost, was a run-down guesthouse behind a mechanic's shop—a one-bedroom shack adjacent to a chicken coop.

The only upside was the owner's brother, Carlo, worked as a cook for the Vanderses, and he promised to sneak her onto the property that evening. She'd wanted to go over earlier, to make the most of her time here on the ground, but Carlo had discouraged it.

"Oh, you want to go there at night, miss. That's when things get wild."

Wild? At an exercise retreat? "Well, I really am supposed to film the workouts."

Carlo shook his head. "If you want to get dirt on these ladies you go at night. Besides, I don't work till eight."

She took his word for it and spent the day on her own, jogging along the beach and swimming in the gentle water.

She'd taken her entry into espionage seriously, and two weeks of Google searches and tracking down former friends (and quite a few enemies) of Sara Strong helped her build a whole dossier on The Workout star, and, frankly, it wasn't pretty. Ivy had even tracked down the woman's stepmom at the Jersey Shore.

Here's what she knew:

Sara Strong was born Sara Anne Schweitzer in Toms River, New Jersey, to an ear, nose, and throat doctor and a secretary who longed to be a Broadway star. While her dad saw patients, Sara's mom, Pam, saw musicals, anything she could get tickets to, on and off Broadway. She'd sheath herself like Isadora Duncan, line her eyes with dark kohl, and take New Jersey Transit the ninety minutes to Manhattan, sometimes bringing Sara with her, even on school days.

When she was eleven Sara's dad announced to their small family of three that he was in love with his receptionist, Kathy. Their courtship was swift and Kathy was pregnant with the first of four of Sara's step-siblings within six months. It wasn't hard for Ivy to track Sara Strong's stepmom down. Kathy was an incredibly active Facebooker who updated her personal page several times a day with inspirational quotes from her idols—Angelina Jolie and Elizabeth Gilbert—and mimosa ice pop recipes. She'd gotten back to Ivy within minutes of her sending a message. According to Kathy, Mr. Schweitzer tried to stay close with his daughter, having her stay with them on weekends, but the girl was wildly protective of her mom, and sometimes it was hard to convince her to leave Pam alone in the house.

With her husband out of the picture, Pam got fat. Fat like you saw on late-night television shows, the ones where people could no longer fit through their front doors. Within two years Pam could no longer walk up the stairs to the bedroom she used to share with her husband and took to sleeping in the small room off the kitchen that allowed her nightly access to the refrigerator. Kathy knew this from the times they'd gone to pick Sara up from the house.

Sara tried everything to help her mom lose weight. She'd cook elaborate healthy meals that went uneaten in favor of pizza and fried chicken delivery. She enrolled both of them in Weight Watchers but found herself at the meetings and weigh-ins alone. She bought the Richard Simmons *Sweatin' to the Oldies* videocassettes, but she was the only one who ever broke a sweat in their living room.

Sara eventually went to Rutgers University for an accelerated program that gave her a bachelor's degree and an MBA in five years, which she then used to move across the Hudson River and into a job working for Lehman Brothers, first as an analyst, then an associate, and finally as a vice president.

Ivy had been able to track down four former Lehman employees who were more than happy to spill about that period of Sara's life. Lehman Brothers was where Sara met Jian. Chinese-born and brilliant, the Harvard MBA was three years her junior but mature beyond his years. Jian's family was practically royalty in Hong Kong, and they were desperate for him to return home and start running his father's electronics empire, but he was having way too much fun enjoying all the pleasures New York had to offer a young, handsome, and disgustingly rich businessman.

Every woman in their office was wildly attracted to his intense self-confidence and the fact that he didn't give a fuck what anyone thought about him. Sara was his boss and used it to her full advantage, often keeping him late at the office when she knew he had plans with other women. She always scheduled their business trips together. The two of them both escaped Lehman before the collapse, moving over to even better jobs at Morgan Stanley. Finally, one drunken night during a work trip to Detroit, of all places, after several rounds of tequila shots with their clients and a visit to the saddest strip club in the world, the two made it official. They were a couple.

Friends of Jian's said that he was smitten with her Americanness and her New Jersey accent, which she turned on high for him when she talked about growing up down the shore, eating fried dough and saltwater taffy.

When Pam died of liver disease, caused by her morbid obesity, Sara brought Jian home to the funeral. It was a closed-casket service.

Jian hadn't told his own mother and father he was dating an American girl. They were hell-bent on him coming home to marry a Chinese socialite, someone with proper breeding. One friend recalled the words "proper breeding" actually coming out of Jian's mouth.

The pair had a fight right in the office, in front of everyone.

The next part was hazy, but what Ivy was able to gather was that Sara was pregnant. Or at least she told Jian she was pregnant. At least one former friend was willing to admit that she didn't think Sara was pregnant at all. But she did tell Jian that she would have the baby on her own, which forced him to propose to her. His parents disinherited him for lying to them. She had a "miscarriage" two months later.

After that the two of them were as happy as a couple whose marriage was constructed on a foundation of lies could be. Jian grew fascinated with the tech industry and began a fund based on placing risky bets in the start-up market. They had huge success early on with the sharing economy, Uber and Airbnb, but as the market began to correct the way it valued its tech unicorns, Jian's returns shrank, and soon he was taking money from investors and depositing it into his own accounts.

By then Sara was happily settled into their eight-bedroom home in Stamford, Connecticut. Friends said that it took her six rounds of IVF before she announced another pregnancy. The day after she told her friends that she was going to be a mom was the day the Feds burst through the door of their house and dragged her husband off to jail.

Sara gained a lot of weight during that pregnancy.

"A lot," one Connecticut neighbor told Ivy. "Like maybe a hundred pounds. She was probably the fattest person in the whole neighborhood. We used to see her sitting in the parking lot of Burger King eating like three Whoppers. It was sad." Sara sold their house at a loss and barely covered their debts and moved back in with her dad and Kathy in New Jersey until she gave birth.

According to Kathy this was around the time that Sara made a new friend, Stella Bard. The pair met in a coffee shop in Manhattan while Sara was meeting with Jian's lawyers.

"I think she was a witch," Kathy said.

"A shaman?" Ivy had asked.

"Yeah, that's the word she used. Isn't that a witch? I know I saw a shaman on *Game of Thrones*."

Kathy had no idea what the shaman did or said to Sara, but she did spark a complete reinvention. Soon Sara was going to the gym every day and eating nothing but lettuce. Her interest in her daughter waned and she began leaving the little girl with Kathy for longer and longer stretches, until finally she left her there for good, promising to come back and get her when she could support the two of them. That had been three years ago.

Sara used her own reinvention story (minus the bit about being an absentee mother) to inject herself into the fast-growing health and wellness world, met Kate Wells, and then developed The Workout. That's where the trail grew cold. Once Sara got famous, no one she associated with would talk about her any longer, especially not Kate Wells. And now Ivy was in St. Lucia, just a few hundred yards away from Sara Strong's famous Workout retreat, hoping to piece together the rest of the story.

Ivy had procured a brown bob wig with blunt bangs that made her look like a Caucasian Rihanna. She texted Kelli a picture, to which her girlfriend replied with a series of sexy emojis. She was the cutest.

A little after seven, Ivy donned the wig and the white maid's uniform the Vanderses required for their staff, like it was still the 1800s or something. All Ivy had to do was avoid Janey, or at least avoid letting Janey see her face. She'd applied a heavy layer of foundation, blush, mascara, and bright red lipstick until she hardly recognized herself when she looked in the mirror. They drove in Carlo's ratty old Buick, which desperately needed new shocks. Every time they hit one of the many, many bumps in the road, Ivy felt like she'd been kicked in the ass.

In addition to the wig, she'd purchased two wireless pinhole cameras. One of them would stay with her, and she paid Carlo three hundred dollars to place the other one inside wherever the workout part of The Workout retreat was taking place. She promised to give him another three hundred dollars if he got any footage. She really was Jane fucking Bond.

Even in the staff areas the Vanders property smelled grand, like rich people, the kind of smell regular people attempted by buying thirty-dollar scented candles. It was a combination of cleaning products without chemicals, fresh linen, and maybe lavender oil. Ivy could smell the odors of the chicken coop clinging to her wig and body.

Carlo strode with purpose and Ivy followed. He grabbed her hand to lead her down the long hallway. Oh no. He didn't think she was interested in him, did he? He was a ridiculous hunk of a thing. She let him hold her hand because it was easier than bumping into walls.

Ivy could hear the party well before they reached it.

"We're at the wrong place," she insisted. This was a health and wellness retreat of middle-aged women, not a bachelorette party. As they got closer Ivy recognized the deep bass beats of Jay Z's *Black Album*. She adjusted her wig, and Carlo handed her a tray of small glasses. Wait a second. Were these shot glasses? He plunked a bottle of mescal next to them.

"They seem to think mescal is healthier than tequila. Silly white bitches don't know they come from the same damn plant."

He gave her a familiar tap on her backside and pushed her toward the sitting room.

Once through the enormous French doors, Ivy had to struggle to keep a straight face. There were twelve women in the room. All

of them looked like they could be clients of SoarBarre: well manicured, tight bodies, perfect hair, definitely wealthy. Most of them
were over forty. All of them dancing, now to Def Leppard's "Pour
Some Sugar on Me," the way wealthy women dance at weddings,
imitating moves they'd seen performed by strippers in movies—
kicking their legs into the air and jiggling their butts down to the
floor, whipping their hair around their heads as they pursed their
chemically enhanced lips.

They were joined by five hot men, locals probably, all of them
shirtless and young. Each of them had an old lady hanging off him,
grinding up on him, their pasty white bodies a stark contrast to the
dark smooth ones.

It took them a minute to notice Ivy, but when they did they
squealed.

"SHOTS!"

"YEEEEE!"

"Bring them here!"

"What are you waiting for?"

"Me first," yelled a brassy blonde wearing a tank top that read
DROP AND GIVE ME ZEN. She snatched an empty glass and the bottle,
pouring herself one and raising the glass in the air.

"To us!"

Drop and Give Me Zen poured shots for all the women crowded
around Ivy. They each slugged one back and waited eagerly for a
refill.

Before she knew it the bottle was empty and the women had
dispersed back to the dance floor. Ivy turned to walk back to the
kitchen and fumbled in her pocket for the camera. Her heart
pounded against her push-up bra and cheap uniform as she tried
to feel for the tiny switch that would turn it on. Ally and Lemon
would appreciate some photos and videos that proved this retreat
wasn't all about wellness and fitness. That would definitely under-
mine everything The Workout was supposed to represent. Finally,
she found the switch and flicked it into recording mode. How could

she film the women without them noticing? She turned to look at them. Drop and Give Me Zen was on the back of one of the men, hollering for him to take her down to the beach. The rest of them were replaying a scene from *Dirty Dancing.*

Fuck it. They think I'm a servant. I'm invisible, Ivy thought. She nestled the camera into her right fist so that the lens poked out between her fingers. She just held her hand at her side as she stood there filming for another forty-five seconds. She was right. No one noticed her except to yell.

"Hey girl, more mescal!" Ivy turned and nodded, which was when she finally noticed her cousin. Was Janey passed out in the corner?

No one puts Janey in the corner.

CHAPTER TWENTY-TWO

B efore she even opened her eyes, Janey knew that there was a needle inserted into the vein on the inside of her right elbow.

She felt the distinct effects of a hangover—nausea, muscle ache, the kind of headache where your brain felt as though it had separated from the interior of your skull in the middle of the night and was now floating, unprotected and untethered.

But she hadn't had a thing to drink.

Yesterday had been yet another epically long day. She'd felt supercharged with energy at the start of it, able to carry thirty-pound sandbags up and down the beach in a series of boot-camp drills that reminded her of that Tamil Tiger Terror class in Brooklyn. Months ago she wouldn't have been able to lift one of those over her head once, much less twenty times. She'd even managed to choke down her bowl of lunchtime clay before heading out for Stella's paddle-boarding excursion, followed by a twilight Pilates class on the beach. For dinner she again found herself back in the room, with the excuse that she needed to take a call from Shanghai to see about those samples. It was morning there, after all. Back at the yurt she'd enjoyed a lovely dinner of sweet potato gratin, a farro and spinach salad, and another filet of perfectly prepared red snapper.

"We caught it today, madam," Carlo, the sweet-faced cook and waiter said when he brought her the tray. "Would you like a glass of wine? I can go down to the cellar and bring you a bottle." Did he wink at her?

"No, no. This looks like heaven. Thank you so much. I have everything I need."

After dinner she'd walked down to the open-air massage table unfolded right at the water's edge, feeling a bit uncomfortable about dropping her robe to stand completely naked underneath the moonlight. As promised Maizee had arranged the massage with Scott. Janey didn't know what to expect. She wanted to enjoy his magic hands on her back and her neck and her thighs and her calves, but not anywhere else.

She'd assumed he must be a local, but Scott was a run-of-the-mill white guy with nice teeth and shaggy brown hair that just brushed the collar of his white linen shirt, unbuttoned to reveal a taut tummy and a thin line of hair running from his navel down to the button of his jeans. "Relax into the table. Breathe for me," he said to her once she lay down on her belly. "In for ten. Out for ten. Let everything go."

As he began to knead at her knotty calves, she audibly sighed with pleasure, but when he moved his magical hands higher up her legs she stiffened and pushed her thighs closer together.

"Your glutes must be killing you," he said in a kind voice. "I think I saw you ladies do more than a hundred squats today. Let me work them out."

Just her glutes. That was all.

"Okay. Thank you," Janey said, wondering where his hands would go after her bottom.

The answer was onto her lower back. He was incredibly professional as he moved his hands away from her buttocks.

"Your psoas is really tight too," he said and wound his entire hand around the side of her body, squeezing gently at first and then more firmly. "They work you hard here."

Janey was never one for a chatty masseur, but she felt guilty when she didn't make small talk. "They really do. Is this your first time working the retreat?"

"Nope. I was here last time. They ship me in from New York for the whole week. I'm a medical student at Einstein actually."

A med student, and a traveling masseur who made middle-aged women feel "really good" on the side.

"And you do this part-time?"

"I learned massage a few years ago, and it's a good way to make money. I've been a broke student for so long, my fiancée may finally come to her senses one day and marry someone without two hundred and fifty thousand in student debt. This helps a lot. I'm sorry. I shouldn't talk about money."

"Don't worry about it. I asked. I'm curious. I really am. I've never met such a well-educated massage therapist."

He laughed a nice laugh.

"There are plenty of us. It's not easy to make a living in New York City. Do you want to roll over? I'll turn around while you do. Not that anyone can see much of anything out here anyway."

So polite!

"Sure." Janey pulled the soft white sheet up to her chest, rolled onto her side, and then all the way to her back, breathing in the briny smell of the ocean.

"I'll bet the tips can be really good," she said. Was that inappropriate?

"They can be. These women sure know what they want, and they know how to ask for it," Scott said matter-of-factly. He worked his hands down to her belly, careful to avoid her breasts. She tensed again when he reached the tops of her aching thighs.

"Don't worry, Janey," he whispered. "I know what you've probably heard. I promise you, the women here *know* how to ask for what they want."

She opened her eyes without meaning to.

"And you do it?"

"You said it yourself. They tip well. I shouldn't be telling you this. But you seem nice. Different from the rest of them. You're not in there doing mescal shots and hitting on men half your age. They'll tip a couple grand for the whole week. I'm not doing anything I'd consider cheating. It's a fairly mechanical thing, really. Just massage of a different kind. But they seem like they need it. They don't get any attention from their husbands. They come here to let loose. It started with one woman last year and then word got around. I paid this semester's tuition and bought an engagement ring with what I made last time." He shrugged. "We do what we have to do."

Janey nodded and tried to keep her facial expression from veering into judgmental territory. "We do what we have to do," she repeated.

He had moved to the base of the table and was kneading her feet between both hands. She could only imagine the things those hands could do. She kept her sadness about the situation to herself.

"You're incredibly talented with your hands, Scott," she said instead. "I'm sure you'll be a great doctor. You've got your bedside manner down."

His voice brightened with the subject change and the compliment.

"I hope so, Janey. It was great meeting you. I'm almost done. I want you to drink plenty of fluids and maybe take a soak in a bath. Your muscles were tight as rocks. I know you're all here to lose weight, but be careful. Don't strain yourself too hard."

He left her alone on the beach to get dressed and was nowhere to be found as she walked back to the main property. Janey was about to take his advice, get some water, and head straight into the bath, when she was intercepted by Suzy outside their yurt.

The imposing woman swayed as she talked and threw her arm around Janey's shoulders. "Hey babe! How was the massage? Did you get your special treat at the end?"

"He gave me an incredible foot rub," Janey said.

Suzy was clearly put out by Janey's answer. "You've gotta come in and play with us tonight. We've got the dance going and the mescal and we'll go swimmin' in a little. Come on."

"Nah. Suzy, I'm so sleepy. Maybe tomorrow night."

But her roommate was strangely aggressive. "Just one drink. Whatchoo don't like us or somethin'?"

She didn't want to come off as a snot. That would make the rest of the retreat unbearable.

"One drink won't hurt me."

"Yayyyyyyyy!" Suzy threw her arms over her head and then grabbed Janey's hand, dragging her to the main house.

The main house was a whirl of debauchery that rivaled a frat party. Where had this group of handsome young men come from? All of the women were clearly intoxicated.

"Can I get you a margarita?" It was Maizee. Janey nodded. She'd politely accept the margarita, sit down for a few minutes, and then quietly slip back to her bathtub.

Maizee snapped her fingers at a waiter carrying an empty silver tray.

"Margs over here, *puh-leeze and thank yoooo!*" she commanded, emphasizing too many of the vowels.

Janey found her way to a fluffy chaise longue in the corner, eager to rest. When the young man brought her the drink, she ran her finger along the rim and put it in her mouth to suck the salt. The salt, Janey had always believed, was the best part of the margarita anyway. She hated a tequila hangover.

All around her, the other women jumped up and down, dancing provocatively with men half their age, groping them in ways Janey couldn't believe, and throwing back shots of mescal as if they were water. She placed the margarita on the ground and closed her eyes for a second.

And that was the last thing she remembered. She had gone to sleep, and now here she was in bed with an IV in her arm and a pounding headache. Suzy, once again looking no worse for wear, was sitting up in bed, her own IV dangling out of her forearm, reading last month's issue of *Architectural Digest*.

"You really ate it last night," Suzy said.

Janey looked at her.

"You were one and done, my dear. Lightweight."

Janey didn't want to admit she hadn't even drunk her margarita. "I guess so," she said, gesturing over to the man in the white coat across the room. He held up a hand, splaying all five fingers.

"He says you have five more minutes. Trust me, you want the whole five minutes."

But why did she feel so awful? It couldn't be a hangover. She must be dehydrated. Scott had said her muscles were all tensed and that she was supposed to drink fluids after the massage. But all she'd had was a lick of salt before falling asleep. Fluids would do her good.

"Did I miss another wild night?" she asked Suzy, not really caring about the answer.

"The best," Suzy said definitively. "I live for these fucking trips. Live for them. We went into town and found a little taverna and made friends with those local boys," she said. Janey could only imagine. "I just got back a couple of hours ago, but I had some clay and some tea before bed and I'm feeling good. That stuff is magical. It's like herbal magic. All those vitamins and minerals. Whatever Sara is putting in there, it's the best energy boost I've had since I stopped taking uppers."

"Sounds great," Janey said, closing her eyes for a sweet brief moment again. This was day three. There were five more days of this. She had to find Stella. She wanted out.

· · ·

"You can't leave," Stella exclaimed when Janey found the shaman sitting on a meditation cushion on the deck of her own yurt.

"I don't feel good, Stella. I had an IV in my arm this morning, for Christ's sake," Janey said with determination. "I can change my ticket and go home tomorrow. No hard feelings. It's not you. It's these women. This place. Sara."

For the first time since she'd met her, Janey saw Stella's face darken. "I know. I'm not sure what's going on. The first time we did this it was magical. Now it is going all wrong, isn't it?" Stella stood, strode over to the bed, and pushed the mosquito netting aside. After brushing the henna dust from her comforter she patted the space beside her. "I think Sara is under a lot of pressure. She handpicked these women for their money and their clout because she's dying to bring in investors to help her expand. And that's not the right vibe at all. I get it. Go home if you need to."

Janey was certain there wouldn't be a refund if she left early. But what was she even paying for? The workouts? The clay? The on-call doctors or the sexy local men?

Janey released a long sigh. "I'm going to go for a walk on the beach. I'll figure it out."

Stella reached over and enveloped her in a bear hug. "I just want to make people's lives better. You know that, right?" The normally confident shaman's vulnerability was unnerving.

"Of course."

Out on the beach Janey needed something to distract her while she walked. She fiddled around with her iPhone, looking for a podcast. If she found the right one, she might even muster up a jog. One TED Talk looked interesting. Who was Gabby Reece again? Janey clicked through. Of course. It was that professional volleyball player, the one married to the sexy surfer dude. The topic of the podcast was learning to love yourself. Well, that was fitting. Janey left her flip-flops underneath a pretty shrub with orange flowers that looked like tiny trumpets and hit play as she ambled toward the waves.

"Do you ever wake up and think, 'Wow, I'm perfect today'?" came the assured voice of the TED speaker through her headphones.

"No," Janey said out loud.

Janey picked up the pace, finding something between a power walk and a light jog, the resistance from the sand straining her calf muscles. "Of course you don't," Reece continued. "I don't. I have friends who look at my Instagram and then say things to me like, 'You have the most perfect life.' I'm the first one to tell you that the way someone's life looks on Insta is bullshit. Real life doesn't come with filters. We are often comparing ourselves to other women who may be younger or more fit than we are. The problem is that every year as we get older we have a larger group to compare ourselves to. Stop comparing. Acknowledge other people's greatness and you will be more powerful and centered. Others will notice and embrace your confidence. There's nothing sexier than someone who is content with herself and trying every single day to be better and improve on her own terms."

The advice rang too true. Janey turned the phone around and snapped a selfie of her smaller but still round belly peeking out over her jogging shorts and without a second thought posted it to Instagram. "This is forty!" she captioned it and then added, "There's nothing sexier than someone who is content with herself." And then she tagged the professional volleyball player.

Writing the words gave her a moment's pause. Wait a second. Janey rewound the podcast and listened to it again. Janey looked at the date of the TED Talk and saw it had taken place more than a year ago. But the words sounded so familiar because Janey had heard them very recently. It was almost the exact same thing Sara had said during The Workout in New York and again here at the start of the retreat.

Sara Strong was an inspirational plagiarist! Janey listened to it a third time to make sure, but there wasn't any doubt. What was up with this woman? Was she a complete fraud? Did it matter if she was? She wasn't claiming to be a doctor or a preacher or a Supreme Court justice. Sara Strong was just a personal trainer with a following of very rich women. What did it matter if she cribbed a few lines from a famous person's inspirational speech? It still left a sour feeling in Janey's stomach. She was just about to dial the phone number for American to find out how much of a change fee she'd have to pay to switch her return ticket when she heard Suzy screaming from down the beach.

"Miranda's had a heart attack!"

CHAPTER TWENTY-THREE

A fter leaving the big house the night of the mescal shots and wild partying, Ivy had gone back to her small room next to the chicken coop and sat on the bed compiling her notes to send over to Ally and Lemon. She plugged the keyhole camera into her laptop to review her footage. Who knew what her bosses would do with this? She'd gotten a thrill out of uncovering the dark underbelly of the retreat, but no matter how rich and how ridiculous these women were, these videos could ruin their lives if they were leaked. And there was the fact that Janey was in the video, all passed out on the chaise longue. She'd decided to wait until the morning to email anything back to the States. Her plan for the next day was to grab some footage of the actual workouts in the hope that those would be useful to SoarBarre and less icky for everyone involved.

That morning, she'd barely arrived at the compound when a maid ran out of one of the yurts screaming. She followed the commotion and came upon a scene straight out of *Law & Order*. A perilously thin woman lay lifeless on a gurney in the yurt, her chest covered in blood. The faux rustic dwelling had been transformed into an operating theater with high-tech machinery, IV lines, and a scrum of nurses in white uniforms. A white man in green scrubs was in the process of applying a defibrillator to the woman.

"MOVE. AWAY. EVERYONE GET AWAY!" screamed the small woman Ivy recognized as Sara Strong. She saw one cook snap a photograph of the scene with his phone and watched as Sara dove through the air to tackle the formidable man and claw his phone out of his hands. She looked like she wanted to spit in his face.

"How dare you!" she shrieked at him. Ivy turned quietly and made for the big house, pulling her own phone out of her pocket and dialing 0 before calmly asking the operator who to contact in case of an emergency. Behind her she could hear other guests gasping in horror as Sara Strong tried to contain the scene.

"Go back to your rooms!" the woman screamed. "Get away from here!"

The operator put Ivy through to the local hospital and she repeated the address twice for the dispatcher, who thankfully understood her despite the pandemonium in the background. She continued through to behind the kitchen, where Carlo was smoking a cigarette.

"The price they pay to look like they do." He exhaled and offered the pack to Ivy. She shook her head. She'd never smoked a cigarette; no one her age smoked cigarettes.

"Do you know what happened?" she asked.

Carlo nodded. "The doctors came to do a quick nip and tuck and something went wrong. Happens all the time. I thought these women were rich. Why do they come here to do surgery? It's cheap, but sometimes no good."

"What do you think went wrong?"

"Who knows?" Carlo said, his eyes falling down onto Ivy's chest. She crossed her arms, knowing the maid's uniform was too tight across her breasts. "They get what they deserve." He took a final puff and stubbed the cigarette out on the ground.

She heard the ambulance siren before she saw the vehicle pull into the gravel parking lot.

"Who called them?" Sara Strong screamed. "Who made that call?"

In the distance Ivy could see Janey jogging up the sandy path from the beach. For a second her cousin's eyes rested on her, and she thought she saw a flicker of recognition, but Janey turned and ran over to join the commotion.

Ivy wanted to grab her cousin and sprint out of this place, escape the middle-aged debauchery together. Neither of them belonged here, but she knew Janey would be pissed if she learned Ivy was spying on her. A man who could have been a police officer or a member of the national guard was closing off the area around the yurt with a roll of yellow and black police tape, and Ivy knew it was only a matter of time before someone pulled her into a room to be questioned and quickly pieced together that she wasn't supposed to be there at all. She slowly backed away, tiptoeing across the lush green lawn. The grounds were like an obstacle course of flowering bushes, palm trees, and bocce courts, and it took forever to get back out to her car, parked alongside the beaten-up used cars owned by the rest of the staff.

For the next couple of hours Ivy let her phone go straight to voicemail. Her bosses were calling every ten minutes or so and texting rapid-fire questions. What did she know? Had she seen anything? Was it true that Miranda Mills had a heart attack at The Workout retreat? Social media was fast. Too fast. Their glee at Sara Strong's takedown was too palpable. She also got a text from Kelli that just said, *Please come home.*

She was almost home. Her plane would land soon.

CHAPTER TWENTY-FOUR

~

The next available flight back to New York didn't leave until
one a.m. Janey tried to close her eyes and rest on the plane,
but it was impossible in the middle seat between a harried
father with a crying baby and a snoring old man.

Jacob had texted her right before she took off to ask how she
was. She said she was coming home. He'd been so excited that she
was coming back early he insisted on picking her up from JFK, and
she felt bad saying no, even though all she wanted to do was go
home and curl up in bed alone. She started composing messages to
explain what had happened at the retreat, but she'd erased them
before she hit send. It was just too strange to talk about over text.
It didn't sound real.

A beat-up old Jeep, the kind with the wood paneling that was
popular with parents in the late eighties, pulled over next to Janey.
She glanced up and saw the Uber sticker in the window, waving the
driver away.

"I'm waiting for someone. Thanks, I'm good. I didn't order a
car," she said, even though the driver had the windows pulled up
and couldn't hear her. Janey backed up a few steps to let the car's
passenger through and then realized the Jeep's engine had stopped

idling and Jacob was getting out of the driver's seat. Of course Jacob was also an Uber driver in his spare time.

"Hey, island girl." Jacob grabbed her bag and gave her a kiss. "It's good to see you!" His normally shaggy locks were pulled high onto his head in a man bun. It was an image she'd never be able to forget.

She mustered a smile and climbed into the passenger seat. "You too."

"I don't know why you cut your trip short, but I'm glad you did. Was the weather bad? Surf wasn't what you expected?"

"None of it was what I expected." Janey stared out the window, her stomach lurching as Jacob eased the car out of the parking lot.

"I hear ya, man. Group vacations are hard. Did I tell you about that one time I went to a surf camp in Costa Rica?"

Janey shook her head. She didn't want to hear about it right now.

"Oh god. Those guys. They picked up these girls in Tamarindo who turned out to be hookers and they robbed all of us blind."

They missed the exit for the Midtown Tunnel.

"Hey, Jacob. Is it okay if I just go back to my place? I'm exhausted."

He reached over and squeezed her thigh. "Oh, I have a surprise for you. I know you're tired. This will perk you up, I promise. You're gonna love it."

He was so eager, so enthusiastic. She was too bushed to deflate his excitement.

Jacob turned onto the Greenpoint Avenue exit. Empty juice bottles rolled over Janey's feet.

"Jacob, I'm really tired."

"I know. We're almost there. This will wake you right up."

She was starting to feel dizzy. Jacob pulled up next to the curb and bounced out of the car toward what looked like an abandoned warehouse. When she caught up with him he grabbed both of her hands.

"Are you ready for this?"

No, I'm not, she thought to herself. I'm not ready for anything but bed. He pulled her through a creaky metal door. All of Janey's senses were assaulted by a riot of sound and light. Furious electronic dance music pulsed in time to brightly colored strobe lights. The room was filled with bodies in various states of dress and undress.

"What the hell is this? Did you bring me to a rave? Is this the surprise? I don't do drugs."

"It's a sober rave," Jacob yelled as he tried to pull her into the melee. "It just got started. Goes from four to seven. It's wild. People come here and dance out all their stress and tension before going to work. I thought you'd love it. They call it conscious clubbing. The only drinks they serve are my juices. How cool is that?"

The room was spinning. A girl dressed as a bumblebee thrust a Green juice into her hand. "Welcome to Morning Glory!" she said and buzzed back into the crowd. Jacob began bouncing up and down to a Fatboy Slim beat. In the corner a tall reedy man led a group of yogis through a series of animated sun salutations. Exercise bikes attached to giant blenders lined one wall.

"Bike-blended smoothies! YES!" Jacob headed toward the bikes. "Isn't this just the coolest way to start your day?"

She needed to sit down. Needed air. Janey sipped at the Green juice in desperation, but it did nothing to calm her roiling tummy.

"I need to leave." But Jacob didn't hear her. He was up on a stationary bike while two women in bright purple spandex loaded beets into the blender perched on the handlebars. "I need to go home." She bent forward and placed both of her hands on her knees as she gulped for air.

Jacob finally cast a worried look her way and hopped off the bike.

He reached her just in time to catch Janey's head before she hit the floor.

. . .

She woke up in a private room in NewYork-Presbyterian Hospital.

"Oh thank god!" CJ's face loomed large above her, Sam, one of the twins, shyly peeking out from behind her back. She lowered her voice to a whisper. "You're not pregnant, are you? I told them you couldn't be pregnant. But with all the men you're juggling these days, who knows! No judgment. We'll raise your bastard baby together!"

Janey's head pounded as she shook it from side to side. "Not pregnant. How did I get here?"

"Jacob called an ambulance. He was here until about twenty minutes ago. He had to go relieve his babysitter. God, he's sexy, Janey. I mean. Wow. Even with a man bun. But where were you? Were you at a rave? I didn't even know you were back from the beach. Is this because of Miranda Mills?"

"How did you know about that?" Janey was surprised by how raspy her voice sounded.

"Everyone knows about that." CJ pulled out a copy of that morning's *New York Post*. A grainy photo of a human being covered with a sheet and carried on a stretcher over the sand was blown up large on the cover under the headline WORKOUT TILL YOU DROP—MODEL IN COMA. Janey grabbed the paper from CJ's hand and winced as she straightened up in the bed. She must have hit her tailbone when she collapsed at that rave. Why did Jacob have to take her to a rave in the first place? What was wrong with him?

www.nypost.com

MODEL IN COMA FOLLOWING FITNESS RETREAT
By Dan Maxwell

Beloved model and handbag designer Miranda Mills is currently in a coma in New York-Presbyterian Hospital after being rushed back to New York City from a fitness retreat in St. Lucia yesterday morning.

Sources say she is in critical condition. Mills, fifty-three, who was a much-coveted cover girl in her heyday, was attending a retreat led by the personal trainer Sara Schweitzer

Yang, better known as Sara Strong, as part of her top-secret fitness program "The Workout." The exclusive retreat held at society maven Maizee Vanders's private beachside home is said to cost the ridiculous sum of fifteen thousand dollars and promises to help participants shed fifteen pounds in eight days.

But sources claim it wasn't starvation or an excess of physical activity that caused Mills to have a heart attack in the middle of the Caribbean. One retreat guest claims that Mills was in the midst of a backroom breast reduction and liposuction the morning of her heart attack. St. Lucia is well known for cut-rate plastic surgery. Investigators are currently looking into whether the doctor who operated on the model was licensed to be performing surgery on the Vanders property.

Schweitzer Yang couldn't be reached for comment. The personal trainer rose to a certain fame due to her famous clientele, which included Academy Award–winner Kate Wells. The two women had a falling-out earlier this year, and Wells released a statement about Miranda Mills through her publicist: "I have no comment on Sara's methods for weight loss or personal wellness. But my heart goes out to Miranda, a truly bright light in our world, and her family during this devastating time."

Janey folded the newspaper and placed it on the table next to her.

"Did you see it go down?" CJ asked. "Was it completely gruesome? Did you know you could get plastic surgery done at the retreat? This is all so crazy."

It *was* all so crazy.

A baby-faced man in a white lab coat strode into the room. "I'm Dr. Knots. I need to have a word with Ms. Sweet."

Janey tried to smile at him. "It's all right, Doctor, they can stay."

He raised an eyebrow and looked at CJ. "Are you family?"

CJ placed her hand on her hip. "I'm her wife."

"Fine; whatever. I'm not a lawyer or a police officer, and this is really none of my business, but how often do you use recreational drugs, Ms. Sweet?"

"Excuse me?"

"The report from the ambulance says you were brought in from a rave at a warehouse in Greenpoint. Is that correct?"

Janey nodded slowly. "It was a sober rave." That sounded ridiculous. "They had juice there." Even more ridiculous. "That's it. I don't use drugs, doctor," Janey said with a measure of force. "What are you talking about?"

The doctor softened his tone, clearly deciding it was best to take a softer approach with his drug-addict patient.

"We ran the tests for traces of Zika and malaria and dengue and other tropical mosquito-borne diseases since you were very recently on a Caribbean island. We didn't find anything. We checked for various other discrepancies and found large traces of amphetamines in your system, likely cocaine. What is happening to you right now is classic withdrawal. I don't know your situation, Ms. Sweet, but I can recommend some highly regarded rehabilitation facilities that can help you."

"I'm not a drug addict!" Janey practically screamed. She felt like she was going mad, like one of those people on reality television who are tormented on purpose by greedy producers who just want to make them cry. None of this made any sense. "Can you run the tests again? There's some kind of mix-up."

The doctor sighed and ran his hand through his thinning hair. "We ran the tests twice. Maybe this was a onetime thing. I don't care. You didn't have any illegal substances physically on you when they brought you in, so no one is going to press any charges. But like I said, I'm happy to recommend a counselor. There are options for you if you need help."

She had speed in her system. She was withdrawing from cocaine? What was this alternate universe she was living in?

CJ looked at Janey and then at the doctor. "My wife does not do drugs!"

The doctor clearly didn't have the energy to argue with an irate lesbian. He looked back down at his charts and then at Janey. "You're also severely underweight, dehydrated, slightly anemic, and you have some problematic vitamin deficiencies. Have you recently changed your diet? Lost a lot of weight?"

Janey thought for a second. How much weight had she lost since that breakfast with Beau? It must be at least thirty pounds. She obediently recounted this to the doctor in the hopes that somehow the weight loss would supersede the drug issue.

"In how long?" the doctor asked.

"Two months."

The doctor made a tsk-tsk noise better suited to an elderly woman. "Not healthy. You shouldn't be losing more than four or five pounds in a month. And frankly, you were probably a healthy weight before." He paused for a moment and stared down at the floor as if he wanted to give Janey more advice but decided against it.

"We should keep you for a few days and get you stabilized. Get some vitamins in you, get some weight back on you." Vitamins. Janey thought back to the vitamins she'd been given in the IV at the retreat. What exactly had been in that IV? She made a mental list of everything she'd put into her body in the past few days. There was fruit, vegetables, fish, clay, and then there was the strange man who stuck a needle in her arm and gave her an IV filled with vitamins in the early morning hours. She couldn't have been given speed at a wellness retreat. Could she have?

"I understand, doctor. I'll stay as long as it takes to get healthy."

When the doctor left, CJ climbed into the hospital bed with Janey. Sam wriggled his way on top of the two women.

"Ooomph. He's getting heavy," Janey said.

CJ rolled her eyes. "I told you."

The doctor had given her some pain medication (no opiates) that should kick in soon and help her sleep.

"Hey wifey," CJ cooed, pursing her lips in a kissy face.

"I have to hand it to you, Chakori." It hurt Janey's stomach to laugh. "You're quick on your feet."

CJ lowered her voice so the little boy wouldn't be able to hear her. "Oh please. I'd marry you any day. So *did* you do drugs in the Caribbean? No judgment. Steven and I took molly last New Year's."

"Of course I didn't. But something strange happened down there." Janey closed her eyes and tried to sort through everything. "Miranda's in this hospital, right? That's what it said in the article."

CJ nodded. "I think so. What do you think happened down there? You don't think they drugged you, do you?"

"I have no idea." She thought back to how this all began, back to breakfast, back to Beau telling her she was fat. She wasn't fat. She thought back to CJ signing her up for SweatGood.

"Why were you so obsessed with my weight, CJ?" Janey asked.

"What?"

"Why were you so into helping me get skinny?"

CJ brushed Janey's bangs off of her forehead. "Honey, I don't give a shit what you weigh. I'm obsessed with what I weigh, but I'm more obsessed with you being happy. I thought you wanted to lose weight to get back at Beau. That's the only reason I helped you. I like revenge. I'm like the bad guy with great hair in an eighties movie. Gain two hundred pounds if you want. I don't give a fuck. More of you to love."

CJ paused for a second. "You know . . . I think it's a lie that all women want to be skinny. I think we just want to be told it's okay to look the way we look."

Her friend's words made her want to cry.

"Get some sleep." CJ stood up. "I'm going to take this super-sized munchkin home soon but I can come back and bring you dinner. Want anything special?"

"French fries," Janey said as she let herself drift off to sleep.

vy, we want to offer you this bonus as a sign of our gratitude for all of your hard work here," Lemon said, pushing a check for thirty thousand dollars across the concrete desktop.

"So grateful, Ivy," Ally added.

Ivy had told Ally and Lemon everything she knew about The Workout. She explained about the crazy classes the staff had described to her in great detail, the drinking and the dancing and late-night parties, and told them she was the one who called for the ambulance for Miranda Mills.

Part of her didn't want to pick up the check they were offering her.

The two women smiled like leopards after a kill, lips stretched tight over their bleached teeth. The Workout was clearly no longer a threat. Their legacy as the most important exercise studio of all time was secure, for now. Ivy reached her hand across the desk to take the small piece of paper, written from Lemon's personal account instead of the SoarBarre corporate account. This was surely something they'd be keeping off the books.

"I hope she gets through it okay. Miranda, I mean. It was awful to see her like that," Ivy said, folding the check again and again until it became a very tiny cube.

"Oh, me too," Lemon said, at least having the decency to stop smiling. "Our thoughts and prayers are with her and her family. We tweeted at them this morning."

"Right," Ivy said, putting the tiny cube into the pocket of her gym bag. "Well. You're welcome, and if that's all I think I'm going to head out for the day. I'm still really tired."

Ally and Lemon rose at the same time.

"Of course," Lemon said. "Get some rest and come in here to whip some chubby bitches into shape Monday morning." Lemon bowed to her. "Namaste, Ivy. Namaste."

She should just quit on the spot, but she didn't have the energy. And who was she kidding; she wanted the check to clear in her bank account before she did anything rash. Thirty thousand dollars was nothing to these women, but it was a lot of money for her. It was enough to maybe invest in something real and good and secure a future for herself that didn't involve screaming at overweight women with postpartum depression.

"Yeah. Monday. Have a good weekend, guys."

Ivy could hardly walk through the lobby. She'd come in through the back door of the studio and had missed this enormous crowd in the front. She recognized some of her regulars, but it was hard to tell who was who, since everyone was dressed in costume. Was that colonial garb? Ivy vaguely remembered seeing something similar on her eighth-grade field trip to Williamsburg, Virginia.

She dodged a woman wearing a tall white wig and carrying a musket.

"What the hell is going on?" Ivy asked Kimberly, who was wearing a long navy soldier's uniform with shiny brass buttons.

Kimberly sighed. "It's the *Hamilton* karaoke ride. Don't you remember, Ivy? We have the original Broadway cast in today—well, Leslie Odom, Jr., is apparently under the weather. But Lin-Manuel is in the locker room right now. It's a fund-raiser for Lemon's kid's school. How could you forget?"

Of course Ivy had heard of the wildly successful Broadway show.

Who hadn't? But she'd been so preoccupied with her crazy mission that she'd blocked out the big day.

"We've raised like half a million dollars," Kimberly said.

"And who are you dressed as?" Ivy eyed her warily.

Kimberly stood up behind the desk and saluted her. "Hercules Mulligan at your service."

At a loss for words, Ivy ducked back down the staff hallway and into the alley behind SoarBarre.

This day was filled with things Ivy didn't feel like doing. Training Kate Wells was the second thing on that list, but Ivy reluctantly rode her bike to the Upper East Side and locked it outside of Kate Wells's enormous townhouse. The tax bill on this place was probably thirty thousand a year. Maybe more.

Kate once again answered the door all ready to work out in a pair of black shorts that stopped just below the perfect curve of her backside, revealing a set of pale white thighs without a speck of cellulite, an achievement for a woman of any age, particularly one with two children. A large white-and-caramel-colored dog perched on his haunches behind his owner.

"This is Bernardo DiCaprio. I didn't name him. The kids went gaga for Leo when we were on location in Namibia for that movie where he and I fall in love after being trapped on Mars together." Kate grabbed the scruff of the dog's neck affectionately. "Bernardo was out with his dog walker last time you were here." The massive Saint Bernard must have weighed twice what Kate Wells did. She couldn't possibly walk this dog herself. A fine line of drool began to fall from the edge of Bernardo's mouth as he turned his droopy eyes to his owner to ask if it was all right to investigate the stranger.

"It's okay, Bernardo," she said and turned to Ivy. "He's been working with Cesar Millan. Amazing progress. He used to just knock guests flat on their back when I opened the door." Kate confirmed something Ivy had long guessed at, that all famous people knew one another and were hanging out together, singing karaoke and training one another's dogs, all of the time. Bernardo immediately put his nose directly into Ivy's crotch.

Kate gave her a warm smile and offered to let Ivy bring the bike inside the foyer instead of keeping it locked outside.

"This neighborhood is going straight to hell," she said as Ivy undid the lock. "We had a peeping Tom the other night just staring in Dusty's window. I had to call the police. And you can't imagine how impossible it is for someone like me to call the police. The papers find out about it the next day. Thankfully there was bigger news today with that whole Miranda Mills story. Did you see that? Wasn't it awful?"

"Awful," Ivy agreed, hoisting her bike to her shoulder and carrying it up the small set of stairs leading into the townhouse.

"Did you read about it?" Kate pressed. Ivy would have loved nothing more than getting Kate Wells to talk about The Workout just five days ago. Now she wanted to put it all out of her mind.

"I did. It's terrible." How was it possible that this whole house smelled of freshly washed laundry?

Kate's taut backside led the way down the hallway and into the kitchen, where she opened the fridge and pulled out a pitcher of fluorescent orange liquid. Ivy looked past her into a small backyard garden where two Asian gardeners furiously clipped the hedges into neat rectangles.

"Turmeric smoothie?"

Ivy shook her head. "But you have one. I had my turmeric with breakfast," she lied. She hated turmeric. It tasted like rubber and turned your mouth the color of a hunting jacket for at least three days.

"I didn't know Miranda well or anything. But I did have some involvement with The Workout back in the early days. And believe it or not I helped organize their first retreat. Of course nothing happened like this. My god. No." Kate poured herself a glass of turmeric and a second smaller glass of a yellow viscous oil and settled into a large wicker chair, clearly not ready for exercise just yet.

"Have you tried mustard oil yet? I try to have at least five table-spoons a day. It creates warmth in your bones and your nervous system to generate natural energy. Since I started on it, I haven't had a single cup of coffee." Kate's perfectly pouty lips took on a sultry sheen from the oil. "Do you want some?" She offered the glass to Ivy.

Ivy shook her head. "Not yet. I think I read about it on Goop. Gwyneth was raving about it." The stuff smelled like a sweaty gym sock.

Kate made a face. "You probably read about it on Lovely first. We do everything before Gwyneth."

"So you organized the first Workout retreat?" Ivy asked.

"I was one of Sara's very first clients, and I helped her create the idea for The Workout," Kate said, her register lowering. "It's so sad. She was so good at what she did. But so desperate for money."

Ivy began to look around the kitchen. It was perfect. No cabinets, just basic wood shelves with white china stacked in serene columns. One of those retro Smeg refrigerators custom painted with the British flag occupied one corner, a stainless steel Bosch range in the other.

"Desperate for money?"

Kate took a long sip of her drink and placed the glass down on the butcher block countertop with a supremely satisfied sigh. "She'd do anything to get rich quick. Anything." This woman wasn't an Oscar-winner for nothing. Kate Wells knew how to build a sense of drama, how to let it linger in the air and then, just when you wanted more, pull away from it.

"Shall we get started? I have everything we need downstairs in the basement."

"Yeah. Can I use your bathroom first?"

Kate pointed to a powder room off the hallway. Ivy splashed water on her face in the hopes that it would help her feel less out of sorts. She was pleased to see a little clutter in the bathroom, an open box of tampons sitting in the corner. She constructed a fake

Us Weekly headline in her head: KATE WELLS BLEEDS—JUST LIKE US. Sunday's *New York Times* was folded on the back of the toilet bowl with the crossword puzzle completely finished and written in pen.

The basement of Kate Wells's house was a fully equipped sound-proofed exercise studio with mirrors on three walls, a ballet barre, weights of every shape and size, a full set of kettlebells, and a closet filled with various other props.

"I know your specialty is circuit training, so I'm ready to do whatever you suggest." Kate smiled. "Should I turn on some music? Anything you prefer? I have it all. Except Madonna. She kissed my ex-husband at a Grammy party and I can't listen to any of her music without wanting to scream. And not in a good way. But, too much information. Right? Oh. Wait. Did you sign that confidentiality agreement I sent over to you? I need everyone to sign that. I have no filter, and you wouldn't believe the things people have leaked to the press over the years. I had a maid who took photographs of all my bras and panties and sold them to the *Daily Mail* for a small fortune. Can you imagine someone paying for something like that? Or being the kind of person who gets paid for things like that? It's disgusting."

Ivy reached into her gym bag for the signed confidentiality agreement, her fingers brushing the folded check.

"Here you go." Ivy handed her the piece of paper with her name scrawled on the bottom. She'd only skimmed it before signing it. Essentially the document forbade Ivy to say Kate Wells's name in public unless she wanted the actress to be able to sue her for the very little amount of money she had, which right now was about $31,500.

Ivy didn't know how to approach her next question, so she just said it. "You know I work at SoarBarre. Do you want SoarBarre-style training, you know, the kind where I yell at you?"

Kate Wells laughed her perfect laugh.

"No, no honey. If I wanted to be abused I'd read the comments section of my blog. Let's just work out."

Ivy was so relieved she wanted to hug Kate. "Let's start with squats. Twenty-five. Grab the ten-pound kettlebell and lift it up to your chin as you're coming back up. Give me ten push-ups in between sets and we'll do three sets. Sound good?" Ivy couldn't help but admire Kate's picture-perfect body as she bent over to pick up the kettlebell. It was amazing what a healthy diet and good fitness could do to a body. She wondered if Kate had ever had plastic surgery. Nothing was too obvious. Her breasts were a perfectly normal size and even drooped a little the way breasts should after having a couple of kids. The thought of plastic surgery made Ivy think about Miranda Mills again.

"What you said earlier . . . about Sara Strong being willing to do anything for money. What did you mean? What do you think happened to Miranda Mills down there?" Ivy hoped she wasn't pushing her luck with the question. Kate nodded to indicate she'd answer when she finished this set of exercises.

Once her push-ups were complete, the actress stretched her legs in front of her and bent over her thighs.

"Sara wanted The Workout to be bigger than any other fitness class out there. She wanted something that would make her rich and famous," Kate said, her breath beginning to equalize. "But at the end of the day it was just an exercise class. She wanted to make it something grander. She needed to make her clients obsessed with it. And so she made The Workout something they absolutely had to have."

What was Kate talking about?

"Mark my words, if they did a toxicology report on that poor model they'd find out she didn't just have a heart attack. Sara was giving her clients speed. She put it in the tea. She put it in the clay. It kept them skinny and it kept them coming back. Those women were actually addicted to The Workout. But they didn't have a choice in the matter."

Ivy's jaw dropped.

"How do you know?"

"I get my blood tested on a weekly basis to check my hormone levels and have my diet rebalanced. My doctor noticed something funny. There were ridiculous levels of amphetamines in my system. I knew right away. I'm also a little psychic. I don't know if I told you that. I just have a more highly attuned sixth sense than most people." Kate stood and grabbed her bottle of water from off one of the weight benches. "I confronted Sara about it. I told her I couldn't work with her anymore. The problem is that she knew a lot about me. She was around when I was having problems in my marriage. That was before I had people sign off before they worked with me. We came to an agreement. We'd part ways; neither of us would air the other's dirty laundry. But I knew this would happen one of these days. I knew it would go too far and someone would get hurt."

Ivy didn't know what to say. It made sense. Those women were amped up out of their minds when she saw them down at the retreat. She'd assumed it was by choice, but maybe not. And Miranda Mills's heart attack most definitely could have been caused by having drugs in her system when she went under the knife. Fuck! That meant Janey had been given speed too.

She had to come clean and tell Janey what she knew.

"Do you think Miranda's family knows she took something before she had the surgery? Do you think it could make a difference?" Ivy asked Kate, who was working on her second set of squats, diligently pulling the kettlebell up to tap her dimpled chin with each movement.

Kate appeared lost in thought. "I hope someone who knew what was really happening called the doctors and tipped them off," Kate said.

Ivy nodded. "Me too."

As quickly as she'd begun discussing the topic, Kate Wells shut down. "I can't talk about it anymore," she said in a clipped tone. "It's just too sad."

"Of course," Ivy said carefully, taken aback by the shift in her mood. "So, next up we're going to move on to plank . . . Do you mind if I run up to the powder room again? I have the tiniest bladder." Kate shook her head as she steadied her arms and legs beneath her in the most perfect plank position Ivy had ever seen.

Ivy walked up the stairs and into the backyard, where the only people who would hear her were Kate's gardeners.

Janey's phone just kept going to voicemail.

CHAPTER TWENTY-SIX

B y the next morning, Janey's room smelled of both French fry grease and lilies from four bouquets Hugh had sent over. He was in Tokyo for meetings until the end of the week but promised to send flowers every day she was in the hospital. She didn't tell him why she was there, had just mentioned she caught a terrible bug down in the islands and was severely dehydrated. He'd called to see how she was doing instead of texting. She'd forgotten what it was like to have someone call her on the phone and she much preferred it to communicating via emoji.

When she received a beautifully wrapped Tiffany-blue box with a large white ribbon she assumed it was another present from Hugh. She opened it eagerly, tossing the paper-thin tissue paper to the floor.

The gift wasn't from Hugh. Inside the box was a silver picture frame, small and oval with a black-and-white photograph inside. Janey had never seen this particular print of her and Beau from the debutante ball in Charleston. She didn't even know it had been taken. It was just the two of them, shot from behind, holding hands and walking through an immaculate southern garden. A wave of dizziness swept over her, and her hands shook so hard she nearly dropped the photograph onto the linoleum floor. Beau's childish script was scrawled on a note card inside of the box.

"Found this the other day. Thinking of you. Xoxo, Beau." The last interaction they'd had was in that boot camp when she'd beaten him in that absurd obstacle course. The sweetness of the note implied something nefarious. It was too random and too calculating to be anything but trouble. He wanted something.

And there it was. On the bottom of the card was much neater handwriting, clearly written by someone else, his attorney most likely. "There are a few things that need to be taken care of in the office. Since you're in the hospital you can give me power of attorney to sign for you." A document folded neatly in the bottom of the box had a place for Janey's signature. It would allow Beau to make decisions for their company in her absence.

She looked at the photograph again and then back at the piece of paper before placing them both on the table beside the hospital bed. She tried to close her eyes, pushing the black-and-white image of her and Beau, so young and so happy, out of her mind. A nurse interrupted her reverie and moved the package and its contents to the far corner of the room to give Janey her lunch. She had the option of a kale salad or fried chicken and she cautiously asked for both, not sure which one would be edible. After looking at her chart the nurse was happy to oblige her.

"Glad to see you're getting your appetite back," she said. "We need to get some weight back on those skinny bones!"

Jacob came by later in the morning, probably on an early lunch break. To his credit, he was sheepishly apologetic for taking her to the early morning rave. He was as handsome as ever in his tight but not too tight Levis and flannel shirt, his chin and cheeks covered in several days of scruff. Even with the man bun gone, the spark between them had finally gone out. She punched the buttons on the remote control glued to the side of the hospital bed, trying to lower the volume on the episode of *Friends* she'd been watching when he walked in.

"I had no idea what happened to you down there," he started. "I only just read about it in the newspapers. If I'd known . . ."

She let him take her hand. His fingers were different from Hugh's. His skin was smoother and softer, and she noticed, for the first time, the dirt beneath his fingernails.

"You couldn't have known. I didn't tell you." There were other things she hadn't told him. She hadn't said that she didn't think it would work out between the two of them, that dating two men at once had been exhilarating at first, but now it was just exhausting. She liked him so much, but there was only so far like could go. It was clear their short-lived affair needed to come to an amicable end. It wasn't the fact that Jacob was the kind of person who wanted to go to sober raves at four in the morning and that Janey was never going to be that person. It wasn't even his singular interest in liquid nutrition or the questionable hairstyles. She'd lost every bit of stability in her life in the past twelve months—her parents, her best friend, her marriage, her job. If she was going to choose to be with anyone right now, she wanted that person to be strong and stable. She wanted to be with a man and not a boy. She'd been prioritizing boys all of her life.

"Jacob?" she began.

He gave her the look of a Labrador puppy whose favorite ball has just been lost in a lake.

"I know," he said. They both sat there in silence, staring up at the muted television screen. From their wild gesticulations, Janey could tell Ross and Rachel were having an argument.

Jacob's breathing grew more relaxed and he unwound his fingers from hers. "We'll still be friends," he announced with his youthful confidence.

They could still be friends. Why couldn't they? Who said everything had to end badly?

"Yeah. We'll definitely still be friends."

Jacob stood and pushed his hands deep into the pockets of his jeans, tilting back on his heels before he leaned down to kiss her forehead in a way she imagined he did every night to his daughter. He left her with a Tupperware of bee pollen and a sweaty pitcher of Green.

After Jacob left Janey got out of bed and padded through the hospital hallways, down to the first-floor conference room, where the doctor suggested (gently, but sternly) that she might enjoy visiting one of the hospital's weight counseling sessions.

"It's a good idea for you. Just a mix of some patients and women from the neighborhood. I could send you to a drug counseling session if I thought that would be helpful, but how about we do this as an alternative?" Janey agreed that this was the better option.

She didn't know what to expect, but what she got was a room of women of all shapes and sizes, ranging from dangerously skinny (not so different from most of the women on the fitness retreat) to much larger. She was late, but the counselor, a cheery man in his mid- to late forties wearing a sweater vest and steel-rimmed glasses, gave her a wide smile and beckoned her to take a seat in the circle. The group was held in a little-trafficked corner of the cafeteria, an irony that wasn't lost on Janey. Maybe it was a form of aversion therapy. The smell of the day's special, meatloaf, mingled in the air with the hospital-grade disinfectant they used to clean the floors.

"You must be Janey. Dr. Knots told me to keep an eye out for a pretty brunette. Thanks for coming. I don't know how much you know about our group, but this is really just a place where we talk about different issues surrounding weight and our feelings and our lives. No judgment here. You can say whatever you want. This week we're talking about confidence. Alice was just talking about what makes her feel good about herself." The counselor gave two happy snaps and gestured over to a woman sitting across the room in a loud yellow top and tight black jeans, a brown felt fedora cocked jauntily on her head. She was tall and broad, like Janey, but bigger. Janey guessed her weight to be more than 250 pounds.

"I'll catch up the new girl," Alice said with a kind smile in Janey's direction. "You all know this already, but I used to be a thin girl.

Well, first I was a fat girl and then I was a thin girl and now I'm a fat girl again, but the difference is I'm a fat and happy girl. I lost more than a hundred pounds five years ago. I was as skinny as Charlotte over there." Alice pointed across the room to a frail-looking woman with a thick cardigan wrapped around her slight shoulders. "The world was my oyster. All of a sudden men loved me. Men who'd never even looked at me before began asking me out on dates and buying me presents. But I felt like shit. If I wanted to stay that skinny I had to take a handful of diet pills every day and only eat lettuce. Just lettuce. Like a rabbit." She made a little munching noise that elicited titters from the rest of the group. "And I didn't feel like me, not the real me. So I stopped pretending and I let my body do what my body wanted to do." She stood up and twirled, gave a little bow. "I don't hide my body anymore. I love it. I'm fat and I'm happy."

The room erupted in applause. Alice was clearly the shining star of therapy, a woman so comfortable with herself that Janey was a little afraid of her.

Charlotte, the skinny girl in the cardigan, timidly raised her hand.

"We don't need to raise our hands, Charlotte. Just jump in if you have something to say." The therapist gave a double thumbs-up in the woman's direction, incongruous in a circle of adults.

Charlotte's voice was little, just like her, barely a whisper.

"Thanks, Alice. You're so inspiring." She looked at Janey. "I know you. I follow you on Instagram. I follow B and Beau too."

Janey was taken aback. She'd assumed this group was supposed to be anonymous. She had nothing to base that on except for a couple of AA meetings she'd attended with Beau the first time he got out of rehab.

Charlotte continued. "I wanted to wear a B dress for my wedding. That's when I started following you. I actually did end up buying one. It's the Eliza. It's beautiful." Charlotte looked around the room. Everyone leaned in closer to the center of the circle.

"I was a big girl too. Like Alice. But I was never very confident.

I used to shop online so I would never have to go into clothing stores and endure the judgey faces of the salesgirls who thought I wouldn't fit into anything. What if I just wanted to buy a hat? Anyone can wear a hat! They always looked at me like they were scared I'd put on a pair of pants and split them right down the back. I would Google restaurants before I met up with friends to make sure there was enough room between the tables that it wouldn't be embarrassing to get up and go to the bathroom. I inspected the chairs at the restaurants too, made sure they were wide and strong. My worst nightmare was a chair breaking in the middle of dinner."

Janey's heart broke for Charlotte.

"I met a guy. Online. That's how I had to date. I didn't meet men in real life. And he was wonderful. I thought he was wonderful. We emailed and talked every day for a year. I sent him pictures of my skinny cousin, who looks like me, but not like me, you know. He was a soldier. Over in Iraq for two years."

The rest of the group nodded.

"But I figured I could look like my cousin if I tried so I drained my bank account. I spent my entire savings on two things. I got a surgery that stapled my stomach and I bought a B wedding dress." She made direct eye contact with Janey as if she were the only person in the room. "The biggest size for the Eliza dress was a four. So the four was my goal. In a year I reached it and David, that was his name, proposed to me. He was still based in Iraq and we talked over Skype, but we never did video. His bandwidth wasn't good enough. Thank god. He had no idea about the surgery or the weight loss or anything. He was about to come home and we were finally going to meet in person. I know what you're thinking. He's not real? Right? The fat girl got catfished. But guess what? He was real! And he was just as handsome as his picture. I wanted to tell him every day about what I'd been doing to get ready to meet him, but I couldn't. I just felt so lucky. He was back for a month when I started getting really bad headaches and fainting. The diet wasn't sustainable. It was bad news. After the surgery I could only eat like four ounces of food a day. That's how I ended up in the hospital. And that's how I found the group. That's all."

More applause. Two women stood and walked over to Charlotte to wrap her in a hug. Now that the girl had called attention to Janey, and the fact that Janey was complicit in an industry that only made wedding dresses for impossibly skinny women, she felt like she had to speak up.

"I'm Janey. Like Charlotte said, I used to work at B, which is a company that makes wedding dresses." This was the first time she said she used to work at B. It rang true. "A couple of months ago someone very close to me hurt me. He told me that there was something wrong with me. And I became obsessed with fixing it. I didn't think much about it. I just started doing anything I could to lose weight. Being judged like that shattered my confidence. And I did a lot of things that probably weren't healthy. And I felt a little sick sometimes." She wasn't sure what else to say. She didn't think her story was nearly as interesting as either Alice's or Charlotte's. This was the first time she'd acknowledged out loud how hurt she'd been by what Beau had said and done. He was a vain and spiteful person, no longer the lively little boy she'd fallen in love with three decades ago. She had to let go of that little boy. She'd let his opinion of her be her own opinion of herself for too long. "I loved the person who made me feel bad about myself. But I don't want to feel bad anymore." She turned to face Charlotte. "I'm sorry. I'm sorry that dress only came in a four. It never occurred to me that we were shattering people's self-confidence. I'm really sorry." Janey meant it. She'd known they were wading into ridiculous territory with their ever-shrinking dresses, but she'd been so focused on growing the business, she hadn't thought about any of the consequences.

Charlotte smiled for the first time since Janey walked into the room. She had a great smile, one that defied gravity by lifting her entire face from her lips to her eyes.

"Stop it. Seriously. Don't be sorry. We're gonna elope when I'm better. And when I walk down the aisle I'll wear whatever fits!"

CHAPTER TWENTY-SEVEN

Janey sank into a deep and restful sleep after attending the therapy session. It'd been a long time since she felt so at peace. She woke to find Stella sitting in the uncomfortable plastic chair next to her bed. The shaman's head hung like a pendulum from her narrow neck as she looked down at the floor instead of at Janey.

"I'm so sorry," she said in a voice even deeper than usual. There was a lot to apologize for. Ivy had left six frantic voicemails explaining all about Sara Strong's narcotic-infused tea.

Janey had a hundred things she wanted to ask her. What did the shaman know about the plastic surgery? Could she tell Janey why she had cocaine in her system? Was she a fraud, just like Sara Strong?

But Stella began talking before Janey could ask any of her questions.

"I'm so sorry," she said again. "You have to believe me when I tell you I didn't know. I didn't know it would be like that. I got carried away with making The Workout a success. Sara has been offering to make me a partner when The Workout expands nationwide and I hate to admit this . . ." Tears rolled down Stella's porcelain

cheeks. "I let the idea of money get the best of me. I know I'm supposed to be above all that. My job in the universe is to be a light, to
move positive energy around the world. But maybe I'm not. Maybe
I'm just a sellout too. I'm scared, Janey. I'm a forty-five-year-old
former model with no résumé and no real skills. I have a wonderful
husband who has a job that he loves that pays just about minimum
wage and two girls in private school. I need college funds. I need a
retirement plan." For the first time since Janey met her, Stella was
a real person.

"Sara was the first person I truly helped. I don't know how much
you know about her history, but she was a mess when I met her. I
felt called to help her transform herself and I watched her transition
from a broken woman who thought she'd lost everything into such a
beautiful butterfly. I was so taken with that butterfly, with the idea
of her, that I was blinded to anything else. Does that make sense?"

Janey stared at Stella's collarbone. She was too thin, much too
thin, emaciated really. But why hadn't she noticed that before?
When had this, a woman whose bones she could see through her
skin, become the norm, the bar for beauty?

"She was your butterfly?" Janey said with a healthy dose of skepticism. She'd allowed herself to be taken in by Stella when she was
at her lowest. She was in a different place now.

A tear slipped down Stella's cheek. "I don't expect you to understand it all. She was my student and I helped her and it made it
difficult to see that she was quickly becoming a negative force in
my life."

"What do you know about the amphetamines?" Janey asked
carefully. A cloud of confusion crossed Stella's fine features.

"What are you talking about?"

There was no point in beating around the bush. "Were there
drugs in the tea? At the retreat. Were you responsible for drugging
Sara's clients?"

Stella shook her head. "Why would you ask that?"

Stella appeared deep in thought. She momentarily allowed her eyes to roll around in their sockets as if she were searching the files in her brain for a very specific piece of information.

"Sara controlled what was in that tea. I don't know what she put in it. I never asked. I had doubts. I've had concerns. But I never asked. Sara wanted to make everyone happy to make sure they would invest their money, and I wanted Sara to be a success. I thought her success was my success," Stella admitted, chewing on the edge of her pinky nail.

Janey wavered for a second before telling her everything she knew. She wanted to trust her. Every cell in her body had wanted to trust this woman from the moment they'd met.

"Someone gave me drugs. I'm going through withdrawal. From speed. Sara was trying to smuggle something into the country. Remember, I told you that. That something was speed. And when she couldn't ship it god only knows what kind of coke she replaced it with."

The horrified look on Stella's face was real.

"That's not possible."

"It *is* possible. The doctor told me he wasn't going to arrest me or anything, but he recommended several very nice rehabilitation facilities."

At that Stella burst out laughing. And, for the first time, Janey could see the humor in the situation.

"I'm sorry. Really sorry," Stella said. "It's just that you're the last person I'd accuse of being in withdrawal from recreational drugs. And I can say that. I wrote a book about being a heroin addict. I was a heroin addict."

Janey sat up and reached for the pitcher of Green.

"You believe me, don't you?" Stella wasn't asking her. She was begging her. "I need us to come to a place of peace."

Only a shaman could get away with saying *I need us to come to a place of peace*. Janey sank back into the hospital bed. What was the point of fighting with Stella? The shaman was just as broken as any of them. Janey reached out her hand. "Namaste."

. . .

The doctors were ready to sign off on Janey's release forms, but there was one final thing she needed to do before she left the hospital.

Janey felt like an intruder walking toward Miranda Mills's distraught family while they huddled outside her hospital room. She'd practiced options for what to say to them.

Your daughter was the victim of a nefarious personal trainer who gave speed to her clients to make them addicted to her class. That sounded insane. But it was the truth.

An elderly woman in a pair of frumpy mom jeans and a lavender sweater and two men a few years older than Miranda sat outside of the model's room. All three shared Miranda's prominent forehead and full lips. Janey recognized them from the newspaper article as Miranda's mother and two older brothers. The men argued in thick Boston accents, not about their sister's medical treatment, but over a questionable trade recently conducted by the owner of the New England Patriots. "Brady can't carry that team forever. They need to groom some young blood."

Janey cleared her throat to announce her presence.

"Mrs. Mills?" The older woman looked up. She had a ghost of Miranda's bone structure, but her eyes were softer, her features less defined and fierce, her nose wider and fleshier.

"Hello dear. Are you here to see Miranda?" Elaborate sterling silver rings adorned her fingers, one in the shape of a butterfly and the other a leaping dolphin. She kneaded nervously at the fabric of her pants.

At first Janey shook her head, then changed her mind and nodded.

"She's asleep now. She came around an hour ago. Maybe you didn't know. She's out of her coma, but the doctors say it's still touch and go. So she needs to rest. I'm sorry we can't wake her up, but if you want to leave a note I can give it to her."

Janey heaved a sigh of relief. Miranda had woken up? Did Janey even need to talk to the doctors? If she was awake then maybe the model was out of the woods. Miranda's mother looked so hopeful that Janey didn't feel comfortable giving her any more bad news than what she'd been dealing with.

"I'll leave my name and number. Please just tell her I came by."

Miranda's mom put one of Janey's hands in both of hers. "She'll be so happy you did. You're the only one who's shown up here besides family. So many people talk to those newspapers and they say how sorry they are on the Facebook, but you're the only friend who has stopped by. I know she'll appreciate it."

As she walked out, Janey passed by the nurse's station and asked for the doctor on duty for Miranda Mills. He was a small and harried man with bloodshot eyes who'd clearly been on call for longer than twenty-four hours. He listened quietly when she told him she'd been on the retreat with Miranda and had some information to share with him. She explained very carefully how she'd learned that the women at the retreat could have been given medications (she was careful not to use the word drugs) that bore a resemblance to amphetamines.

"Thank you, ma'am. I'll do you the favor of not asking how you came by this information. But we had an anonymous caller tell us something similar. It wasn't completely anonymous, I suppose. The initials were KW. Do those mean anything to you? Oh nevermind."

Janey capitalized on the doctor's exhaustion and excused herself. He didn't call after her or follow her.

She hoped Miranda was on the road to recovery.

. . .

Back at the apartment, Janey pulled *City Walks of New York* off the shelf, thumbing two-thirds of the way through to a page Lorna had turned down. As she opened the book to a lovely stroll along the Hudson River in the West Sixties, a beige vellum note card fell out and fluttered to the floor. Janey and Boo Radley reached the piece of paper at the same time, inspecting it together. Janey felt a tug of emotion at seeing her mother's initials, LMS, Lorna Marie Sweet, atop the personalized stationery with the profile of an elephant on the top. Lorna loved elephants. "They're a matriarchal society, you know," she'd say whenever anyone complimented her on her note cards. "Strong women can do anything."

When the book first arrived, Janey remembered being surprised there was no note. Lorna must have tucked it inside instead of just leaving it in the package the way she usually did. Lorna never used emails or text messages, but this was the first note Janey had found since her mother's death.

My sweet, Sweet girl,

Quiet couple of weeks here at home. Daddy's been off on one of his bird-watching trips. After all these years of marriage I can't make myself like birds. I don't know the difference between a kingfisher and a cuckoo bird and I don't ever care to.

I saw Miss Elsie at the store the other day. You remember Miss Elsie, right? Your third-grade teacher? She asked me about you. I said you were doing great. I didn't mention the divorce. Did you know she's a lesbian now? And such a pretty girl too. Shame. She asked me about Beau too. Third grade was when you met Beau, wasn't it? That boy just worshipped you back then. You have always been that boy's muse, and I don't know what he'd be without you. He worshipped you, but he also wanted something you had, maybe it was money or status or maybe just a mama who took care of him. I loved that little boy, but I never trusted him. I don't think I've ever told you that, but maybe this cancer is making me melancholy.

My mama always used to tell me that behind every great man is an even better woman. I love your father to the ends of the earth and back, but I know that has been true for our marriage. Your daddy has me and Beau has you. But I want more for you than to be the great woman behind any man. You'll never spread your wings as long as you work with Beau. I don't know if this will make sense to you, and you might write this off as the ramblings of an old lady, but I hope it gives you something to think about. I'm also enclosing my latest recipe for zucchini bread. All those young skinny ninnies joining the Rotary Club these days want me to make it low-carb and sugar-free, so I just lie and tell them it is, but this recipe contains more sugar, butter, and flour than any other yet. What they don't know will make them happier!! Give it a try if you have some time. All the love in the world.

Your mama.

CHAPTER TWENTY-EIGHT

~

I t was another full week before Janey felt good enough to lace up her sneakers and actually go for a walk. At six a.m. she pulled on her grey track pants and favorite worn-out Princeton sweatshirt, made her way to the coffee shop, ordered her usual double espresso, and sipped at the strong liquid as she made her way over to the High Line's northern staircase. The snows of the previous month were a memory and the first flowers of spring poked their heads from beneath the old railroad trestle.

Janey broke into a light jog for about a mile before settling down on her favorite bench in a wild patch of elephant grass just above Fourteenth Street. She turned on her phone to find a new email from Ivy with the subject line *HOLY SHIT!!!!!!!!!!*

In it there was a link to a *New York Post* story describing in great detail the capture of Sara Strong.

Federal agents had searched Sara's apartment, finding several kilograms of high-grade pure Colombian cocaine in her closet. But Sara was nowhere to be found. For a week, the authorities tried to track her down by attempting to triangulate her cell phone calls and monitoring her credit cards, but Sara was sneaky, and they came up empty-handed until yesterday. Maybe she'd gotten too cocky. Maybe she was just hungry. Whatever caused Sara Strong to order

$200 worth of gorditas at the Taco Bell in Duluth brought about her downfall. She charged the fast food to her MasterCard and was found by the local police within the hour. There was a second story on Miranda's emergency evacuation and miraculous recovery. Apparently the movie rights to Miranda's story had already been optioned by Paramount. Kate Wells was considering taking on the role.

Janey put down her phone and stretched her legs, tilting her head up to let the sun stream down onto her face.

Her phone rang right on time. Ronald Applebaum, the Sweet family attorney, was never late. It was time to deal with Sweet Chocolate. She never should have let it go this long without making some kind of serious plan for the company. In hindsight she shouldn't have kept Sweet on the back burner since she'd graduated. This was her family's legacy. It should have meant more to her, and it was time for her to rectify that.

She had a plan. A good one, one that she'd concocted with a little help from Hugh, who had just returned to the country with a large package for her.

"I bought you hiking boots. I'll get you a Sherpa when we get to Peru," he said, before handing her plane tickets for a trip to Lima and an itinerary for the Inca Trail later that year. She didn't mind him planning ahead.

After days of poring over the notes of every minute from every meeting of the Sweet board of directors since Reginald had passed, she'd decided the best course of action was to initiate a nationwide search for a new president of Sweet Chocolate, someone without the last name Sweet. She wanted someone smart, young, and hungry who would work with her, as the company's chairwoman, to lead Sweet Chocolate into the twenty-first century. She was excited about endearing the Sweet brand to a new generation, one that was more health conscious but still loved their chocolate. Sweet could still be an indulgence, but they could make it with less sugar and with organic ingredients.

Janey got right to the point with Ronald and assured him she could come down to Charleston as often as it took to get things on track. After that she wanted a direct role, if not an everyday one, in the company's future. She also wanted access to her trust, the one due to her if she ever came back and ran Sweet Chocolate. "I'll be running Sweet," she insisted. "Just not on a daily basis. I'm fulfilling the terms my father requested for me to obtain access to the funds." Janey took a deep breath. She'd begun to feel a determination that had been lost to her for months, maybe even for years. She had built a successful business once and she could do it again. She wanted the money to fund the kinds of projects she was passionate about.

She'd help Ivy get her boot-camp fitness studio off the ground. With all of the press she'd gotten as the star of SoarBarre, it wouldn't be hard for her cousin to build up a client base.

Alizza's designs inspired her. There had to be a way to take affordable bridal to a whole new level. Janey wanted to help her craft an app that would let the bride design her own wedding dress, couture on demand for all body shapes and sizes at reasonable prices. Janey felt unfamiliar pinpricks of excitement as she described the plans out loud.

She could hear the attorney furiously taking notes. He was one of the few people Janey knew who still covered yellow legal pads in endless scrawls of ink. "We can make these things happen." He paused. Janey could hear a dog howl in the background and the clink of ice cubes in Applebaum's bourbon breakfast. "We do have to talk about B."

She'd never signed the document Beau sent her in the hospital. Janey closed her eyes and breathed into her diaphragm. When she opened them she looked down the length of the High Line. An older couple, both of them grey haired and slightly hunched against the morning chill, sat laughing on a nearby bench. She was slim and pretty. He wore an Italian-cut camel hair coat and a loud scarf. Their connection clearly wasn't a romantic one, but it was obvious they loved each other very much. *That could have been us,* Janey thought. But it won't be. Life has to move on.

Ronald continued. "I got a call from the company's general counsel yesterday. Beau is selling the company, Janey. A large Chinese conglomerate called Xi Fong has put in a sizable offer for B. The decision is Beau's since he's the majority stakeholder. But from what I can gather, this is something that's been in the works for half a year. If I had to bet the bull's balls on the farm, I'd say he made a deal to get rich right quick while you were out of the picture."

She wouldn't take that bet. He was right. Beau was a vain little son of a bitch, but she knew in her heart that pushing her out of the office had nothing to do with what she looked like. He wanted her out of his hair so he could do what he liked with B. That's what those papers in the hospital were about too. Beau loved money more than he loved Janey. She had packed the photograph from the deb ball into its box and mailed it back to him in the office without adding a note or her signature.

Janey accepted the news from Applebaum with a sense of detachment. She should have been livid, but the anger didn't come. Was it relief she felt? The idea of staying on at B, propelled by an unhealthy sense of obligation and inertia like a poorly made marriage, would have been impossible. Three months ago she never would have let Beau get away with this. She never would have allowed him to sell everything they'd built to a faceless international corporation. Things were different now. She was different now.

"When is this happening?"

Ronald Applebaum shuffled his papers around. She knew he didn't have a computer on his desk. His secretary still transcribed all of his emails.

"Next Monday morning. Should I tell them you'll be attending the meeting? They have to pay you out whether or not you show up."

"No. Just get me the time of the meeting. They don't need to know I'll be there."

CHAPTER TWENTY-NINE

hank god for Net-a-Porter. Janey's standard black suit
wouldn't do for this meeting. She chose a flattering navy
blue Roland Mouret stretch crepe sheath dress that hugged
her curves. She was never going to be a size 2, or even a 4 or a 6
again, and that was just fine with her. It was amazing how easily
weight found its way back when you weren't starving yourself or
forcing your body to burn calories in cruel and unusual ways. She
didn't choose the dress to please Beau or even to impress him. Just
the opposite. She chose it because it made her feel confident and
fabulous.

Hugh picked her up in his town car and drove her downtown to
the meeting, which was completely unnecessary, but welcome. He
didn't attempt small talk. He just held her hand.

Anna, the company's vice president of delight and Janey's mole,
met her at B's reception desk. Janey handed the woman an enve-
lope containing a glowing letter of recommendation.

"I called Vera and Ralph and I put in an excellent word for you.
Send them your résumé and you'll have a new job in no time. I
removed any reference to delight," Janey said to her. "I'll talk to the
rest of the staff shortly. No one has to stay if he or she doesn't want
to. Is everyone here?"

Anna nodded and pivoted on her heel to point Janey in the direction of the men waiting in the conference room. Janey made a quick stop to prepare herself an espresso from the obscenely elaborate and confusing professional machine Beau had custom-designed in Milan.

"Don't get up," she said to the Chinese executives gathered around the table when she walked into the conference room. *"Wŏ shì Janey Sweet. Suŏyĭ, hĕn gāoxìng jiàn dào nĭ. Wŏ shì CEO."* She introduced herself as the company's CEO in passable Mandarin. Those language apps and long walks down the High Line had really paid off.

Beau had yet to make an appearance. This meeting wasn't supposed to start for another five minutes, and of course he'd be another five late. Janey made small talk in English, mentioned how much she loved visiting China, asked after the men's plans for the company. They were nice enough, but these were businessmen who could care less about good design or quality craftsmanship. Hugh had filled her in on their backstory. He'd once negotiated a deal with them for All-American Juice, one of the first companies to bottle cold-pressed juice out of Brooklyn. It was now produced in Bangalore but still bore the "All-American" brand. This was the same company that now owned two famous Kentucky-born whiskey brands, a majority stake in the largest beer company in the world, almost every popular denim brand, and several American cosmetics companies. The situation was just as she'd suspected. They planned to mass market B dresses all over the world, a strategy Beau had always rejected in the past in favor of small production, hand craftsmanship, and high quality. But Janey knew Beau had been dazzled by their offer, by the money, by the fact that he thought he could pull this off behind her back. The sale price was even higher than Ronald Applebaum had been told, making it clear once again that Beau had intended to shortchange her on this deal.

She should have asked Anna to take a picture of the moment Beau realized Janey was sitting in the conference room. Through the glass she saw him mouth "What the fuck?" to Natasha, B's lawyer. Janey could see the older woman trying to calm Beau down by rubbing his shoulders before he walked into the room. On his other side was a newer and younger version of the tall and beautiful Alizza. Was Beau manufacturing muses in a lab these days?

"This is our designer, Beau Matthews," Janey said, knowing that in the mind of these executives the title of designer was much less important than her title of CEO.

"Tā shì yīgè xiǎo nánrén!" one of the men said, eliciting a burst of laughter from the others. Janey thought hard on the words and then laughed along with them. He had said that Beau was much smaller than he expected. She replied in Mandarin that he *was* quite petite, which encouraged more chuckles.

She opened the cardboard box she had picked up on her way to the office.

"I know you gentlemen have traveled a long way. I would like to offer you a delicious new American delicacy. This is the bruffin, a delicious combination of brioche and muffin, created right here in SoHo." Their guests eagerly grabbed at the pastries.

Janey took control of the meeting before Beau could get in a word. She told the men from Xi Fong that she expected to spin the news of their acquisition to the press in a way that would be beneficial to every employee of B. She expected her employees to be well compensated and was happy to forfeit her own earnings to make sure they were all given large payouts from the sale. She was sick of CEOs who sold out their companies and left their staffs to flounder. Her people had helped her build this thing and they deserved to be compensated. Besides, she didn't need the money. Beau sat there frozen, his eyes the size of saucers. When she finally allowed him to get a word in edgewise, his voice was small.

"And you'll be staying on with the company, Janey," he said. It wasn't a question. "As CEO."

She looked over at the men the way a parent would look over the head of a child.

"That's not necessary. These gentlemen know exactly what they are going to do with B. None of you need me involved. I'm proud of everything we accomplished, but this is not my baby anymore."

She stood and smoothed her dress over her hips. For the first time since she'd arrived in the office she stared straight at Beau. His beady little eyes were filled with rage, a twinge of fear, and something new. Maybe it was respect? She didn't know. This would be the only closure the two of them would have. Beau would be a very rich man after this sale, but he'd never achieve the same level of fame that he had with B. It would be a long time before their paths even crossed again, and when they did Janey would be with Hugh, finishing up a half marathon with him and his two daughters in Central Park. She'd see Beau as they walked hand in hand to the West Side. Beau would avert his gaze and Janey would smile in remembrance of their shared history.

A sense of ease settled over her as she thanked everyone in that conference room and reached across the table to snatch the last bruffin. Janey nodded to the Xi Fong team and promised to be in touch soon with her strategy for dealing with the press.

She walked toward the doors and bit into the pastry, smiled, and air kissed Beau's cheek, her mouth filled with the delicious sweetness.

ACKNOWLEDGMENTS

We couldn't do this without the A-Team! Suzanne Herz, Judy Jacoby, and Todd Doughty, your talent at making everything look so wonderfully easy when we all know it's not; your positivity; and your kindness impress us every day.

We've been blessed to work with Jenny Jackson as our editor. Everyone should have someone in their lives who helps to make everything not better but brilliant   whose integrity and professionalism infuse everything they do.

Thank you super agent Alexandra Machinist for pushing us fearlessly.

From Lucy: Gin Boswick, Tracey Taylor, Hailey Lustig Prince, Ann Caruso, Amelie Lonergan, Aliza Griscom, Mallory May, Plum and Alice and Tom and Valerie Sykes, Sara Costello, Elana Nathan, Lloyddee Nathan, Amanda Foreman, Dee Poku, Stephanie March, Alexandra Scott, Dria Murphy, you are my Earth Angels. The gift of your friendship and constant belief in me, an unconventional storyteller/writer, is magic glue. Thank you to Kara "UberFly" Liotta, who whips and works us hard but most of all made getting fit so much bloody fun. Massive shout out to the most supportive hubby, "Marathon Man," and Dad ever—Euan Rellie. My two fantastic boys, Heathcliff Rellie and Titus Rellie, who make me feel like every day is Christmas—love you more than the stars and the moon.

From Jo: Emily Foote, Sara Chadwick, Christine Ryan, Kim Rittberg, Danielle Antalffy, Glynnis MacNicol, Rachel Sklar (and the entire Li.st), Jaclyn Letschert, Jackie Cascarano, Brad dePeyster, Ursula Rouse, Leah Chernikoff, Dan Wakeford, Ben Widdicombe, and Rebecca Prusinowski, thanks for being the best squad a girl could ask for. Thank you, Nick, for marrying me while knowing I would need to write two books in the next nine months, and bringing me sunshine and pandas when I needed them the most. I couldn't do any of this without you and I wouldn't want to.